To Lucie
May God bless you,

Tish

Lost Children of Cush

D1784391

LETITIA MASON

ISBN: **1548221333**
ISBN-13: **978-1548221331**

Rev 1

DEDICATION

This story is dedicated to the women of South Sudan,
who have loved their families through conflict,
separation and famine.

Cover art created by Cally Mead,
and formatted by Howard Mason.

CONTENTS

LETITIA MASON

ACKNOWLEDGMENTS

I would like to thank my husband, Howard, for his patience during the writing of this story and my son, Alex, for his encouragement; my mother for her enthusiasm and Jon, Shell, Emily and Jamie for inspiring my first childish attempts at story telling. Thanks are also due to Ruth Sander and Thomas Oldman for their reading and editing; and to Jan Ransom and Flame International for taking me to South Sudan. Finally I owe a debt of gratitude to Ruth Brandt of Creativity, Inspiration and Muses, Susanne Irving of Creative Communicators and Nikki Salt of M3 Corridor for their constructive criticism, encouragement and helpful suggestions.

1 A GIANT STIRS

Ah, land of whirring wings which is beyond the rivers of Cush; …
Go, you swift messengers, to a nation, tall and smooth, to a people
feared near and far, a nation mighty and conquering, whose land the
rivers divide. [1]

The dark waters boil and part. Ripples spread outwards
and islands of floating hyacinth undulate. A dark hump
emerges and two protuberant eyes scan the river bank,
passing briefly over the people standing on the wooden
jetty. The hippopotamus shakes its head from side to side
and emerges from the shallow water opening its jaw to
reveal flabby pink gums and a picket fence array of teeth
enclosing the fathomless pool of its throat.

'It could swallow me,' I muse, standing less than a hundred
metres away, 'and if those jaws closed I would be broken
up and swallowed into its belly!' I glance at the rest of the
group who seem mesmerised, grasping their phones in
disbelief and taking as many pictures as they can. I tap my

---

[1] *Book of Isaiah* chapter 18

own phone to camera and focus on the animal. The hippo has hauled its bulk up the steep bank and closed its jaws engulfing bushes lining the river. Papyrus reeds sway and shiver as swathes of vegetation disappear down the vast throat. It is a prehistoric grab devouring everything in its path, primeval Africa destroying the camouflage that is its own protection. Hunger satisfied the hippo slithers down the bank, flattening the mauve water hyacinths flowering at the river's edge and submerges once more. A break in the succession of floating islands allows wavelets to spread to the opposite bank several hundred metres away, their crests lit by the setting sun. Then all is still again and the fading light shines serenely on smooth water and the flat, drifting mats of vegetation.

I hear a communal sigh of relief and awe and then the sardonic tones of my boss, Andy, murmuring at my shoulder.

'You could pay thousands for a safari package and not see that, Jane.' I meet his eye and grimace; we are not on a holiday but a reconnaissance trip to find out more about the plight of young people and particularly girls in war ravaged South Sudan, the world's newest nation.

'That animal kill more people than lion.' I hear Bishop Michael say. I glance at his creased face and wide set eyes, sometimes sharply focused but now warm with relief that the party of Europeans under his protection is unharmed.

'I have never seen this one before,' breathes Pastor Peter, the Bishop's Peace and Reconciliation Officer, his dark face glowing with wonder. He is a tall man, who walks with a limp, perhaps an injury from the decades of civil war.

'It is a sign of the Lord's favour,' pronounces Pamela, the mission leader who initiated this expedition to the White Nile. Andy and I exchange raised eyebrows but say nothing. It is through Pamela that we have been able to meet local people in this forgotten corner of South Sudan close to the Ugandan border.

'Shall we continue?' she adds. The bishop nods. Pamela steps forward and turns to face the group.

'This stretch of river has been used for millennia for the slave trade, extracting people from southern Sudan, the heartland of the ancient kingdom of Cush, and taking them north to Egypt and south to Zanzibar. Who knows what misery this river has witnessed; but we are here this evening to atone for what has passed and to pledge to work together to eliminate slavery in the future.' Pamela strides forward, her sandy grey hair layered for practicality rather than style, her slight figure erect and taut. I stare down into the dark waters of the river as it passes the jetty. The jutting vertical timbers create swirls and eddies that hint at the depths beneath and I wonder what is down there beneath the surface waters. How many destroyed souls lie on the river bottom, how many coins won through corrupt means, how many weapons dropped in the fight to preserve this terrible trade in human life? I stare at the swirling reflection of my own face, grey in the fading light, dark curly hair ruffled by a light wind and brown eyes that stare erratically back at me as the eddies shift, decay and re-form. I do not see there the clues to how my life will change.

Pamela is sprinkling salt crystals on the water below the jetty and reading a passage from Isaiah. Her words boom out through the still air and die away as the sun drops beneath the horizon into the velvet darkness of the African night.

'The LORD *has chosen and sent me to tell the oppressed the good news, to heal the broken hearted, and to announce* **freedom** *for prisoners and captives.'* Pamela reads from her Bible and then prays aloud:

'Oh Lord, our nation fought hard to abolish slavery under General Gordon. Forgive us that we withdrew and allowed this trade to continue.' I look apprehensively around the group wondering how this Euro-centric view of the matter will be received. The bishop steps forward, raises both hands to the sky and looking out across the water speaks in a voice that is a deep drum beat.

'I am the descendent of a chief. I repent of the sins of my ancestors, who sold our people into slavery.' I make no sound but inwardly gasp. It is a matter of historic record that African chiefs sold their people into slavery but to hear it spoken of openly is as shocking, as if the bushes destroyed by the hippo had sprung upright again. We stand as still as the wooden posts of the jetty while currents of unspoken thoughts swirl and settle.

'Father God, we thank you for this place and we declare the love of Christ for all who live here,' continues Pamela and adds 'Shall we say the Lord's prayer? Our father in heaven, hallowed be thy name, thy kingdom come, thy will be done on earth as it is in heaven....' The voices of Pamela, the Bishop and Pastor Peter ring out across the water. Andy and I mumble and falter as we try to keep up. My grandfather was a missionary and my parents took me to church every Sunday but it is many years since I have said this Christian prayer. The archaic words stick on my tongue but are strangely comforting, cloaking me with a sense of familiarity.

The chirping of crickets is audible in the undergrowth and mosquitoes are starting to bite; I slap at my legs as I feel them drawing blood. There is barely enough light to find our way back to the car and bump and bounce along the rutted dirt track to Nimule. I ponder the significance of what I have witnessed – an English mission worker and a South Sudanese bishop talking to a river and sprinkling a few grains of rock salt into the water in February 2015. How can that change what has happened through the centuries? Representatives of two nations have made a public declaration that nobody heard. Yet I feel in the depths of my being that something has changed; as significant as if the fault lines of the Great African Rift Valley had shifted and realigned.

That night I wake in total darkness sweating and distressed by a dream. I am back on the river bank but this time standing alone staring into the depths. The waters stir and from the centre of the channel, where the current swirls like a snake uncoiling, the head of a giant emerges black and glistening. It stands and strides to the water's edge. Dark weeds wrap around the body and festoon the head, trailing behind as it passes up the steep sandy slope. It looms over the papyrus reeds, which bend and bow in its wake. At the crest of the bank the figure glances down in my direction, holding my eyes for a fraction of a second and then stomps across the bush, each foot falling heavily, for the ankles are bound; iron chains, rusted by centuries under water, drag and impede progress. A young girl cowers in terror as the giant strides past, trampling her home underfoot; and a boy goat herd stumbles through the bush on bare feet, racing to catch up with youths fleeing the menacing presence. The huge head turns and looks back at me. I wake up terrified, stifling a scream and lie trembling on the thin foam mattress, sweat pouring off me in the tropical night, and soaking the cotton sheet I have wrapped around my legs and abdomen for modesty. I am sharing a tukul with Pamela. I remove my ear plugs; I can hear her steady snores from the bed a couple of feet away. I want to hear clearly and bring myself back to some sense of reality. What is the giant? Who are the children? My eyes adjust and I begin to see the pattern of the cloth that our hosts have pinned under the grass roof to keep out lizards and mice. There is a faint rustling above my head and the sound of a cow in the patch of wasteland behind our small hut chewing the cud. I breathe deeply, try to make my body relax and reflect on the last two days.

Andy and I work for the Olaudah Trust, set up to prevent trafficking along the White Nile. We arrived in Juba on Sunday evening to attend a three day conference on protecting children. We left at seven yesterday morning for the three hour drive to Nimule over pitted tarmac roads. Pamela's organisation, Doves of Peace, has worked with the New Jerusalem Church for several years and we had made an arrangement to meet with them yesterday afternoon.

Bishop Michael is a lean elderly man with deep lines at the corners of his eyes. He has led the diocese through two generations of civil war and must now deal with the many scars of a scattered people. Most of his flock fled to Nimule when the Khartoum government's Sudan Armed Forces bombed the Torit headquarters of the Sudan People's Liberation Army.

'There are children wandering in the bush,' the Bishop told us. 'If we do not take them in they sell themselves into slavery or become child soldiers. We have twenty four orphans living in the cathedral compound in Torit.' He was matter of fact, resigned to dealing with each situation as it arose; I held my breath as I reflected on what he was telling me. What would it be like to be a small child wandering in the intense heat and relentless sun of the South Sudanese bush, picking a way over stones cracked by heat, tormented by insects, watching for water lurking underground, and constantly alert for snakes and lion?

Supper was provided by the Mothers' Union and as I ate the goat stew, rice and beans I heard Pastor Peter's story. His family was captured by northern forces during the fighting. He was shot in the leg, looks after his mother whose back was damaged in the same incident, and lost three sisters who were taken as "wives" for the soldiers who shot him. Only one of them has returned.

'We need peace,' he told me. 'Dinka and Nuer peoples must lay down their weapons and learn to live as brothers.' but "cattle raiding" the local euphemism for tribal fighting, still continues along the Torit to Nimule road. 'Many people are in camps in Uganda because they are afraid to return home.' Peter tells me.

Yes, there is much to reflect on in this land of great beauty and natural wealth, where fighting has destroyed so much and ancient disputes have yet to be settled.

Was the figure I dreamed of a portent? It was primeval, like the hippopotamus. How much damage is done by its vile cloak of mud and weed, dragging detritus in its wake? Should I be comforted that it staggered away towards the interior of this vast continent or will it be back, stirring up the currents of rivalry in this region of Sudd, the land the tributaries of the Nile divide?

At home I would get up, wander about a bit to calm myself and record the dream in my audio diary. Here the generator went off at ten, the moon has set, I am sharing a room and there is only a mud partition between me and other sleepers in adjacent tukuls. There is total silence now except for the whirring of insects and the occasional snore from Pamela. I fumble for my bottle of drinking water, put my ear plugs in and will myself to go back to sleep.

....

27 Feb 2015 9pm East African Time

Dear Fi,

I am at Nairobi airport with a four hour wait for my flight. Andy is staying over for a meeting and going back via Dubai tomorrow.

The trip has gone well; Bishop Michael has invited us to Torit next time to meet people from the surrounding villages and hear their stories. He introduced me to a wonderful man, Peter, who is the 'Peace and Reconciliation Officer' for the diocese. He is tall with a wide craggy face and a mop of shaggy hair. His job is to recruit people from each District to attend UN funded conferences on reconciliation but there is no money and no-one can afford to travel. He is not paid and lives in the refugee camp in Nimule.

There have been some funny moments – there are many children, all very curious and keen to practice their English.

'Good morning. Hoow are youooo?' They say. We have tried various responses but the only one that gets a reaction is to repeat. 'How are you?' which throws them into paroxysms of giggles.

The bishop took us to "Gordon's Lookout" one evening, a mountain promontory overlooking the White Nile. Then we drove down to the riverside past a derelict garrison, built by General Gordon, and saw a massive hippo feeding on the river bank.

There is plenty of meat and fruit in Nimule because it is near the Ugandan border. In Juba there were mangoes and pineapples, so I have kept my vitamins up.

I will give you a call when I have caught up on sleep.

See you soon. Jane x

Nairobi airport is a halfway house – the transition from the open air lifestyle of South Sudan, its mud huts, water carried in plastic jerry cans, and latrines. I love the beauty of the unpolluted sky, the sense of community as everyone gathers under the trees to eat and talk, but daily hygiene is a struggle. There are few shops and they sell an identical range of basic items, frequently laid out on the dusty footpath at the side of the roads. Nairobi airport in contrast is clean and well ordered with a handful of small gift shops and cafés. There is even a shower if you don't mind paying for it. I make do with a wash down in the toilets – this is more luxurious than the "showers" in Nimule where a large bowl of water to throw over myself in a grass enclosure must suffice.

Once on the flight there is a subtle change of pace. I accept the hot flannel offered by the steward and watch as he moves smoothly down the cabin. The stewardess on the opposite aisle moves in tandem, her sleek black hair scraped into a bun and her make-up immaculate. Their synchronisation, and the red and black uniforms and smart waistcoats, speak of the corporate world of the global economy.

'Chicken and rice or beef stew?' asks the steward

'Chicken please.' I'm looking forward to a change of diet.

'And to drink?'

'Orange juice please.' This too is a luxury. Mangoes, papaya and citrus fruits grow wild in the lush forests of western South Sudan but not in the east, and with no processing plants the only "fruit juices" available are brightly coloured fizzy drinks imported at inflated prices from Kenya.

We eat and the trays are cleared with another burst of synchronised efficiency. My neighbour cloaks herself in a blanket and reclines her seat but I cannot settle. I gaze out of the porthole and watch tiny orange points of light flickering in the darkness below. Trade routes have extended across the empty space of the Sahara for centuries taking camels, goods and people from north to south, east to west. The latest stream of migrants will be somewhere below us, spending everything they have to reach the departure points along the North African coast, hoping for a new life in Europe.

I put on an eye mask and try to sleep but my mind is active, going back over the events of the last few days and haunted by the dream of the immense figure. Who is it? The Dinka speak frequently of spirits in the water and fear to go near the river courses at night, but what I experienced was not an ethereal spirit but something powerful. I love my job but it can be tough to make inroads against attitudes and patterns of behavior entrenched over centuries and I feel inadequate for the challenge of the work, tired and alone. The soft towelling lining of my eye mask catches a tear as it forms; its hot wetness is strangely comforting and I sleep.

………………………………..

'Cabin crew to your seats.' The engine noise changes as the pilot starts his descent. We circle for several minutes; the undercarriage comes down with a soft clunk and we land at dawn on a grey Saturday morning. The exit walkway is carpeted, the lighting white and even, no flicker of a generator straining to keep going. There is a faint smell of chlorinated water and scented disinfectant. I walk out into clean, sanitised Britain, six thousand miles away from the chaotic and dangerous world of South Sudan, and take the tube home.

I live in a second floor flat in a Victorian terrace in Bethnal Green, near the Museum of Childhood. I intended to renovate it with wood floors and contemporary furniture but somehow between travel and the pressures of work it never gets done. The main room has a large sagging sofa covered in throws which I have brought back from different parts of central Africa. My bedroom has a huge brass bed, which came from my grandmother's house. One day I will polish it but for now I am just grateful to sink into its metal embrace. The kitchen is basic with a work surface along one wall and a glass door opening onto metal steps. These lead down into the garden and give welcome access to the south facing lawn and the garden shed where I keep my kayak.

I shall do my washing and tidy up and then take a walk in Victoria Park or along the South Bank. I watch a magpie strut along the roof as I drink a can of cola. He is self important and brash and his graphic plumage and officious manner seem to mock my inefficiencies as a home maker. My mobile rings.

'Hi Andy, where are you?' I answer.

'Dubai. Jane, I need to talk with you first thing on Monday? I want you to go to Bristol next week; something's come up. You can check the stuff for the anniversary display at the Record Office while you are there. Enjoy your weekend.'

Enjoy your weekend! Well, he has just put a damper on that. I really need a week at home to sort myself out. I love this job and the travel. I have always been a bit of a nomad, a quester after alternate modes of life and different ways of doing things. But Mum and Dad are complaining that they haven't seen me, and I need to clean the flat before they come. My friend, Anna, had a baby three months ago; I'm to be a godparent at the christening in April and I have not even met little Poppy. I was looking forward to giving Fi a call and seeing if she fancies going to a film or a concert. Bristol! As far as I know the Trust has no business there. Why has Andy suddenly decided I need to go?

There is a loud bang on the front door, which makes me jump. I mop up spilled cola and go to answer it galvanised by further bangs and shouting. It is the son of the family who live on the ground floor. He is a tall lad of about sixteen whose physical strength often seems to outmanoeuvre his mental capabilities. He hands me a rectangular box tied with string.

'For you,' he says and grins.

'Thank you, Musa. Shalom.'

'Shalom,' he mutters, ducking his head and retreating down the stairs two at a time. I hear him bang the front door below. My heart sinks as I untie the parcel. Six brightly coloured carnations lie in the box – anorexic dolls in gaudy dresses. I take out the note tucked into them and read.

'You are my sunshine in the rain. J.' Jay is a single friend of Anna's who has moved to Blackheath recently and who, she assured me, just needed to be taken out. I met him at Waterloo and led him up through Covent Garden, along to St. Paul's, over the Millennium Bridge and back along the South Bank, where we had a drink looking out over the river. He talked about his work as an IT specialist, which I had expected, but Anna had not warned me that he had a romantic streak and as we walked back to Waterloo in a light drizzle he began to stroke my arm.

'You're the most beautiful girl I have ever been out with,' he murmured. This may well have been true, I doubt if he has much experience. 'You are the girl of my dreams, will you marry me?'

I walked as fast as I could back to Waterloo with Jay pawing my arm all the way; headed into the thickest part of the crowd and then down the steps to the underground before he could follow me. The last time I saw him he was peering through thick spectacles, jostled by passers-by. I wonder if Musa's mother would like the flowers. It would save me the trouble of trying to keep them alive while I am in Bristol. Anna means well; she is revelling in domestic bliss and wants me to join the fun but I could never be tied down to a house in the suburbs and the school gate. If I marry it will be to someone who understands my need to travel and explore; who will be interested in unravelling the puzzles of other cultures. I return to the kitchen and gaze out over the bare branches of the overgrown garden wishing I was back in Nimule. I tip the dirty washing out of my rucksack, load the washing machine and run a shower. The terror of the dream about the giant has faded but the questions remain.

.

2 A GENEROUS GIFT

When I arrived I was carried on board a fine large ship, loaded with tobacco &c. And just ready to sail for England.[2]

I'm feeling refreshed after a weekend of catching up. The March wind is stirring the leaves as I stride along the pavement. I've promised Mum that I'll fix a time to meet her and Dad for a meal as soon as I know when I will be back from the Bristol. I've phoned Jay, thanked him for the carnations and told him that I'm going to be away. Musa's mother was delighted with the flowers. I've even phoned Anna and arranged to meet baby Poppy. My brain is starting to function again and I'm full of ideas for the Trust's twenty five year anniversary in November.

The Olaudah Trust was set up in the 1990s by Mike Trent, a geologist exploring for minerals in Sudan. When oil was discovered in Unity Province he stayed on for several

---

[2] *The Interesting Narrative of the Life of Olaudah Equiano. Or Gustavus Vassa, The African,* Written By Himself, A Public Domain Book, London 1789

months mapping the whole area. Many of the families in Khartoum had servants who were Dinka and Nuba peoples and he realised they were captured in southern Sudan and brought down the Nile to the capital. The name comes from Equiano Olaudah, a freed African slave, who wrote for the nineteenth century abolitionist movement. Mike has been frustrated that the Trust has not been able to achieve much because of the constant fighting between southern rebels and the Sudanese government. Sadly Mike was diagnosed with cancer two years ago and Andy, a government policy maker looking for a change, was appointed.

The underground spews me out at Elephant and Castle. The rain is heavy as I walk down the Walworth Road, past the shops and Burgess Park. The Trust has offices in a Georgian house, once the home of a wealthy merchant but now owned by a charity working with the homeless, who let us have two rooms on the top floor. One is large enough to fit four desks, for me, Paul, my fellow field worker, and Ellie, Andy's personal assistant. The fourth desk is for interns, who join us in the summer months. There is a small park in centre of the square, where spring bulbs are beginning to show through the soil, their sheath-like leaves spattered with mud thrown up by the raindrops. I shake the rain off my coat as I enter and push a hand through my hair.

'Hi Ellie, had a good weekend?' Ellie must have come through the rain as well but her long brown hair is smooth and tidy, her angular face alert and smiling. She is as meticulous in her work as she is in her appearance.

'Hi Jane, how was Juba?'

'Very hot and slightly scary but the conference was

worthwhile and we had a good trip to Nimule. Is Andy in yet?'

'Not yet, and Paul's popped out to get some milk.'

I hang my soaked jacket and settle down to catch up on emails. Our window looks out onto the street and I watch the rain drip steadily off the slate roofs of the houses opposite into the lead gutters and think longingly of the warmth and sunshine of South Sudan. Paul enters the building and we hear him coming up the stairs.

'Hi Jane, welcome back, good trip?' He is younger than me, with three small children; lean and muscular, he probably biked here, even in the rain.

'Yes, fine thanks. Have I missed much?'

'The pressure's mounting on the anniversary event but otherwise all good.'

We work companionably until there is a crash on the stairs and the door flies open. Andy bursts through trailing wet garments and an umbrella in one hand, and clutching an overstuffed laptop bag in the other. He is a large man, with sandy hair and a full beard trimmed to an acceptable limit between wild eccentricity and individuality. He is overweight, which combined with his height gives a shambling lackadaisical impression but the blue eyes above the plump cheeks are sharp and purposeful. He is an affable man but there is an ambition beneath the laid back outward appearance that chafes against slow progress. On the rare occasions when he mentions his family they all seem to be solicitors and accountants and I wonder what made him take a different route.

'Morning all,' he says. 'Jane, give me ten minutes to log on and then we need to talk.' He passes through our area to his small office. Paul, Ellie and I exchange glances.

'You in trouble, Jane?' murmurs Paul.

'No I'm not, but he's asked me to go to Bristol this week and he knows I'm not keen.'

'Bristol? That's new.'

I finish an email to Pamela thanking her for arranging the meeting with the bishop and then pick up my tablet and poke my head round Andy's door. His desk just fits against the wall leaving room for a couple of battered armchairs on either side of the window overlooking the square.

'Come in, Jane, shut the door and take a seat, you had a good journey back?'

'Yes, not bad, I had an elbow jabber in the seat next to me but otherwise OK.' He gestures for me to sit down in one of the arm chairs while he remains at his desk, making me feel at a disadvantage in the lower chair.

'Jane... Bristol?'

'Andy, I really don't think it is necessary. There is plenty of material here I can use.'

'This isn't about the Record Office' he explains. 'Have you heard me mention David Hamilton? He is a friend of Mike's and a generous donor. Now he wants to do more.' Andy leans forward on the desk, his eyes narrowing as he holds my gaze by the intensity of his own.

'He wants to give us a house in Bristol. He rang me last

week. He'd like us to go down as soon as possible to have a look.'

'Why me? Why not you or Paul?'

'I'm in meetings with potential funders all week. Paul has a heavy caseload. Jane, you've been telling me for months we need a safe house for trafficked women, this could be it! Just keep him sweet till I can meet with him and don't mention it to the others. Ellie is making an appointment for you with the Record Office, let them think that's why you're going.'

Ellie and Paul are incredulous.

'You can access the Bristol slave records online, why do you have to go there?' queries Paul as we stand in the galley getting drinks.

'I'm to meet a Mr Rory Odhiambo tomorrow afternoon.'

'Something going on,' mutters Paul, as he picks up his coffee and returns to his desk while I stand with a glass of water staring out of the window at the rain and wondering how I let Andy's piercing hazel eyes persuade me to take this on.

I deal with the most pressing of my backlog of emails and go home to pack my bag again. By four in the afternoon I'm on the Great West Road making good time to the M4 before it gets congested. The rain is falling heavily and the windscreen wipers on my ancient Fiesta labour to keep up. The monotony of the route and the rush to get ready earlier in the day are catching up on me. I push on, fighting fatigue by playing jazz music on the radio. I'm staying in the suburbs of south Bristol and it is going to be difficult to find the place. I feel a flood of self pity well up inside me. How did I end up like this? My parents are both lawyers and assumed that I would follow them on the same path through endless exams and placements until I qualified. But I knew I could never do that. My dad was brought up in Kenya. When I was a child I loved to hear him talking with my grandfather about the Great Rift Valley, watching hippos in Lake Victoria and, when Dad was in his early teens, climbing Mount Kenya. I must have inherited some of my grandfather's wanderlust. I did an internship with the Trust one summer and stayed on. I never thought I would still be in the job ten years later. I suppose I had a vague idea that I would build up my career and then marry and have a family, but how and who? I have tried to explain to Mum that I want to marry but it must be to someone who can accept my travel and the work I do. She does not understand me and it has become a taboo subject between us.

The rain is easing as I follow my elderly Sat Nav's directions through central Bristol and onto the Bedminster Road. I park at the back of the South Bristol Bed and Breakfast where a plump lady greets me and introduces herself as Mrs. Jackson. She has dyed blond hair cut in a wavy bouffant style. Traces of a Somerset accent are overlaid by clipped and deliberate annunciation which gives her voice the strangulated tones of a pilot handling a difficult take-off. Her brown dress sculpts over her ample curves and the hem undulates as the jersey fabric eases and stretches. Her bust is pronounced and adorned by a necklace of beads in the curious brown, black and gold stripes of tiger's eye. Her smile is wide and friendly but the grey eyes are two swivelling daggers, swift and furtive. A list of house rules is posted over the desk in the hallway adjacent to the mirror. After an effusive welcome she insists that I read and sign a copy:

- No smoking indoors
- No noise after 11pm or before 7am
- Wet shoes to be removed in the entrance porch
- No mobile phones in the breakfast room
- No pets
- Rooms vacated by 10am
- Cars left in car park at owner's risk
- Additional guests must be checked in
- Hot bath £1 extra

It doesn't sound very welcoming but Mrs. Jackson is pleasant, and sympathetic about the traffic.

'Now you unpack, dear and you'll find a nice cup of tea and a cake in the breakfast room.'

'I'm afraid I don't drink tea, Mrs. Jackson.'

'How about a cola or lemonade? My other lady and the two gentlemen are just finishing.'

I hadn't expected to meet other residents but the thought of a cola is welcome so I hastily unpack and make my way to a pleasant room with a large bay window curtained in flowered chintz, and chat as best I can until it is time for bed.

....

I sleep surprisingly well despite the busy traffic on the main road outside my window. The decor is loud and intrusive, red curtains with matching lightshades and buttermilk yellow walls, but the bed is comfortable. When I open the curtains sunlight is sparkling on the damp pavements and glinting off the windows of the nineteen thirties semis opposite.

I'm meeting David Hamilton at his office near Temple Meads station at ten. I decide to walk following a footpath along the Malago, which is little more than a scruffy stream. It's cold in spite of the pale sunshine but the air smells soft and fragrant. Terraced houses line the path, and on steep grassy banks small early daffodils are already opening their flowers.

Hamilton Insurance Ltd occupies an impressive mirror-glassed office block, which slopes outwards at the base, giving me slight vertigo. I negotiate the revolving door, cross the marble floor feeling sea sick and clutch the front desk, my sweaty palms marking the smooth surface.

'Good morning, I'm Jane Taverner; I have an appointment with Mr. Hamilton.'

'Take a seat please and someone will show you up.' The black suited receptionist indicates an area by the windows. I sit on a leather covered sofa and flick through the pages of a magazine called "Hamilton Investment Monthly". There are pages of small print, tables and charts interspersed with photographs of smart offices. Why does the boss of all this want to help the Olaudah Trust?

'Hello, I'm Sophia. Mr. Hamilton will see you now.' A small woman with blond hair wearing a straight black skirt and white satin blouse shakes my hand briefly and moves rapidly to a glass gate at the back of the hall, heels clacking loudly on the hard floor. I follow her into the lift and we rise to the top floor in silence; a black suited mandarin and a creature of the African bush at a loss to know how to address each other.

'This way please. Have you travelled far?' Without waiting for an answer she heads down the corridor her heels making a line of faint hollows in the carpet.

'I came from London last night.' I respond but she is already tapping lightly on a door with an engraved sign saying "Chief Executive".

'Miss Taverner for you, Mr. Hamilton.' And she is gone, closing the door firmly behind her.

David Hamilton is of average height, with iron grey hair thinning on top. He has a razored cut that contrasts oddly with his wide, puffy cheeks. Hazel eyes, a small neat nose and thin lips are set in a broad face with a pale brow. He is not a handsome man and the slight paunch and fleshy hands suggest that he is not a particularly fit one but there is a latent energy about him that reminds me of a leopard I once saw stretched along a tree branch, satiated and relaxed but ready to leap in an instant.

'Good morning, Jane, thank you for coming, I gather you have just returned from Juba. Was it a useful trip?' His handshake is light but firm, the eyes cool and appraising.

'Yes, Andy and I attended a conference on the protection of children.'

'Good work, but not I think a high priority for the Juba government?'

'No, winning the tribal conflict seems to be the main concern.'

'Andy has explained the position?'

'Yes, briefly; you have a house available, which you are

considering offering to us.'

'In essence, yes. Would you like a tea or coffee before we start?'

'Tea, please.' I dislike both tea and coffee but sometimes it's diplomatic to accept. He presses a button on the desk, gives an order and then stares ahead, hands in front, palms facing each other and fingers pressed tightly together.

'I own Avon View House in Leigh Woods to the east of Bristol. It has been in my family for several generations. When my wife and I returned from Nairobi we built our own home in the grounds.' I suppress a gasp; this is clearly a larger property than the terraced houses I passed as I walked in this morning.

'No-one in the family is in a position to maintain the old house but we don't want it to pass out of our ownership. We would like to lease it to the Olaudah Trust for a peppercorn rent. I understand from Andy that you need a hostel?' The quality of intensity that struck me initially increases – the ears of the leopard are alert, scanning for the slightest sound.

'Yes, we have a number of women who have been trafficked from central Africa and forced to work as prostitutes or in the film industry. They are deeply traumatised and have no papers and little education. We have to place them in bed and breakfast accommodation in London while we sort out documents for them and provide them with basic training. This can involve legal proceedings and take many months. We have a smaller number of men who have been in forced labour. It's becoming increasingly difficult to arrange accommodation.' I pause as Sophia enters with a tray laden with china cups and saucers and tiny shortbread biscuits, and hands them round. David Hamilton's eyes have not left my face the whole time I have been speaking but it is impossible to gauge his reaction. I hope I'm making a good impression.

'The house needs substantial renovation.' he says, 'A family member has offered a small grant but the Trust would need to find funds to complete the work.'

'I will report to Andy and the trustees who will make the decision about whether this is something we can take on. I would need to see the property, Mr. Hamilton, in order to assess whether it would be viable for us to convert into a hostel.'

'How many people do you need accommodation for?'

'It varies, depending on the referrals we get from the Salvation Army and Social Services. We currently have six young women and two men. The maximum I've known is last summer when we had seven women and three men.'

His eyes consider me over the desk top. I feel the power of his personality probing into the depths of mine. He springs to his feet and goes to the window leaning against the sill and gazing out. I know that he is weighing up whether to go ahead with his offer of the house. Will he trust me? He turns decisively and returns to the desk.

'It's unfortunate that Andy isn't able to be here.' I open my mouth to reiterate Andy's emailed apology but he flattens his hand and spreads the short fat fingers to pre-empt me. 'But you have explained the need very clearly; I suggest that we arrange for you to view the house.' He is about to press the buzzer again but there were one or two things I need to clear up.

'Mr. Hamilton I'd like to understand more fully your reasons for leasing the house and why you have approached the Olaudah Trust.'

'I've already given my reasons. It is surplus to requirements but must stay in the family.' His eyes as they lock into mine are firm and direct. I can feel my palms sweating. He continues:

'I met Mike Trent in Kenya some years ago. My wife is from northern Uganda and we were concerned about children in her home village being abducted by the Lord's Resistance Army. They were being brutalised and forced to fight; young girls taken as "wives" for the leaders. Mike and the Olaudah Trust worked with us to help keep these children safe. We were forced by family circumstances to return here five years ago. We hope that Avon View House will be a way of continuing to support the work of the Trust.'

'It's a very generous offer, Mr. Hamilton, and we are grateful that you have considered us.'

'We'll discuss the matter further when you've seen the building.' He presses the buzzer and I'm fearful that I have already undermined his goodwill.

'Thank you for seeing me, Mr. Hamilton.' We shake hands and the inscrutable Sophia escorts me out. She consults a diary in her phone and allocates a time of two the following afternoon, giving me the address and postcode.

'Have you worked for Mr. Hamilton for a long time?' I ask as we go down in the lift.

'Five years. He's a good boss,' she volunteers. 'Tough but fair.' She sees me back through the glass gate.

'Enjoy your day,' she says but there is no indication that she means it as she turns back towards the lift and I wonder what it would be like to work in these polished, impersonal offices. I cross the foyer feeling discouraged and am spun through the revolving door and deposited onto the chilly pavement.

I buy lunch at a corner café and dial Andy's mobile.

'Hi Jane, make it quick, I'm about to go into a meeting.'

'I've met with David Hamilton; quite tricky. How well do you know him?'

'He's supported the Trust with regular donations for years; I've met him at supporter's events – that's about it.'

'Well I'm going to the house tomorrow. It's on the outskirts of Bristol and sounds a big place. How much do we want to take on?'

'Look, Jane, don't worry about that for now; just take some photos and write a report for the Trustees; I'll take it from there. Why was it tricky?'

'He was pleasant but I think a little put out that you could not be there. I did my best to show appreciation. The Hamilton Investment office is an impressive set-up.'

'Keep your cool and collect the facts. Don't make any commitments. I've got to go.'

'OK, bye.' But he is already gone and I drink my cola slowly and wonder if Andy has thought this through. It could mean a move to Bristol. I doubt if the Trust could afford to run an office in London and a hostel in Bristol. Has Andy deliberately sent me to meet David Hamilton because he does not want to get involved at this stage? My hands clench about the glass and I stare vacantly ahead.

'Is everything alright?' The man behind the counter catches my eye.

'Oh I'm sorry, just thinking. Can you tell me where Temple Meads wharf is?' Ellie has told me the easiest way to the Record Office from here is by water taxi. I finish my sandwich, locate the wharf and sit under a harbour side shelter looking at the high rise offices of banks, insurance companies and accountancy firms on either side of the water.

When the ferry docks I avoid the stuffy cabin and sit on the benches around the deck along with a family party on a day out. We leave the new offices behind and pass between the cliff-like frontages of former warehouses. A high stone wall encloses the waterway, with glimpses of a derelict church beyond. Brightly lit canopies shelter riverside restaurants and boats converted into bars.

As we move into a more open stretch of water the children point excitedly at four cranes higher than a church tower ranged alongside a building labeled the 'M Shed'. I gaze at the SS Great Britain in dry dock nearby and the retired warships, converted barges, and dilapidated cargo vessels lining the quayside. The sunlight catches a row of brightly painted terrace houses on the hillside above, and beyond are stretches of green countryside. At the end of the expanse of water two red brick warehouses dominate the skyline; one of these, according to my research last night is B Bond depository, which holds the Bristol Record Office.

The boat ties up at Hotwells Wharf and I follow others out onto a cobbled street.

The lobby of the renovated depository contains an overloaded bike rack. Inside there is a busy traffic of pushchairs, wheelchairs and family parties visiting the "Create Centre" display. To my right is a modest cafe whose customers are overflowing onto chairs and tables in the entrance hall. On the left signs indicate "Toilets" and "Record Office". I turn my back on the café, pass down a slight ramp and continue through a hallway to the Search Room, a panelled room with massive concrete pillars down the centre. A poster showing "Brunel's Clifton Suspension Bridge" hangs between two arched windows. The skeletal branches of sycamore trees dance and shiver outside, deflecting the sight and sound of traffic streaming past on the dual carriageway. In this towering depository twenty-first century life dare not intrude on the quiet atmosphere of accumulated knowledge.

I wait at a chest high reception desk. A dark skinned, loose-limbed man with a long nose set in a thin face appears. His hair is razored at the sides but dark and curling on top and he has a neat goatee beard. His mouth is wide but his lips are pressed together giving his face a lean unhappy look. He keeps his arms pinioned firmly to his sides.

'Good afternoon, you must be Miss Taverner. Rory Odhiambo. I hope you parked legally? We've very little space.' His voice sounds clipped and strained.

'I came by water taxi.'

'Ah, good. Before we start I must ask you to leave your bag and coat in the lockers outside. Only pencils may be used in here; pens are not allowed.' I go out again, feeling slightly humiliated, and when I return he is hidden behind the reception desk engrossed in a computer screen. I lean forward over the counter.

'Ah.' He stares fixedly at me, apparently trying to recall who I am. Then he becomes business-like again.

'Errm, I understand you're looking for material on the trade of Bristol in the eighteenth century? Can you tell me precisely what you interested in? We hold many different sources.'

'We want to produce three panels for the Olaudah Trust twenty fifth anniversary in November, one showing how slaves were brought to England in the eighteenth century, the second showing how the transatlantic slave trade was abolished in the nineteenth century and the third showing how slavery continues today and what we do to prevent it. My colleagues in London are working on the second and third panels. I am looking for suitable images for the first one and permission to take copies for public display.'

'Well we have several archives that may help you – records of the families who lived here, such as the Smyths at Long Ashton; we have the company reports of Bristol businesses; and the ship muster rolls –lists of people on each ship as it left and returned to harbour.'

'Will they include the number of slaves on board?'

'They will show how many are on board for the first and last leg of the journey but not for the middle passage across the Atlantic. You may log onto one of our computers or you can access our open Wi-Fi "B free".' I look at his face to see if this is a joke but Mr. Odhiambo clearly disapproves of this frivolous appropriation of the B bond warehouse address.

'If you want to copy or photograph anything here is the list of charges, and the guidelines for using the Search Room,' he continues, handing two sheets of paper to me. 'If you wish to use material for publication you must notify us and further charges must be met.' His face is stern.

'I'd also like to find out if there are any records for a Victorian house called "Avon View" and a family called Hamilton,' I say.

'When you log in there is a search function. Here.' He brings it up on his screen and types in "Hamilton". A list appears and he explains how I must fill in a form to request the records I want.

'Thank you.'

'I'll show you to a desk,' he says. I had hoped for more help than this. He seems very unfriendly.

I look at the other researchers near me, listening to subdued scribbling as one occupant takes notes in pencil; another is making a list on the back of an envelope. I open my tablet, log on and bring up a screen listing thousands of ships, with scanned images of original documents in illegible writing. I find a painting of the *Juba*, which sailed in 1787, collected over two hundred slaves in West Africa, sold those who survived the thirteen week passage across the Atlantic, sailed back towards Bristol and sank in the Irish Sea. In spite this disaster the voyage was profitable due to the amount paid for slaves in the Caribbean.

After a while studying the lists I glance up to see Mr.

Odhiambo staring at me fiercely, brows drawn together. What am I doing wrong? I am not using a pen or making a noise. I raise my eyebrows inquiringly and he looks down at his computer screen again.

I scan the collection in search of the Hamilton family but find nothing relevant. I catch Mr. Odhiambo observing me again. Does he do this to everyone or is it something about me? I save the notes I have made and go to reclaim my bag and coat.

'Miss Taverner?' A different archivist raises her head as I pass the reception desk. 'Mr. Odhiambo left a package for you.'

'Thank you,' I say, hoping it is nothing unpleasant. I place the pack of photocopied documents in my leather messenger bag. I bought this bag in Entebbe a few years ago and it is a prized possession, made of cowhide with Luo tribal markings punched into the edges of the flap and substantial metal buckles. It lacks the finesse of Italian leather but has developed a glossy brown sheen that reminds me of the dirt roads and animal smells of East and Central Africa. I put the strap over my head; I can feel the weight of Mr. Odhiambo's package as it rests against my thigh.

I walk over the bridge, through Grenville Smyth Park and cross Ashton Road; the white metal grandstand of Ashton Stadium is visible in the moonlight. The Smyth family were obviously major benefactors of this part of Bristol. I stop for a pizza and hope, as I climb the hill and turn out into the main road, that Mrs. Jackson will be offering soft drinks and cake again.

The neat bay windows of the South Bristol Bed and

Breakfast are obscured by the flashing blue lights of two police cars. Mrs. Jackson, vibrant in a deep pink jersey dress and matching beads is standing, left arm on her hip and right hand raised to shield her eyes. She is watching two dark figures being brought out of the house next door handcuffed and held firmly by a policeman on each side. They are bundled into one of the cars and the door is firmly closed as I reach Mrs. Jackson.

'Well!' she exclaims. 'I always said there was something not right about those two. This is a respectable neighbourhood.'

'What have they done?'

'Drugs. My other half heard talk in the pub. He's a builder,' she explains, 'knows all the locals. Now dear, tea and a piece of cake?'

Later in the evening I open the package from Mr. Odhiambo and lay the papers out on the bed. One is a letter dated 1796 and barely legible, from a Mr. George Hamilton of Orchard Street to Rogers and Co threatening legal action if the sums owed to him following the return to port of the merchant ship *Phoenix* are not paid immediately. The second is a newspaper article from the Western Daily Press dated 1891 and referring to Avon Banking House, director Mr. David Hamilton, and the growth of new businesses in Bristol. Then there is a folded A3 sheet of photocopies of dance programmes, photographs and concert notes all at Avon View House at various dates in the nineteen twenties. Finally there is a scrawled note:

'My colleague, Matt Williamson, has recently completed research into Bristol families for an exhibition which will tour the Bristol public libraries. He has pieced together a history of the Hamilton family from the sixteenth century to the present with the help of Anka Hamilton, who still lives in Bristol. If you can come tomorrow after three he will be able to tell you more. With best wishes, Rory Odhiambo'

I stare down at the barely legible photocopied fragments of the past in amazement. Mr. Odhiambo was curt, verging on rude, and I had dismissed him from my thoughts. Now I am looking at tantalising evidence of real lives and my thoughts start to race. Who is Anka Hamilton? Could we use the Hamilton's story in our panels? I hear Andy's mellow voice saying

'Keep your cool and collect the facts. Don't make any commitments.' I must visit the house and take one step at a time. I could ring the Record Office and ask to meet Matt Williamson on Thursday. It would delay my return to London but might give me a fuller picture. I want to find out more even if it means staying in Bristol another day.

3 FAMILY SECRETS

Colonial slavery shaped modern Britain and we all still live with its legacies. The slave-owners were one very important means by which the fruits of slavery were transmitted to metropolitan Britain.[3]

What an astonishing sight – the Avon Gorge! In the middle of Clifton village in north Bristol a deep chasm, carved through limestone and red sandstone by ancient rivers, cuts through the suburb like the lash of a whip, coiling and turning, separating the early port from the twentieth century container docks just visible at Portishead. How the city's merchants must have watched here for their ships to round the corner on the high tide and sail into the quiet waters of Bristol harbour.

I return to my car, set the Sat Nav and follow it into Church Road, a private world of Edwardian elegance on the edge of Leigh Woods, built around the quintessentially Victorian parish church of St Mary's. I follow a sharp bend

---

[3] *Legacies of British Slave Ownership* https://www.ucl.ac.uk/lbs/

into Sandy Lane and come to two brick pillars labelled 'Avon View House'; but the high wooden gates are closed and barred. There is a second entrance beyond where a gap between low sculpted bushes leads to a wide gravelled drive sweeping between well-kept lawns. The land drops to banks of rhododendrons on my right and rises steeply to a line of trees on my left. The drive curves and the house comes into view - a startling contrast to its neighbours – a contemporary structure of glass and steel, one end soaring across the bank of rhododendrons, the other disappearing into the sloping hillside. I pull up opposite a front porch roofed by a single slab of slate, supported by thin metal pillars. At one end water cascades through a narrow V-shaped notch into a pool below, at the other a white door set with orange and yellow glass opens and David Hamilton is extending a hand in greeting.

'Jane, I heard your car, you found us OK?'

'Yes, though I nearly turned into the wrong drive.'

'I should've warned you. Come in. Glycella, my wife, will be here shortly, my mother is coming over from the Coach House, and we'll have some coffee.' I follow him across a spacious sunlit hall to a reception room where three floor to ceiling windows look out onto lawns edged by shrubs. He is wearing chinos and an open necked shirt and looks more relaxed than when we met yesterday but he still has that latent leopard-like energy as he pads across the wooden floor in leather moccasins.

An elegant woman with very dark skin enters the room through a door at the far end.

'You must be Jane, I'm Glycella.' Her voice is strong and rich, like chocolate. She is taller than David, thin, and immaculately dressed in camel and red with a toning scarf. Her hair is straightened and held in a gold clasp at the nape of her neck. Her eyes are a deep liquid brown flecked with gold, set in a smooth forehead. She has the lithe compact movement of the supremely fit. She extends a manicured hand; I feel the coolness of her skin and regret my tendency to moist palms when stressed. But I smile, and behind her social poise I detect a touch of sardonic humour in her eyes.

'Thank you for inviting me here. This is an amazing house.'

Glycella bends her head in acknowledgement and gestures for me to sit on the wide leather sofa.

'I call the porch Glycella's folly,' comments David, 'It's her tribute to Murchison Falls near her homeland in Uganda.

A woman enters with a tray and places it on a large sturdy coffee table.

'Thank you, Agnes, will you join us?'

'No, thank you, Mrs. Hamilton, I'll be late picking my granddaughter up.'

Glycella pours the coffee into white china cups. They are square with solid handles and as she hands mine to me I struggle to balance cup on saucer without spilling the coffee. Thankfully I have no inclination to drink it so I place the cup safely on the glass coffee table. The door behind me opens and I turn to see an older woman enter the room. She is slightly stooped and using a stick. Her long white hair is caught in a bun high on the back of her head with soft pin curls somehow looped into it. She wears several necklaces and a brightly patterned scarf that drapes across the front of her suit and is caught into the hand holding the stick. She is an arresting figure, colourful, haughty and austere. David rises to help her but she waves him away and limps forward with careful dignity to an armchair by one of the windows. He greets her with a kiss and brings her a cup of coffee.

'Mother, this is Jane from the Olaudah Trust. My mother, Anna Katarina.' A suitable name for an exotic person I reflect as I rise to shake her hand. Full of years she is still beautiful with high cheek bones and slanting grey eyes. Her skin looks fragile with many fine lines but she is carefully made up and has the alert air of a bird.

'Good afternoon, Mrs. Hamilton.' I extend my hand and she holds it for a long moment looking at me carefully. I know she is sizing me up, seeing my nervousness, my sense of being out of my depth. I gaze back keeping my smile as steady as I can. She is clearly held in respect and affection by her high-powered son.

'Jane's come to see the old house, Mother; part of her job is to look after the young women the Olaudah Trust helps,' explains David.

'Ah yes, David has told me about the good work that you do.' She releases me and I return to the sofa, as she explains in decisive tones:

'Avon View House was my home until two years ago. David, Geoffrey and Isabelle were brought up there but it is too big so I've renovated the coachman's cottage. I'm near the family but have my own entrance,' she adds with a twinkle.

'You don't want to be too close to our two imps,' David laughs.

'Our sons are twelve and nine,' adds Glycella, 'and very mischievous!'

I smile politely, apart from Anna's Poppy my life is a child free zone and I find conversations that linger over children difficult. I'm here to find more about the house, so I ask:

'Does anyone live there at the moment?'

'No. Geoffrey, my brother, and his wife divorced three years ago and Geoffrey isn't in a position to keep on such a big place,' replies David. His mother is in my peripheral vision and I note the sudden down turn of her mouth when Geoffrey's name is mentioned. For a moment the tranquil grey eyes are troubled and her brows draw together in a fierce frown. David is continuing:

'Glycella and I built this home on part of the land when we came back from Kenya five years ago. None of us wish to live in the old house but we're looking for a way to bring the building back to life.'

Anna Katarina's expression is serene again as she adds:

'It was always a house of fun when David and the others were young, so many parties, concerts, events. We hope to see it used for good again.' Whatever troubled her has passed but there is a strange inflexion on the word "good" as though she was underlining it.

I feel uneasy; there are deep currents of emotion here that I do not understand and a sense of grief, unexpressed but visible in the shadows in the older Mrs. Hamilton's eyes. I look towards Glycella for clues but she seems unaffected.

'We appreciate your generosity in considering us for this gift,' I say, feeling that I must smooth an awkward moment, 'but the decision lies with the director and trustees and I will report fully to them.'

'Let's show you round before the light goes,' says Glycella. 'Anka, will you come with us?'

Anka – Anna Katarina Hamilton! It is David's mother who is helping the Record Office with the research into Bristol families.

'No dear, it's too chilly for me,' says the elder Mrs. Hamilton. 'I'll stay here.'

I follow David and Glycella out of a side door up a path curling through fruit trees to the top of the lawns, where it opens out onto a gravelled walk with a wide border full of daffodils. A curved brick wall winds in and out providing alternate shade and exposure for the leafless stems of roses and other climbers. At the near end of the wall is an octagonal brick summer house with a steeply tiled roof. The Hamiltons lead the way through a wrought iron gate next to it and along a narrow path through a shrubbery. The dense leaves shut out most of the light but I can make out the red brick wall of a substantial building through gaps in the canopy. We emerge onto a wide gravelled turning circle. It is muddy, colonised by grass and traversed by ruts and narrow tyre marks.

'We've had some trouble with boys on bikes,' explains David picking his way across the ruts. 'That's why we had to close and bar the main gates.' We turn to face the house and I'm dumbfounded. It's a three story building, red brick, mellow with age and encrusted in places with yellow lichen and marked by dark stains of damp. Pairs of sash windows on two floors flank a generous porch with a tiled roof supported by white painted columns and two stone steps to a double front door with a long narrow window above it. The roof is tiled in slate with five gable windows. On the left side an extensive wing juts forward, topped by a square tile-hung turret with casement windows and a weather vane in the shape of a ship's pennant on the pinnacle of the roof.

David leads the way up the steps and opens the front door with a shove, which leaves particles of paint pattering onto the stone floor. He and Glycella show me many rooms in this bewildering mansion, from the main bedrooms on the first floor to the small attic rooms where glimpses of the Avon Gorge are visible through the trees; from the high ceilinged ball room to small closets and pantries. I make notes, take photos and listen to their commentary; my brain struggling to absorb the layout, assess the potential and suppress my concern about how the Trust would manage something as magnificent and demanding as this.

We return down the wide main staircase with its solid oak banisters and carved uprights. The newel posts are shaped like ships' prows, sailing out onto the hall floor, which is tiled in brown and rust coloured squares; the centre piece is a compass design in black and white encircling a mosaic of sailing ships leaving a harbour.

'My ancestors made their fortune from merchant shipping,' comments David. 'By the time this house was built they had migrated into banking and insurance but my great grandfather liked the nautical connections and my father and grandfather saw no reason to change anything. Geoffrey had great plans ....' There is a quiet 'Tccch' behind me and I catch Glycella's down turned mouth and darkening eyes. It is clear she is not comfortable with the mention of "plans" within the family.

We emerge from the chill of the house into hazy sunlight. It is a warm day for the time of year with softness in the air that hints of spring. Bird song fills the garden and a pair of enthusiastic blue tits dive and swoop between the overhanging trees. I breathe deeply.

'What a beautiful place; it must have been wonderful to grow up here,' I say.

'Yes, it was in many ways but times have changed.' responds David. Glycella makes no comment but the speed with which she dives back into the shrubbery suggests that it would not be her choice of home and she leads us back into the landscaped and groomed lawns of the new Avon View House.

The older Mrs. Hamilton is still ensconced in the drawing room.

'Glycella wants to finalise some papers for tomorrow,' says David, 'and I've a call to make. We will leave you with my mother and she can fill you in on the story of the house.'

I sit down obediently, overwhelmed by thoughts and feelings; which jump between excitement and anxiety. I must stay calm and find out as much as I can.

'Well, my dear, it is a substantial prospect for you?'

'I don't know what to think, Mrs. Hamilton, I had no idea it would be as big. Is there no one in your family who can use it?'

'For many years it was the home of my eldest son and his

wife but they've divorced and Geoffrey has been forced to move away.' Something about the way she says this with an emphasis on the "forced" makes me wonder again what happened. 'When Geoffrey left David and Glycella returned from Kenya with their two boys but they had their own money and built the new house. If Geoffrey had stayed on he would have dealt with everything. I carried on for a while but it's too much for me. If the Trust took it on there would have to be some repairs. I believe David has some funds set aside but the rest would be your responsibility.'

'It must've been hard to move out of such a beautiful place.'

'I hated leaving. I came to the house with David's father, Gerrard, when I was in my early twenties. We lived in what had been the servants' quarters to begin with and then as Gerrard's parents, David's grandparents, became frailer we took over the main house; David, Geoffrey and Isabelle all had eighteenth birthday balls and we had a fundraising concert every Christmas.' I see her eyes twinkle and come alive with memories of the past.

'They were wonderful years,' she continues, 'but life is different now. Glycella has her own career as a family lawyer. They go back to Kenya and her family in northern Uganda in the holidays. Her grandfather was a chief and her family is still very powerful. They have their own lives and I am fortunate that I can stay where I have lived for so long and see my friends.'

'How does David's sister feel about the house?'

'Isabelle is happy to leave the matter to David. She and her family live in Gloucestershire and are well provided for.

My husband left each of the children money and David and Isabelle have invested wisely.' I daren't ask what happened to Geoffrey's money.

'Now tell me about your work and your plans for the future,' she continues.

'I have just returned from South Sudan where I was working with local bishops to identify where trafficking is taking place. I have a caseload of women who have been trafficked from Central Africa to the UK. Sometimes they've been taken into Arab families, and a handful are then brought to the west. Others are sold down the Nile to the Middle East. Numbers are small and we cannot support more than a handful at a time but their stories are helping us build a catalogue of evidence to show how the slave trade along the Nile operates. I am part of a group of organisations in central and east Africa working to eliminate slavery.'

'And how do you support these young women?'

'They're not all young, some of them have been enslaved for many years and are only able to seek help because the police receive a tip-off. We arrange trauma counselling and medical support, teach them skills that will provide them with legitimate work, and find somewhere for them to live until they become independent. At the moment we use hostels or bed and breakfast accommodation but it is becoming difficult to find spaces in London and often we are moving them repeatedly, which delays recovery and self-sufficiency. I've one woman who has been moved three times in the last four months.'

'You're looking for somewhere to provide a more permanent home?'

'Yes, if we had our own accommodation we could be more effective and they would find comfort and support from each other.' She nods and I carry on:

'It's the Trustees' decision of course. I've taken photographs and will explain to them your family's generous offer.'

'Well, my dear, I hope they feel able to take it on and make the house useful again. Now help me up please, I'd like to get home before it is dark.' She rises to her feet levering herself up with one hand pressed into the side of the chair. I stand beside her, an outstretched arm at the ready as she straightens up. Her chin juts out and her thin lips set hard with determination as she takes her stick and walks carefully across the room. I wonder how easy she will find it to allow the family home to become a hostel.

....

My phone rings at eight on Thursday morning just as I am packing my overnight bag.

'Hi Andy.'

'Hi Jane, how's it going?'

'Fine, I had a good meeting with the Hamiltons yesterday. I've taken photos of the house. I'll write it all up when I get back.'

'Right, I need you back here immediately; we've had a girl referred to us and she's in a bad way. She was originally from Uganda but the police brought her in following a raid in Camberwell. She has no papers. They want her picked up by midday.'

'Andy, I can't. One of the archivists at the Record Office is researching Bristol families and has some information on the house the Hamilton's are offering us. I've already had to reschedule the appointment to ten this morning. We don't want to offend the Records people in case we need permission to publish some of their documents.' I hold my breath while Andy weighs the matter. I already seem to be viewed with suspicion by Mr. Odhiambo, though I have no idea why, and to change arrangements again with his colleague would be unfortunate.

'OK, but get down there early and get straight on here as soon as you can,' urges my boss. 'You need to be picking up your caseload from Paul now,' finishes Andy and closes the call. There it is again, that constant drive that underlies Andy's laid back exterior. He is not an easy man to work with. I'm pleased I held my ground.

I hastily thrust the rest of my possessions into my bag. Mrs. Jackson is in the entrance hall as I come down the stairs. She is wearing lilac boucle jersey and a large crystal pendant which bobs to and fro on her bosom.

'Goodbye, Miss Taverner. We'll see you again?'

'Yes.' I reply, though I'm hoping that Ellie will arrange a cheap hotel if I have to come back.

There is a light drizzle as I drive to the B Bond warehouse, where thankfully there is a parking space. I wipe my feet in the entrance and choose my route carefully through the mass of wet bicycles and abandoned umbrellas. I have the papers from Mr. Odhiambo's package in my hand.

Matt Williamson is a pleasant man with a solid jaw and sandy coloured hair. He invites me into the small glass panelled room behind the reception desk, closes the door and opens up the large folder he has brought with him.

'Rory tells me you're interested in the history of the Hamilton family?' he says.

'Yes, and of Avon View House. The Hamiltons are offering the organisation I work for use of the house and I'm trying to find out as much as I can before I report to the Trustees. I met the family yesterday. I am grateful for any information you can give me.'

'Well, we have few complete histories of Bristol families except for the Smyth family at Ashton Court and the Pinney family. My research has involved piecing together as much as I can from our records about families who were influential in the eighteenth and nineteenth century development of the city. I've been able to find a number of papers on the Hamilton family and Anna Katarina Hamilton has helped in filling in the gaps and opening up new lines of enquiry.' He pauses.

'I met Mrs. Hamilton senior yesterday,' I confirm.

'As a result of her assistance,' he continues, 'we have a more complete record of the Hamiltons. There are still gaps and periods where the story is supposition rather than history but it has enabled me to pull together a brief summary, which, together with copies of the records, will go on display as part of our touring exhibition over the summer months.' I nod again. 'So, I have here,' he continues, 'a file containing photocopies of the evidence, with transcriptions and explanatory notes. Each record is labelled so that you can call up the original if you wish. At the end there is a brief history of the family and another for Avon View House.' I look at him and am at a loss for what to say. The meticulous detail of the folder in front of me means I don't need to spend more time here foraging through archives.

'It must have taken many hours to complete this.' I comment. There is a faint beading of sweat on the end of his nose and he rubs at it thoughtfully with the back of his index finger.

'It was helpful to have input from a relative. It showed me where I needed to look and Mrs. Hamilton gave me access to pictures and records which were being held in Avon View House at that time.'

'Where are they now?'

'After Mr. Geoffrey Hamilton was convicted they were moved to Bristol Museum and Art Gallery.'

I thank him and turn to the folder but my head is buzzing. Geoffrey Hamilton, convicted! Mr. Williamson conducts me to a desk and leaves me to look at the folder but I cannot do that yet. I turn on my tablet, log into the Wi-Fi and search "Hamilton Geoffrey conviction". A string of URLs pops up: *Geoffrey Hamilton of Leigh Woods sentenced to three years in prison for fraud and insider dealing; Bristol family fraud, Geoffrey Hamilton Chief Executive of Hamilton Investments one risk too far….; Judge passes severe sentence on defrauding financier.* The date is May 2010.

Five years ago David Hamilton's brother was sent to prison for fraud and ordered to pay a substantial fine. Five years ago David and Glycella came back from Kenya! I am staring blankly at the poster of the Avon Gorge just as Rory walks past the desk. His sour mouth is a thin line and a frown appears above the bridge of his narrow nose.

Quickly I look down and start to read the summary at the back of the folder Matt has given me, scanning it quickly. My hunch was right; in the eighteenth century the Hamiltons worked their way from being agents to owning their own ships. They held a plantation in Barbados, and when slavery was abolished in 1833 they received a substantial pay-out in compensation, which they used to build up a loans and insurance business. In effect they received a double portion – the wealth generated by their slaves and the compensation pay-out.

I go to the desk to get copies of what I need. Rory appears from the inner office and I thank him for arranging the meeting with Matt.

'You're very welcome. Please let us know if there is anything else we can do to help.' The contours of his face change dramatically as his mouth curves up under his narrow nose and the corners of his eyes crinkle. I can't help smiling in return.

What an extraordinary man. At first I thought he was the most unpleasant person I've ever met but he and Matt have given me more than I dared hope for. If Andy and the Trustees approve the proposal for Avon View House we could build our first panel for the anniversary around the story of the family.

And Rory Odhiambo has a very nice smile.

4 A CHILL WIND

Orchard Street: James McTaggart, sometime captain of the slaver, "Africa", built a house in this lovely street, which was first laid out in 1717.[4]

The house creaks and rustles as the chill March wind blows up the Avon and across the neglected garden, dividing around the red brick walls and streaming down the drive before eddying under the Clifton Suspension Bridge and into central Bristol.

Leaves, left uncleared, dry and curl, swirling about the walls looking for new places to hide. Cracked paint on the windows, once a sparkling white but now grey with mould, flakes under the savage onslaught. A section of guttering, broken free from its bracket, hangs from one screw, flapping against the wall with vindictive jabs, and the house shudders with each blow of iron on brick. In the

---

[4] *Slave Trade Trail around central Bristol*, Bristol Museums and Art Galleries 1998

once elegant ballroom a slab of plaster breaks off the wall and crashes into the fireplace, sending up a shower of dust over the wooden boards. The building shakes as tree branches, untrimmed for years and hanging low, chastise the roof tiles and drip moisture into cracks, opening them up to further damage. As the temperature falls ice forms, expanding and forcing masonry apart, and causing cracks to appear in the upper stories. The uncurtained windows look out over the rutted gravel with blind incomprehension. Water runs down the wall where a drainpipe leaks, leaving the damp mark of a tear rolling down the grimy frontage.

How could so much have changed? A century and a half ago the house was vibrant with new life, and dreams of a bright future. A young couple brought their coach and horses to a halt in front of the wide oak door and entered arm in arm.

'Welcome, my darling Grace, to your new home.'

'Oh Arthur, it is wonderful. How pleased I am to be out of those cramped rooms in Orchard Street.'

Their large family, eight children born in as many years ran along the corridors to the nursery, laughing and shouting as they whipped the wooden rocking horse to make it go faster. The house adapted to their needs as they grew up and was extended to include a ballroom and billiard room, modern plumbing, and Mr. Crapper's flushing toilet, one of the first houses in Bristol to have this luxury. The high ceilinged rooms resounded to the noise of weddings and parties as the children married. At the turn of the century the house embraced new fashions gaining a front porch and a veranda along the south facing windows of the drawing room.

Through the generations many Hamiltons enjoyed the spaciousness and comfort but left little mark on the fabric except one grandson of Grace and Arthur - Robert, an ebullient man with a love of the sea. The house nurtured him as it had many others but this one never grew up, moving with unruffled ease from the toys of the nursery to the yacht he kept moored at the fish quay in Portishead. He and his German wife, Olga, filled the house with their passions and to everyone's surprise she developed an interest in the very English hobby of garden design.

'Olga!'

'Yes, my sweet?'

'Hudson is designing a new staircase for us.'

'Robert, it looks just like two ships with balustrade and prow sailing out into the hall.'

'Yes, that is what I intended; and I have asked him to set a compass design into the hall tiles.'

'Robert, would Hudson be able to make me a gazebo at the end of that curvy wall, so that I can design the planting for the long border and for an orchard? And Robert, I think it would be wonderful if we had a fountain in the centre of the drive!'

During the early twentieth century the house basked in their lavish hospitality: rooms were filled with flowers, curtains and drapes constantly updated in the latest style. Young men and women arrived for house parties in open topped automobiles, which tossed gravel against the porch walls as they swept round the fountain and braked abruptly to the squeals of their female companions. Those were frivolous times brought to an end too quickly by war. Curtains faded and were not replaced, servants left and there was no coal for the basement boiler. Local businesses folded as clients withdrew their custom; Hamilton Insurance hit hard times and money was scarce. The ballroom wing was closed and the servants' rooms on the second floor became storage areas for the debris of past generations. The house was requisitioned as accommodation for nurses working at the hospital based in Ashton Court and the family moved back to the Georgian property in Orchard Street.

When Armistice was declared the house sank into neglect. The only sounds in the corridors were the eldritch memories of the past, held captive in the brickwork, caught in the moonlight on a clear night, or chattering in the drafts that eddied through the empty rooms.

House and garden slumbered through the lean years of the Depression, rousing briefly in 1940 when the War Office held it as a transit camp for wounded soldiers, then collapsing back into dilapidation as a triumphant nation faced the reality of too many mouths to feed, too little work for returning soldiers, inadequate housing and elderly people left frail and neglected. But all was not lost, Robert's only surviving grandson, Gerrard, returning unscathed from flying spitfires, went late to university and met a wealthy young Finn of Russian extraction, Anna Katarina, whom he brought back to Bristol when he finished his degree. They married in 1951 and joined Gerrard's parents, Charles and Isabelle, and grandfather, Robert, in the narrow town house in Orchard Street.

One fine day in 1952 Robert, Charles and Gerrard penetrated the overhung drive of Avon View House in a battered Daimler, pulled up in front of the roofless porch and made a thorough inspection.

'It's a bit neglected, but nothing that a lick of paint and some new tiles wouldn't correct.' said the ever optimistic Robert, waving the stick that he now leaned on heavily and nearly losing his footing on the rutted gravel.

'There's been damp penetration in the floor boards,' muttered Charles, prodding the floor with a brass topped walking stick he had picked up out of the ceramic umbrella stand in the hall and staring at the jagged hole he had made.

'They've bashed my boats!' Robert cried indignantly, running a trembling hand over the ships' prows at the end of the staircase, inevitably vulnerable to damage from people passing in a hurry.

Young Gerrard stood silent, gazing in awe at the cavernous hall, the dirty but still visible compass mosaic in the floor and the elegant sash windows, drawing light into the room in spite of the overhanging branches outside. He had never lived here, knew only the cramped quarters of Orchard Street, and was visibly shuddering at the scale of the work needed but the house wrapped warm brick walls around him and gave him space to breathe beneath the high plaster ceilings, damaged but still beautiful. He made his way up the staircase, treading carefully to avoid rotten steps. Sash windows at either end of the long corridor lit the motes of dust rising from the wooden boards and with them the fleeting touch of ancestral memories were loosed. Wooden skirting boards, their characteristic double curve pockmarked by the careless passage of heavy boots entranced him and whispered that this was where he and Anka should bring up their children.

A plan was made and the house endured a maelstrom of activity as damp floorboards were lifted and replaced, damaged skirtings patched and painted, leaking roof tiles realigned and the whole of the main building painted and refurbished. The wing would have to be left till later. On a bright May morning in 1955 the family came home, Robert frail now but elated to see his precious house revived, Charles and Isabelle relieved that the work was finished, the bills paid, and that the resurgence of the insurance business had covered the costs.

'Now you will be my princess,' promised Gerrard as he swung his young wife over the threshold and placed her gently at the foot of the stairs. And so it was, the house entwined itself around Anka's heart, and the garden welcomed her into its arms and there grew such a close bond between mistress and mansion that it became impossible to tell what was Anka's own creativity and what was the house stimulating her imagination. Either way there was a sense of jubilation as once again the rooms and corridors filled with voices.

Opening the house absorbed all Anka's energy for a while; the parties she and Gerrard gave in the sixties were renowned; bringing in rock stars and television celebrities, they filled the downstairs rooms with music and dancing. The neglect of previous decades was forgotten and the house basked in the warmth of thronging crowds, groundbreaking music and fine dining. At last new young lives arrived with the birth of David and Geoffrey in the early sixties, and the upstairs floors rang to the sound of their infant voices chirruping along the corridors and chasing their pet dog in and out of the bedrooms. Four years later chubby Isabella stomped determinedly after them.

'I want to play.'

'You're too young.'

'I want to,' and she would set up a wail that summoned Nanny to take her back to the nursery.

Life settled into the pleasant pattern of earlier decades. Robert, Charles and Isabella in their turn joined the row of ancestors in the church graveyard. Children played, grew, married and left, David for Nairobi and Isabella for nearby Gloucester. Geoffrey stayed on, married to Estelle and with three children. Now it was the turn of Gerrard and Anka to make way for the young family. The insurance business had boomed under Gerrard's cautious management and Geoffrey's innovative flair. The ballroom was renovated and the billiard room and floors above converted into a separate apartment for Gerrard and Anka, giving Geoffrey's three boys the run of the main house; until disaster struck.

The house sighs as an erratic gust of wind sucks air out through the cracked windows. Memories of the happy home of the post-war decades disappeared in a single phone call that dreadful day in 2010 when Estelle, picking up the receiver on her way through the hall, was asked by investigating police when her husband would return. He came by taxi from the station half an hour later and was intercepted on the drive and arrested for fraud. He was not allowed into the house, either to say goodbye, or to pack belongings, and left a distraught Estelle sobbing on the porch steps. Even when Geoffrey returned on bail she was inconsolable and it was Gerrard and Anka who worked out a rescue plan. They contacted David and Glycella in Nairobi and, once sentence was pronounced, brought Geoffrey to see that he had little option but to sell out to his elder brother to raise funds to pay his fine and the reparations due to the business. Only the house witnessed what happened the day that Gerrard collapsed, his heart overloaded by the worry of rescuing the business and maintaining some sort of stability for Estelle and the children. He was found stretched out on the sofa in the former billiard room, now an elegant lounge, one hand clutched to his chest, the other gripping tightly to the window sill as though somehow the building could give him strength to carry on.

David and Glycella, snatched from busy and fulfilled lives in Nairobi, struggled. There were not enough hours in the day to settle their boys in new schools, carry out all that needed doing in the house and rescue the business after Geoffrey's mismanagement. They were battered by Estelle's incessant demands. Though comfortably settled in a modern home nearby she continued to regard the house as her own and to help herself to any item she needed. It was Anka who finally brought things to a head.

'This is no good for the family,' she announced one day, her voice heavily accented, lilting, but with an edge of the icy tundra where she had been brought up.

'David, your wife needs her own space and I am too old to cope with this draughty house. I shall go to the Coach House.'

She used her own inheritance for the refurbishment and moved there within six months. David and Glycella held lengthy discussions but eventually decided to build their own home in the area beyond the orchard and what had once been a sheltered kitchen garden. A year later they too moved out and in January 2012 the house was empty and neglected.

'What are you going to do?' asked Anka, seeing the home where she had brought up her children abandoned.

'Once we have built our own house we will make a plan,' said her son. Glycella said nothing but the amber light in her eyes flashed dangerously. There was no quintessentially English mansion in her family background. The photograph in her wallet was of her grandfather in a chief's headdress and her childhood memories were of a substantial modern home in a gated estate on the outskirts of Kampala. The leaf buds were forming on the apple trees in the orchard and the thorny stems of the rose bushes were beginning to swell but the essence of England, which Gerrard had flown his plane to defend, was not part of her DNA. The oak front door of the house slammed shut and the shockwave reverberated along the corridors and through the rafters.

Decay set in once more as the rot soaked into the floorboards, mould grew in deserted bedrooms and damp leaves accumulated at the base of the walls. Only in summer was there any life as three boys cycled up the drive, tentatively at first and then more boldly. One of them was a familiar face: Robert Hamilton, Geoffrey's eldest son, brought up to think he would one day own all this, now clinging onto his dream through assurances to his three friends that it belonged to the Hamiltons. They dug trenches in the drive and built ramps and ditches to run their bicycles over. They collapsed under the trees when it was too hot to cycle and rolled tobacco and cocaine, purchased by Robert's mother for her own use and purloined by him from her bedroom. They lay in a dreamy bundle on the grass unaware of the powerful oversight of the once grand house. Only the youngest, Camarg, seemed sensitive to the atmosphere of his surroundings, gazing up at the windows with wide eyes, following the movements of the invisible figures that had once danced across the ballroom floor or sat under the elegant veranda.

'Who lived here?' he asked one day.

'My great great great great grandfather built this house,' Robert announced. 'My family have always lived here, except during the war.'

'Why don't you live here now?' asked Paul, his other companion.

'Oh, my Dad's away and my Mum wanted somewhere more modern. Mum says we'll come back here when Dad's back.'

The house shudders as a strong gust shakes the chimneys and rattles the tree branches against the windows. For three years now it has withstood the onslaught of wind and rain, while the lives of the family are too full to address its growing problems. There is a leak in the chimney breast on the wall facing the orchard. Last summer the boys broke a pane of glass in the verandah while playing cricket and water drips steadily from the roof onto the floor, rotting the base of the drawing room windows. The fountain in the centre of the drive is blocked but the water has not been turned off and so it oozes steadily making the top part of the drive a quagmire.

The building needs people but only Anka comes to the old gazebo between the fruit walk and the wall of the kitchen garden to sit and watch the birds sheltering in the shrubbery. Neglect never endured before. The red brick walls and tiled roof are strong. The house waits patiently, ready to welcome whoever needs its spaciousness, and the enchantment of its position in the woods above the Avon Gorge.

5 NINA AND MARIA

The Salvation Army is a First Responder, which means that we can make referrals....... and offer support to those that have already been referred by another agency.[5]

Clear conditions and light traffic on the way back to London allow me to update my audio diary and mull over the prospect of the Trust taking over Avon View House. The building would give us a secure base for our clients to rebuild their lives, but it would be a major undertaking and stretch our capacity. I must try to get my impressions in order so that I can present an accurate picture to the trustees.

At Swindon a light drizzle sets in and by Newbury it's raining heavily. I begin to worry about what is waiting for me in the office. Paul has been keeping an eye on the three women I am supporting but I need to see them. First though I must make contact with the new girl the police

---

[5] http://www.salvationarmy.org.uk/referring-victims

are holding; then write my report on the house and plan my display panel for the anniversary. I'm longing to have some time at home, but that will have to wait, and I haven't phoned Mum back, I'd better do that this evening. Oh no! I have a hair appointment later. I pull off at Reading services and postpone it - not knowing then how this decision would bring Maria into my life, or the impact she would have on the Olaudah Trust and all who met her.

Ellie has reserved the parking space at the office for me so I leave the car and take a bus to the police station. They were expecting me at noon and it's now gone two. I ask for the officer on duty; it's Anna Grainger, we've met before.

'Hi, Anna, sorry I'm late.'

'Don't worry, Jane, we took the girl in during the early hours of yesterday morning and she has been with one of my police sergeants since then. I'll show you the referral form before you see her. We carried out a raid on a restaurant; we've had our eye on it for some time because the neighbours complained that it was a brothel. Then we had a report of a starved child being seen at the window but never outside. We arrested three men and took in several girls.' A young man enters with a folder, which Anna opens and scans.

'This girl's name is Anena but she is known as 'Nina', no surname; her country of origin is Uganda; she says she is from the Acholi tribe; she is approximately sixteen years of age but doesn't know her exact birthday. The boxes ticked on the form include: *physical symptoms of exploitative abuse; withdrawn and refuses to talk; shows signs of physical neglect; indications of psychological trauma; no passport or other means of identity.*

'These girls have been serving the hotels and bed and breakfast places close to London City Airport. Nina's not in good shape,' adds Anna. 'Shall we go and see her?' She takes me to a sparsely furnished cell where a small figure is huddled in a blanket. The police woman sitting with her looks up and smiles.

'This is Sergeant Gemma Anderson; she has been looking after Nina,' says Anna. 'Jane is from the Olaudah Trust.' We shake hands; Gemma turns to Nina and says:

'Nina, Miss Taverner is going to find you somewhere to sleep tonight.'

Nina's hair is matted into a dense wiry cap. Her eyes are bloodshot and unfocussed. Her face is streaked with salt lines where tears have dried. Under the blanket she is wearing a skimpy nylon dress, which does not cover her thin shoulders or angular knees. The plastic uppers of her high-heeled shoes are scuffed and dirty. I crouch and take her hand gently, noting the cracked finger nails and dry skin. She is almost certainly on drugs of some kind to dull the pain of what she has been forced to do.

'Nina, I'm Jane. We're going to see a doctor, then find you a place to sleep.' Her eyes gaze impassively back; she is too shocked to respond.

'Do you understand?' I ask her. Her head nods once and her eyes flicker into life for a second.

'Has she had some food?' I ask the sergeant.

'She ate some breakfast and a bit of lunch.' Our eyes meet over the girl's head. We can both see that she is malnourished and suffering from drugs, abuse and neglect.

It takes me an hour to find a hostel able to take her. The doctor's surgery is busy but our local practice has dealt with similar cases and gives us an appointment in the early evening. Nina seems completely passive as the doctor examines her and confirms that she has been taking amphetamines and cocaine. She will need prolonged treatment. Her eyes are hollow and do not meet mine or the doctor's. She answers questions with monosyllables: 'Yes', 'No', 'I don't know.' Her recovery will be slow but there is an occasional flash of fire in her eyes, particularly when the men she worked for are mentioned, and that bodes well; she is deeply traumatised but not broken. There is still a strong spirit in her.

I drive Nina to the hostel and discuss her dietary needs with the manager. We agree a programme of bland but calorific foods to build her up. She has very limited English but with the help of the Camberwell Salvation Army we find someone who can speak Luo, a language similar to Acholi. She was born in northern Uganda but her family come from South Sudan and as far as we can ascertain fled as a result of the Lord's Resistance Army raids in the first decade of this century. They are poor and she hoped to get work as a nurse in Kampala and send them money. I ask how she got to Kampala.

'An uncle.' My Luo translator explains that this means an older man, not necessarily a blood relative.

'Did you know the uncle?' he asks.

'Yes, he comes to market; and his wife.'

'So your parents knew him?'

'Yes, he buys Ma's mangoes. He says he can get me work.'

This is a common story; an unscrupulous trafficker, winning the confidence of poor parents with the promise of a job for their child. The Ugandan government has measures in place but cannot keep pace with the growth of the trafficking trade.

'Ask her what happened in Kampala,' I prompt.

'Small room, no food. Girls gone.'

'You were on your own?'

'Yes. Uncle say I am his daughter. I say "No". He say he kill my parents. I do what he say. I do not like what he do.'

'He said you must pretend to be his daughter or he would kill your parents?' checks the translator.

'Yes. He says I am his favourite "daughter". We come on aeroplane.'

'You come to the UK by plane?'

'Yes.'

We are recording this conversation, with Nina's permission, so that the police have evidence against the traffickers.

Over the next few days I start to look into Nina's future security. I am constantly reassuring her that she is safe, that the traffickers will not find her again, but the sudden change in her circumstances is overwhelming. She has not been out on her own since she left her family; she has been manipulated and controlled. She is still terrified that her parents have been or will be killed. I long for her to be able to tell her story but few of the victims we help can bring themselves to talk freely about the pain of their former lives; most close a door and move on. I leave her huddled in the corner of her bed, the blanket around her shoulders, frightened and disorientated.

………………………………..

A week later Nina is beginning to settle; she has put on weight and her hair is combed and pushed up into a slide, which lifts her whole face. She has struck up a friendship with a girl from Eritrea; they speak to each other in Arabic. She is on prescription drugs, which will gradually be reduced. I take her to an English class, but she completely freezes and is unable to take part so we leave after half an hour. She will learn from the other girls at the hostel and I'll try again next term. I've let Anna Grainger know that she has her first appointment with our lawyer next week.

In between helping Nina I've written my report on Avon View House for the trustees. On Monday Andy, Paul and I spent the day finalising the displays; we are using the story of the Hamilton family and some of the Society of Merchant Venturers' material so I'll need to go back to the Record Office for permissions.

I'm in the hairdressers slightly early for my appointment and enjoying a few minutes quiet. I've been coming to Lucille's for years; it's a small salon in the next street to the office. Shelly, who usually cuts my hair, is away so I'm with another girl, Mary.

'Miss Taverner?' A tall, dark woman in the Lucille's pink apron stands in front of me. 'I'm Maria. How are you today?'

'I'm fine, thank you, I'm booked with Mary,' I know this

woman; I have seen her sitting at a desk in the small glassed-in office behind the reception desk.

'There is no Mary. You are with me,' she says. 'Shelly is away this week. Please come this way.' She smiles and I follow her to the line of sinks. Her figure is thin and agile; there is dignity about the way she moves that is striking.

Maria drapes a pink check nylon cape over my shoulders and tips my head back against the basin to wash my hair. I stare up at the swirling circular pattern in the plaster of the ceiling. Her hands are firm but gentle and her touch is relaxing as she pushes her fingertips into my scalp, wraps my head in a towel and leads me across to the mirrors.

'Just a trim, Miss Taverner?'

'Yes, please, I've been away – it needs it! Not too short at the sides, I don't like it spiky!' She starts combing through. It feels soothing and I lean back in the swivel chair and watch her face in the mirror. It is long with a high smooth brow and prominent cheeks like plums; rising up when she smiles so that the creases under her eyes deepen. Her skin is as dark as the black Hamburg grapes my father grows.

'You've been travelling?' She smiles again and parts my hair, pushing one side into a comb.

'Yes, work not holiday; I came back from Juba two weeks ago.' The fingers holding the comb falter for a fraction of a second and there is an intense expression in her eyes as they meet mine in the mirror, then she concentrates on her scissors, chiselling my hair into shape.

'Do you work in Juba?' she asks.

'No, my office is in the next street but I go to South Sudan several times a year.' She continues cutting in silence and I see her ribcage heave as she draws in a deep breath and asks:

'You know people in Juba?'

'Yes, people working for the aid agencies, one or two of the commissioners, bishops.' In the depths of her eyes there is alertness as if a light has been switched on.

'Do you have friends in Juba?' I ask in turn.

'No.' She pauses, and stands as if mesmerised, scissors in hand. Her eyes are focussed inwards.

'No,' she reiterates. 'I come from Torit, South of Juba.'

'You have family in South Sudan?' I probe.

'I haven't seen my family for many years.'

'Many people I meet in Juba have lost family members in the fighting. There are many sad stories.' Her features relax but there is sorrow in her eyes and stress in her rapid breathing as her hands resume their work.

'I pray each day that I will see them again,' she says.

Those I meet in South Sudan have endured catastrophe and family loss on a scale unimaginable in the west. The face reflected in the mirror shows a strength and stoicism that is characteristic of the South Sudanese Dinka but may conceal deep pain.

'Maria, I would love to hear about your family. Why don't you pop over to tomorrow and we can have a chat?' I suggest. What am I saying? I have enough to do but there are moments when a remark seems to have heightened significance. Maria brushes the hair from the nape of my neck with hands that are trembling slightly.

'We're on the left at the end of the Square, The Olaudah Trust.' I hold my breath, my eyes on hers. If this woman has a story to tell about South Sudan I want to hear it.

'I, er… I can usually take a break around eleven when the girls are all here,' she says.

'Fine, we'll have a chat.' Light words, but something important is happening. Will she come?

....

'Ellie, I may have a visitor today at eleven; her name is Maria.'

'OK, Jane. Andy's office will be free if you want to take her in there.'

I spend the morning finalising the report on Avon View House and then working on my panel for the anniversary. By mid morning I have forgotten the conversation in the hairdressers yesterday, but as I lift my head and gaze absently out of the window I see a tall dark figure in a black coat turning into the street.

'Maria.' I breathe and Ellie looks up.

'Your visitor?'

'Yes.'

Maria hesitates at the front door, reading the posters in the window. She takes a step back and starts to turn away, then hesitates and turns back again. I rush past Ellie, tumble down the stairs and open the door – she's standing there.

'Maria! Come in.'

'It is convenient?'

'Yes, of course, come on up,' and I lead her up the narrow stair case.

'Ellie, this is Maria.'

'Hello Maria.' Ellie shakes hands and then offers, 'Can I bring you a coffee, or tea?' Maria accepts a tea and follows me into the inner office where I take her coat and invite her to sit in one of the chairs in the window. I ask how long she has worked at Lucille's. She tells me she has been there ten years and is now the manager.

Ellie enters, hands her a mug of tea and retreats, closing the door behind her.

'Tell me about your family,' I say.

'I lost them many years ago when I was a girl.' The hairs at the nape of my neck start to tingle. Maria must be in her thirties; that would mean she was separated from her family in the 1990s at the height of the fighting between the Khartoum government and the Sudan People's Liberation Army rebels. An idea begins to form in my mind, but I need to talk to Andy first.

'What happened?' I ask, keeping my tone as light as I can.

'I was captured by government soldiers and taken to Juba and given work as a servant. I never saw any of them again.'

'How did you get to the UK?'

'There were bombs and my mistress decided to visit her brother in London. She said I must come to look after the children and work for her brother and his family. We were here for several months then she went back and left me here. I escaped but was caught by criminals. The police came and I was taken to prison because I had no papers.'

'That should not have happened!'

'After a long time, they gave me papers. They helped me to get the job at Lucille's and I have worked there ever since.'

'Have you tried to contact your family?'

'I had no money left after my rent and food. Now I have a phone but I don't know where to call.'

'Maria, we may be able to find out something through our contacts in South Sudan. Would you be happy to work together on this?

'Yes, I would like that.' Her eyes are alight with hope.

'I must talk to my boss; he is away this week. Where can I contact you?'

We exchange phone numbers and I promise to be in touch soon.

....·

I'm in the office early on Monday morning to sort emails before I check on Nina and my other girls.

'Hi Jane, Andy wants to see you urgently,' says Ellie when she arrives. 'It's about Avon View House.'

I've almost forgotten about the Hamilton family and my visit to Bristol. I try to stretch my brain from the daily crises of supporting Nina and the other girls to long term plans.

'Jane, come in and take a seat.' Andy gestures with one hand towards the armchairs in the window. The spring bulbs in the square are in full flower, the daffodil heads blowing in the wind, and the hyacinths leaning over onto the grass. The sun picks out tulip buds, upright and tightly closed waiting their turn in the parade.

'How is the Ugandan girl?' Andy asks.

'I've been worried because she was so thin and ill but she's picking up,' I respond.

'Well done. Now, Avon View House – the trustees have considered your recommendations. They agree we should take the next step but with further investigation of the conviction of Geoffrey Hamilton and the financial arrangements. They were impressed by the thoroughness of your report and your research into the past history and background of the family. Well done, Jane.'

'Th... thank you,' I stutter. 'I had valuable help from the Record Office.' I feel a bit stunned. I had not expected approval, or for things to move so quickly.

'They want a further meeting with the Hamilton family as soon as possible. You and I will go. Ask Paul to cover anything that is likely to come up with your caseload.' I nod. I can see that he is keen to push on with the house project fast but has he considered the impact it might have on all of us?

'And well done on your design for the panel for the November anniversary event,' Andy continues. 'Go ahead and get the permissions for use of the archive material as you suggest.'

'I'll do that while we're in Bristol.'

I decide to seize the moment and raise my other concern.

'Andy, I have been talking to a woman called Maria who was trafficked here fifteen years ago. She is managing a local hairdressing salon, speaks good English and has an interesting story. She has asked for support in finding her family in South Sudan. I thought our contacts there might help. In return I could ask her to share her story. We have so few firsthand accounts of being trafficked.'

'I've no objection, Jane, but watch that it does not take time from your other work. Why not record the story and ask Ellie to type it up or perhaps one of the interns could take it on when they come in July?' As I nod he rises and the discussion is over.

Ellie apologises that the budget does not cover the cost of a Bristol hotel so it will be back to Mrs. Jackson's again. I leave her sorting out dates and ask Paul to pick up any crises while Andy and I are away. I phone Maria's number and leave a message asking if she can meet me in one of the cafés in the Walworth Road. Then I make a list of the permissions needed from the Record Office – a picture of a sailing ship, a copy of the summary of the Hamilton family history, a picture of Avon View House in the 1920s. I'm wondering if Anka has photos of her husband's family at that time. There will be a paragraph about the gift of the house and the plans we have for it, with a link to the final panel on trafficking and the work of the Trust. I'm deeply engrossed in my plans and sketches; Ellie has to remind me that it is time to meet Maria.

The wind gusts along the pavement blowing scraps of paper and dust and, in spite of the spring sunshine, I'm glad to enter the warmth of the café. Maria arrives a few minutes later, black coat buttoned tightly to her chin.

'Hallo Maria, what will you have?'

'Black coffee, please.' By the time I've returned with the coffee and a cola she has shed the coat to reveal a blue jumper and gold scarf, pinned with a blue brooch with the letters "MU" on it.

'What is your brooch?' I ask.

'It is my Mother's Union pin. All our mothers belonged when I was a girl. There's a branch at my church and I help with the young families.'

'Oh, right.' I pour my cola into a glass. 'Maria, I have spoken with my boss. We have contacts in South Sudan who may be able to help us search for your family. Where have you tried before.'

'Nowhere, I was afraid I would put them in danger. I didn't know who to trust.'

'But you are willing to trust me?

'There are good people, Jon and Sara, who have helped me for many years. They said I should contact the Olaudah Trust. But I wasn't sure. Then I overheard you with Shelly and I decided to talk to you.' The dark eyes look at me serenely but beneath that gaze I sense strength of purpose – a woman who had listened and watched and waited until the moment came.

'Let me take some details of your family. Tell me as much as you can about your parents and where you lived.'

'My family are Dinka. We come from the Bor region, north of Juba. My Baba is Joseph Kuol Deng, he was a teacher in Torit, south of Juba, until he joined the Sudan People's Liberation Army, the SPLA. My mother is Peninah Akol, she was a midwife in the hospital in Torit. There were seven of us: my older sister, Deborah, my two older brothers, Aaron and Peter, my younger sister, Rachel, brother Joel, and my little brother, Daniel, who died. Our family compound was in a village on the other side of the river from the centre of Torit, near the police station.

'And when did you last see them?'

'The Sudan Armed Forces bombed Torit and marched across our land. They burned our huts and let our cattle loose. My father and brother were away fighting. My mother, my brothers and sisters and I ran into the bush and hid in caves. We tried to reach my uncle in Nimule but the soldiers stopped us. They shot my mother and beat my brother. Deborah and I were taken to Juba. I never saw any of them again.'

'What is your uncle's name? Perhaps the rest of your family did make it to Nimule?'

'He is Amos Kuol Bol.'

'Maria, we will do our best to find them.' What else could I say in the face of her courage and longing? But I feared for her. There are so many tragic stories in South Sudan of families split apart over three generations of fighting, soldiers maimed, men, women, and children traumatised.

'Do you remember your childhood and what happened to you in Juba?' I ask her.

'Yes, I do now. For many years I did not remember but I went to someone for help with my headaches and then I began to remember what happened.'

'I would like to hear more. How would you feel if I made some notes? Your story may help other women. Would you be able to do that?'

'I want to help.'

'Would you be willing to let me record it so that it can be written down accurately?'

'Can I talk with Jon and Sara first, please?'

'Yes, of course, you must be sure about this. Let me show you some of the work we do.' I show her our website and tell her of my work with other aid agencies to develop educational resources in child safety and human rights, and of the work we do in this country supporting victims of trafficking.

'Maria, let us meet in two weeks' time in the office – that is the eighth of April, – and I'll tell you what we are doing to trace your family, though it may be a long time before we hear anything definite. If you think of any other details that would help to identify them let me know.' I see her down the stairs and say goodbye.

'Good meeting?' asks Ellie.

'That is a very strong and courageous woman.'

....

Two weeks later Maria and I are together again in Andy's office, my tablet is charged and ready to record on the table in front of us.

'I've contacted the Red Cross and Pamela from Doves of Peace,' I tell her. 'Now all we can do is wait while they make enquiries for us.'

'Thank you, Jane.' Her voice is calm but her hands shake and some of the tea Ellie has brought in for her spills.

'I'm very sorry, Jane, have I damaged the equipment?'

'No, it's fine, Maria,' I say, mopping the splashes off my tablet as quickly as possible.

'How has your week been?' I ask, giving myself a moment to think.

'It's been busy. I have been trying to attract new clients and it's going well but it makes more work in the evening!'

'Yes, I know the feeling, in my work there are forms to fill in for everything!' We laugh together and her tension eases.

'How shall we do this, Maria? You can tell me your story and the tablet will record it and then one of our interns will type it up. Does that sound OK?'

She nods 'How shall I start?'

'Do you remember anything about your childhood before you were abducted?'

'Oh, yes,' she sighs. 'I remember those happy days.'

Her eyes mist over and her posture changes; I am seeing the emergence of the young girl she once was. She starts to speak and her voice takes on a singing timbre which echoes with the sound of drum beats, the crackling heat of the overhead sun and the soft whirring of insect wings.

Maria tells her story, with many breaks when the effort of recalling painful memories overwhelms her, but she always wants to carry on. The story that follows is not as she first told it to me, but the version we produced, with the help of a journalist, for the Trust's twenty-fifth anniversary. It is a story of dignity and courage in the face of brutal treatment; it has had a profound influence on the development of the Trust.

6 MARIA IN TORIT

*I was made chief of girls because I was lively, I was bright,
I was not clumsy or untidy. I was not dull, I was not
heavy and slow. I did not grow up a fool, I am not cold, I
am not shy. My skin is smooth, it still shines smoothly in
the moonlight.*[6]

Life is so good in Torit; it is always warm and sunny in
the dry season and in the wet season the rain is warm and
soothing on the skin. At night there are tiny insects that
glow in the dark and light up the grass, and the stars shine
brighter than here. Ma's tukul, where Joel and Daniel
sleep, stands in the centre of our compound, with two
smaller tukuls, one for Deborah and one for Rachel and
me on either side. Peter is training to be a clerk in the

---

[6] *Song of Lawino 4,* Okot p'Bitek, poet's translation from the Acholi,
1966, reissue 2013

government offices in Torit and he sleeps there. Our compound is so pretty. There is a bamboo fence surrounding it and banana trees growing in one corner. There is a big lemon tree which hangs over the fence. When the rains come and the river is full we can grow good crops. We have a few cattle here but our family has herds near Bor so there is always milk and meat.

In our village there are only women and children, and a few youths like Peter, waiting until he can join Baba and Aaron as a soldier. There are many soldiers at the barracks from all over southern Sudan but we do not see them except when we walk past on the way to the town. The soldiers keep us safe from the Sudan Armed Forces. They are fighting for our people to be free.

In the evenings we play by the river. Sometimes we collect lemons from the tree at the edge of our compound. We hurl sticks into the branches until the green lemons come tumbling down, tickling our noses with their scent. I gather as many as I can in my skirt and take them to Ma.

Rachel sleeps late and we get into trouble with Ma if the water is not ready for cooking and washing. I wake while it is still dark and lie on my back to watch the gap between the walls and the grass roof. I like to listen to the insects in the roof and watch the lizards run down the walls and across the mud floor. The cock crows, getting louder with each cry, and I know it is time to get up.

'Wake up Rachel!' But she just groans.

'The cock is crowing, get up!' She opens her eyes and rolls onto her back peering sleepily at the light. When I am sure she is awake I pick up my mug and toothbrush and go to the latrine and washing enclosure. I shower in the water left there last night. It is cool and refreshing – the only time of day when my body is not sticky with sweat. I dress as quickly as I can, leaving the last of yesterday's water in the plastic bowl for Rachel. I can hear Ma's radio and her voice in the big tukul singing praises to God for bringing us safely through the night. She will need water soon for washing Daniel, and filling the kettle. Joel is already on his way to the side of the dirt road, where the trees grow tall, to collect wood for the cooking fire before he lets the goats out. 'Hurry up, Rachel,' I plead as she emerges from the tukul and hastily washes herself. There is splashing and a gasp as the cool water hits her warm skin. At last she is ready and we walk to the river with the empty jerry cans, hurrying before Ma starts shouting at us. We say a prayer to Jesus to protect us because there are many evil spirits in the waters.

We make three trips to the river and back carrying two cans each, though Rachel's are not full because she has seen two rains less than I have. We place the cans near the cooking area where Ma is tending the fire. Then we can rest and take our breakfast from the big pot of millet porridge that has been cooking slowly as the fire heats up. We wash this down with milky tea with three spoons of sugar followed by a small sweet banana. We wrap the cooled leftover porridge in banana leaves for our lunch and then Rachel, Joel, and I set out for school. Deborah has swept the compound with a brush made of twigs, moving her arm in rhythmic semi circles that make even patterns on the dusty ground. All the seeds and leaves that blew off the trees yesterday are brushed into the long grass and the compound looks neat and tidy again. It is a shame to spoil it but we must cross to the gate, leaving a trail of rounded footprints on Deborah's neat patterns.

Miss Aringa, our teacher is waiting for us in the school doorway. She is an Acholi from a village to the south of Torit.

'Good morning, Maria, good morning Rachel, good morning Joel.' She greets us in Arabic. We have been learning English but now the government in Khartoum says that all our lessons must be in Arabic and we must obey their law. Our elders do not like this so our fathers and brothers are fighting. We are Christians in southern Sudan although many people follow the old ways of the ancestral spirits.

For our first lesson we draw a map of Sudan and our neighbouring countries: Egypt, Eritrea, Ethiopia, Kenya, Uganda, Democratic Republic of Congo, Central African Republic, Chad and Libya. We mark the cattle herds, forests and the oil fields. We draw the Bhar el Jhebel, the White Nile, which flows from Nimule and goes north to Juba and Khartoum.

After the morning break we learn singing and dancing; I am the leader. I have to make sure everyone keeps time with the drum. I make my steps big so the little ones can see what to do and follow me. On Sundays I lead in the cathedral and we dance down the aisle. If someone does not keep time then the whole group trip over.

We stop at midday and eat our lunch under the trees. The air is heavy but the movement of the leaves keeps us cool. The trunks are fatter than a water barrel and their roots have spread out making little corners for us to sit. I am with my friend, Nyanga, who tells me about her brother who has been lost since the last fighting and has just returned. He was with the SPLA forces further north.

'What happened to him?' I ask.

'He was captured by the government soldiers. He had to work in the brick yards in Khartoum until he ran away and went north along the river towards Egypt. It has taken him many months to get back. He hid in a dhow taking dates to Khartoum and then walked many miles at night, sleeping in the bush during the day.'

'Your Ma is so happy!'

'We all are. But it is strange to have him in the village. He does not have a garden or cows and there is not enough for him to do in my uncle's workshop so we have to share our food. Ma says we may have to be careful with our stores if the rains come late. He will rejoin the soldiers soon.'

We watch the banana palms; their leaves are frayed and brown now and hang like tattered clothes around their narrow stems. If the rains come the new leaves will rise up and bunches of fruit will grow but if the rains are late the trees become too parched to grow new shoots. Our mothers are waiting to go with the little children to the fields to plant millet and soon there will be many sacks of grain but if the dry season continues then some of the little ones become too weak to walk and life becomes hard and the little children get sick with big tummies. My brother Aaron left the village to find food in Ethiopia and to train as a soldier last time the rains came late.

As we finish our lunch there is a faint sound of drumming a long way off. We listen and wonder what it means. Then we hear aeroplanes and the sky throbs with their engines as they fly past our village and on towards Torit. The doors in the belly of the planes open and big cylinders drop from the sky over our town. As we watch there is a noise like thunder and smoke and dust fly up from the centre of our town and roll out towards us. Our teachers come hurrying out from the school building.

'Government planes are bombing Torit! You must run home to your families! Run now!'

Rachel, Joel and I run home as quickly as we can. The noise of the planes dies away but I am terrified that more will come. If one of those cylinders came down on us there is nowhere we could hide. There is a strange smell in my mouth and nose that makes me cough and choke. Rachel's eyes are streaming. What has happened to all the people who live in Torit?

'God be praised that you are home,' says Ma. She is wearing a dress and her necklace instead of her apron. Usually we change out of our uniform as soon as we get in but she says, 'Maria, take Rachel and Joel with you and fill this cloth with lemons.'

'But Ma, we've only just got here!'

'Go. Now!' She gives us a large cloth and we go out to the corner of our compound where the branches of the lemon tree hang down.

'Come on, Ma is beckoning.' We tie the corners of the cloth and carry it between us.

Ma has gathered our household items and food into bundles. She gives a large one to Deborah and smaller ones to Rachel and me. She has prepared some pancakes and we sit on the floor and eat.

'Ma, what is "bombing"?' I ask.

'A bomb is a metal case packed with powder that makes an explosion – like when a log explodes on the fire but much bigger.'

'Why are the planes making bombs fall on Torit?'

'They are government planes bombing our forces. Peter will be home soon and he will tell us more.' I watch a line of soldier ants coming up the mud wall of the tukul. They fan out investigating, returning, and spreading out again. Then one of them finds something. They swarm over it carrying it back down the wall to the tiny hole in the corner where they disappear.

Through the square window of the tukul I watch the sun sink into the dense leaves of the lemon tree. Small fluffy clouds on either side glow pink; the light fades rapidly and the crickets sing in the soft darkness. Ma does not light a lamp but clears away the last of the pancakes wrapping them in banana leaves and placing them in the top of her bundle.

There is a soft thud as a heavy object falls against the hut wall and Peter enters. He is thin and muscular, two rains older than me.

'Ma! You are all OK?'

'Yes, we're fine, what is happening?'

The drums are saying there is fighting to the north of us,' he reports. 'Some elders say we should flee but others want to stay and fight. They say the mujahedeen do not come this far south. There are rumours that government forces allied with the Nuer tribe are looking for Dr Garang and the SPLA.

'What do you think we should do?' Ma asks.

'Flee,' says Peter. 'The explosions have left craters in the centre of Torit. Shops have been destroyed and people have died. A bomb has hit the cathedral compound.'

'Baba and the SPLA will come for us.' I had seen eleven rains at that time and I thought my father could protect me from everything.

'Maria,' Ma said, 'your father is not with the SPLA in Torit. Your father always said that if the government attacked the town we must flee. We will leave now and go to the caves,' says Ma.

She pushes aside a heavy water pot and scrapes some soil away with a cup to reveal a small wooden box in the floor. She lifts the lid and takes out some dirty folded papers and puts them inside her dress. Then she hands us each our bundle and, putting her own on her head, holds Daniel firmly by the hand and gestures to Peter to lead the way. He picks up the machete and long stick that he left at the door and we follow him to the back of the compound. He breaks down the bamboo fence with the machete and climbs through. Ma follows with the tightly packed bundle on her head and Daniel's hand in hers. Deborah holds her bundle with one hand and beckons to Joel, Rachel and I, then she goes through last. Peter closes the gap in the fence, masking the broken canes as much as he can.

We follow him into the bush straining to see his dark figure striding ahead of us. We are picking our way through dry sticks and thorn bushes but if we make a sound Ma and Peter glare at us so we tread carefully, peering ahead, our eyes wide, straining to see in the dark.

Suddenly the ground shakes. There is shouting and the noise of trucks grinding their gears and heavy boots tramping through the village behind us. Loud explosions hurt my ears and make Daniel cry but Ma clamps a hand over his mouth and I can see the whites of his eyes. There is a crack as something whizzes through the air falling with a crash and a smell of burning. The sky lights up with orange flames devouring the wooden walls and grass rooves of our tukuls. I can hear people screaming and feel the heat of the fires on my back. The animals have been let loose and a cow blunders past wild with terror. Goats are bleating piteously and people are crying and running. The smoke grabs at my throat and makes me want to cough but I try not to make a noise. I hold Rachel's hand tightly and we struggle on holding our bundles with our other hands so that the tangled branches do not snatch them from our heads.

We walk for a long time and the night becomes cool. Our home has been burned and I do not know where we will go. There is a pain in my tummy. We rest for a while and then walk on again through the night. I have never been this way before but Peter strides ahead and we follow.

There are rocks in the path and it is difficult to walk. There are night spirits in the air; I can feel them tearing at my hair and brushing my cheeks trying to get in through my mouth. I sing my favourite song, "Jesus number one, Jesus number one…" under my breath to frighten them away. We rest for a while and then walk again. Ma points to me to let go of Rachel and help Deborah with Daniel. I want to tell her that my feet are hurting on the rocks but I take my little brother's hand and lift him over the bigger boulders. Peter bends low onto a narrow track that passes beneath a thicket of thorns and creeper. He swings his machete and his pack beneath him with ease but Deborah, Rachel and I struggle with our bundles. My feet are bleeding now and I can see a dark mark on the rocks behind me. Ma stops me and wraps her scarf around my foot. She indicates for Deborah to do the same for the other foot. Peter waits impatiently and then creeps forward again. We do this for a long time and my back hurts from bending beneath the branches. I am so tired that I can think of nothing but my feet, trying to find the softest place for them to land. The sky is black, dotted with a sprinkling of stars. Then the light changes to indigo and then to grey. Peter turns left at a boulder taller than a tree and disappears. We see his hand beckoning in the ghostly grey light, and follow him into a small crevice between two rocks opening out into a cave. It is deep and full of stones but there are smoother places between the boulders. Ma says a prayer to protect us from evil spirits and then lays cloths on the ground and gestures with her arm for us to lie down and go to sleep. I am thirsty and she gives me a lemon to suck. As I slide into sleep I hear her voice murmuring with Peter and Deborah.

'...Nuer ....government forces...' (Peter)

'...get water before dawn...' (Deborah)

'...hire a truck... Nimule...' (Ma)

'...when you are safe...' (Peter)

Peter is eager to join our father and brother in the army but he will not leave till we are safe.

I sleep.

When the first pink light of the sun comes through the crack between the boulders I see Ma is not wearing her necklace.

'Did you drop your necklace?' I ask. She shakes her head.

'I've given it to Peter with some US dollars your father left. He has gone to find a truck to take us to your uncle's house in Nimule.' She beckons us close to her and then she says a prayer.

'Thank you, Lord Jesus, that you have brought us through the night. We ask that you will watch over us and guide us safely to Nimule.'

'I'm hungry,' Daniel says.

'Me too,' adds Joel.

'There will be lots to eat in Nimule,' says Ma. 'You need to save a space for all the food we will eat. Maria, take them to the back of the cave and play games with them.'

'Will the bad men hurt us?' Rachel asks.

'Not if they do not hear us,' says Ma.

We spend two days in the cave eating the lemons and the pancakes that Ma carried in her bundle. She sends Joel and me out each morning before dawn to collect water from the stream and we make that last all day. She gives us lemons to suck if we want more and the sour taste makes my tongue curl but they smell clean and hide the funny smell of the cave. The days are long and we spend them playing games with stones in the dust and listening to Ma tell stories about Jesus and how the soldiers captured him and killed him but he came to life again after three days. We cannot see him but his Spirit is here with us in the cave and the angels watch over us.

It is difficult to keep Daniel and Joel quiet but I use stones to outline a wrestling ring and we play "silent wrestling". Then I make pits in the dust and we play count and catch games with lemon seeds and stones. Rachel and Deborah join us and the games become more complicated. Deborah became a woman three rains ago. After the last rains she was married to Seme from the next village but he is in the SPLA so she has come back to live with us and help Ma. She has no time for play but today there is nothing else to do. She helps Ma share out the last of the pancakes and then she tells us a story about how Jesus travelled through the countryside as a preacher with his followers and told people that God loved them.

In the night Daniel is ill. He says his stomach hurts badly, and he is being sick. Then he starts to have diarrhoea. Ma lays him on her lap near the latrine place. I watch the narrow line of moonlight that comes through the entrance move slowly across the ceiling as I listen to Daniel cry and Ma nursing him.

In the morning he is very quiet. I want to cheer him up and make him laugh and play but he is too ill. My stomach feels as though it has a big stone in it and I am worried that we will be here forever and that there is no-one to help Daniel.

'What is going to happen, Ma?'

'Your brother will be back soon and we will go to Nimule,' she replies. Her voice croaks like a frog.

'Will Baba come and help us?' I ask.

'Your father is too far away. We must ask Jesus to help us.'

She makes us all stand by her and closes her eyes and then she says,

'Thank you, Lord Jesus, for bringing us safely through another night. Please help us.'

All that day Ma, Deborah, Rachel and I help Daniel drink sips of water. By night fall it is all gone and Joel and I have to go outside to fill the jerry can again. Then Ma sits with Daniel cradled in her arms. His body is like a bundle of dry sticks. Ma rocks to and fro and as the light fades the tears roll down her cheeks. She is praying constantly for Jesus to heal him; when she does not pray aloud her lips move in silent prayer. Rachel is crying too and Deborah sits down with us near Ma and explains that Daniel needs medicine and a hospital but we cannot go there because of the fighting. The pain in my stomach tightens into a hard knot. I feel angry – why do they destroy our homes so that my little brother has to walk through the night?

Why is my Pa away for so long? My hands have curled themselves into fists and I shove them under my dress. I want to be at home not trapped in this horrible cave with my uniform torn and dirty. I want my brother to be well and my Ma not to be crying. I want Baba and Aaron and Peter to fight the bad men so that we can live in our compound and pray in the cathedral, and sing and dance and be happy again.

'Deborah, Maria, Rachel, Joel.' Ma is calling us and she reaches out her arms to us.

'My dears, your little brother will not be walking with us anymore. He has gone to be with Jesus. Her words feel as though someone has punched me. I feel very hot. I want to fight.

'No, Ma, no!' I start to scream and ululate. This is our custom when someone dies.

'Maria.' Ma takes my hand and unclenches the balled fist. 'We will mourn later; you must not make that noise now in case they find us here. Do you understand? You must be brave and quiet like Rachel.' I look at my sister and see that her face is very pale and her eyes are filled with tears but she has her hand over her mouth and does not make a sound. Joel is standing on one leg with his hands hanging loose and his eyes are looking at something far away.

'But Ma,' I whisper. 'Baba said we were safe in Torit.'

'I know, Maria, we did not expect the government forces to come this far south but the Nuer tribe have betrayed us and let them pass over our land. The SPLA has split into two groups that no longer agree. We must be very quiet until we can get to Nimule.' I understand that the government soldiers will kill us if they find us but I do not understand why Daniel died when we asked Lord Jesus to help him.

'Why has Daniel died, Ma? We prayed to Jesus?'

'I know, Maria,' she says quietly, 'but Daniel was too little to walk so far. We had to get away before the soldiers came. You understand that. He is safe now with Jesus.'

Ma carries Daniel's thin little body to the back of the cave, lays it gently down and covers it with a cloth. Deborah pulls some threads out of the cloth that was tied round her bundle.

'We can make a special belt for Daniel.' She says and shows us how to wrap thread around the stones as if they were beads. We lay the belt we have made over the cloth. Ma puts her arms around us and tells a story about Jesus letting little children come to him. She says a prayer and we say 'Amen'. We do not play now; we sit near the front of the cave and wait for Peter to come. We must not make a noise or the bad soldiers will find us. I want to cry but the tears have become hard and sunk into the bottom of my stomach and there is a deep pain there. I sit quietly, hugging the stone of tears and listening to the insects outside getting louder as the light fades from gold to pink and then to grey.

Peter returns just after dark. He has hired a small truck and driven it along a track near to the cave. Ma tells him about Daniel, and Peter is weeping. I have never seen my brother weep before.

'I tried to be quicker,' he says, 'but no-one has trucks to sell and government forces are everywhere. I had to hide throughout the day. Our relative was able to get an old one for us but we must hurry in case others come and want to take it.'

We wrap up the bundles, lighter now without the pancakes and lemons, and follow Peter out of the cave. My legs feel weak and unsteady and it is an effort to hold my head up to keep my bundle balanced. The grass on either side of the path is dotted with pin prick lights: glow worms in the grass mirror the stars above. I am terrified that planes will come and bomb us but Ma says they will not come over the bush. I wonder where my little brother is. Will Jesus look after him?

There is a rustle in the bushes and Peter shows us a small truck with an open back. It is rusty with metal trim hanging off. The windows are half open and a smell of tobacco and goats comes from the inside of the cabin. The back has a wooden floor and metal sides and is covered in dirt but Ma and Peter urge us in. When we are all lying in the back Peter cuts bamboo and places it across the back of the truck as a lid over us and then he piles more bamboo on top; each cane is as thick as a man's forearm.

'If we are stopped,' I hear him murmur to Ma, 'we are taking a load of bamboo to the New Jerusalem compound in Nimule.'

'Did you hear that?' whispers Ma through the bamboo. 'You must lie still if we are stopped and not make a sound.'

'Yes, Ma,' we murmur. We hear Ma and Peter climb into the front of the truck and the engine start with a splutter. We lurch and bump down the rough bush track towards the main road.

Nimule is a town close to the border with Uganda. My Uncle Amos lives there in a large compound with high mud walls and wooden gates. Each tukul in his compound is made of bricks with a metal roof and window openings with shutters that fit snugly when you close them so no light comes in. There is a "western toilet" next to Uncle Amos's tukul. He told me that toilets in England have a handle you pull and water rushes in but I do not believe him. There is a bucket to pour water down the toilet and uncle says he has fewer tummy pains with this toilet.

I have many cousins in Nimule. When we are staying there I sing and dance with their youth band at the New Jerusalem Church where my uncle is a preacher. There is always plenty of food in Nimule; my cousins and I walk along dust-filled streets between the bamboo fenced compounds to the market and buy fruit and vegetables from Uganda. My aunt keeps a cow in a nearby enclosure. Thinking of food gives me pains in my stomach. We have not eaten for three days except for lemons and pancakes. My head is pressed up against Rachel's as we lay flat under the bamboo cover and I can just see her eyes in the dark. I point to my mouth to show that I am hungry; we smile but do not say a word in case bad men hear us.

Ma stops the truck and comes to the back, pulling aside the bamboo.

'We have to turn onto the main road and there may be patrols and check points,' she says. 'Be quiet, and do not move. If they look into the back of the truck keep still.'

'Yes, Ma.'

Peter appears and hands us bottles of soda and samosas he has bought from one of the roadside tukuls. We climb down and eat and drink eagerly, watching the moon rise, then he pulls the sticks back over us and we are on the move again. We lurch and bump so that our heads and hips hit the bamboo and bounce on the wooden floor. When we turn onto the main road the truck lifts up and down through potholes big enough to swallow us.

We stop and I hear someone ask Peter questions in Arabic. Then there are footsteps at the back of the truck and we lie very still. Something jabs into the bamboo over us. A knife comes slashing through and Joel manages to roll aside in time without making a noise. The engine starts up again and we move on. My mouth is cracked and dry and I feel sick rising up my throat but I swallow it down and look across at Deborah, who frowns at me. I am very scared. What would happen if bombs came now? They would blow our truck off the road. I will scream if I think about it so I decide to remember good times in Nimule and my friend Emmanuel. He is a Dinka from

Bor; he stays with his aunt, who is a friend of Ma's. He is a year older than me and a good drummer. I dance and sing while he drums and others follow us. I dream of Emmanuel while the truck bumps and jolts down the road towards Nimule and safety, but while I sleep the evil spirits plan to trick me out of my dream.

7 'WIVES'

In March 1992 the Sudanese government recaptured Bor,
Torit and Kapoeta from the SPLA. The army had now
retaken nearly all the ground the rebels had won in the
1980s.[7]

Men are shouting; the truck sways sideways, stops and a
heavy object crashes down onto the bamboo. One of the
canes twists and fractures into long splinters, which graze
Rachel's thigh. She is so frightened that she wets herself;
when she sees it running down her leg tears squeeze out
of her eyes but she stuffs her fists into her mouth and does
not make a sound. We stay still while the bamboo is

---

[7] *Emma's War; Love Betrayal and Death in the Sudan* by Deborah
Scroggins 2004

prodded, staring at each other, ears straining. I can smell the sweat of someone leaning over the truck and it makes me feel sick. The bamboo is removed, moonlight filters into our secret place and I am looking into a narrow face with hard eyes and a thin nose, thrown into relief by the light of a torch. I know from the green army uniform and cap with an eagle badge that he is a government soldier. He stands at the end of the truck gesturing with his gun. I reach for my bundle but he growls something and waves the gun so I leave it and quickly push forward on the rough wooden floor, slithering down to stand between Deborah and Rachel with Joel in front of us.

Ma and Peter appear round the end of the truck pushed by soldiers. Peter stumbles and they jab him forward. Ma walks silent and upright but her eyes are flashing with anger. They use their guns to make us stand in a line beside the truck. Deborah is breathing heavily next to me and Rachel is crying silently, I can see her shoulders heaving with sobs out of the corner of my eye. Peter and Joel stand stiffly to attention and Ma's lips are moving. I know that she is praying. I pray silently too:

'Lord Jesus, please help us.'

There is a small office adjacent to the road. A spotlight above the door reflects light off a wire fence extending on either side topped with spirals of barbed wire. Another on the far side of a large compound sheds a pool of light onto a row of huts with corrugated iron roofs. Between the left hand end of the huts and the office soldiers holding torches are bent over a row of army vehicles. At the right hand end of the office there is a cylindrical water tank which blocks the view of the rest of the compound but I can see the top of two thorn trees above it. The office door swings open and a short, fat man comes down the steps. He holds a cane with a handle carved into the head of a crocodile with jaws open, gums drawn back and jagged teeth revealed. He walks up to Ma.

'Salaam taki, Mama, where are you going?'

'Salaam taluka. We are going to Nimule to sell bamboo.' The man snorts, and then strides towards the rest of us swinging the cane by the midpoint so that the crocodile jaws jut towards us. He looks closely at Deborah, then he struts towards me and lifts my chin into the light with his stick. I do not want to look at him so I stare past him at the thorn trees. He lowers the cane and moves on to Rachel. Her face is wet with tears and her eyes are red; her skirt is sticking to her legs where the thin fabric is still damp. He passes on to Joel who stands very straight, but his shoulders are shaking. The man returns to me and holds out his cane by the bottom end and hooks the crocodile handle round my back and pulls me forward. He holds my shoulder so tightly it hurts and pushes me towards one of the soldiers, who grabs my wrists and starts to drag me to the doorway. I do not want to go. I hear Ma give a wailing cry that comes from deep in her throat and she runs towards me.

'No! No! No!' she screams. 'You cannot take her!' I try to run to her but the soldier picks me up and carries me up the steps of the office. I hear a scuffle behind us and shouting. As I am carried through the door there is a loud explosion and I hear Peter cry out in pain and Ma screaming and shouting.

'My daughter! Don't take her! Kill me.' There is laughter and more gun shots. The door bangs shut and the soldier carries me inside and drops me on the floor. I hear the key turn in the lock, and he is gone. I go to the window and look out through the metal bars. Peter is doubled over, a soldier holding a gun to his head. Ma is lying quite still in the dust with her legs splayed out and a dark stain on her dress. There is a smell, like the bombs, that makes my throat hurt. Deborah, Rachel and Joel are standing as if they were trees struck by lightning, their limbs dark and still, their eyes open wide and their faces pale. I push my right arm through the bars and scream:

'Maaaaaa!'

A soldier comes from the corner of the building and hits my arm with his gun. He slams the metal shutters closed and drops the catch into place. The room is very dark. I keep my ear pressed hard to the gap between the window bars. I can hear soldiers' boots scraping in the dust and the officer with the cane shouting in curt angry bursts. There are scuffling noises and a soft thud, and another, then the tramp of boots. Someone climbs into the truck and drives away; I see the headlights through the narrow crack in the shutters and smell the exhaust fumes as it passes under the window. There is silence except for goats bleating in the bush and the wind rustling the thorn trees.

I squat in the corner of the room holding my arm with my dress to stem the blood. I can feel the lump of a bruise developing. I pray to Lord Jesus. The soldiers have shot my mother and brother and older sister. I am afraid they will shoot me so I crouch down in the corner and cry silently. What are they doing to my family? I do not know what to do so I stay in the corner and say 'Lord Jesus. Lord Jesus. Lord Jesus.' over and over again.

There are heavy footsteps; the door opens and a light is switched on. The short man enters the room and crosses to a large wooden desk. He places his cane on top with the crocodile jaw pointing directly at me, sits down and starts to sort through papers. He does not look at me. I stay very still looking at him. There is a knock on the door and a thin man in a brown tunic comes in.

The officer points at me.

'Take her for a wash, Ahmed.' The man comes over and pulls me towards the door.

'No! Leave me alone,' I shout and wriggle away from him but he takes hold of my arm and twists it till I am forced to go with him. He glances at the officer and says something and they both laugh.

Ahmed pushes me outside to the water tank and gestures for me to wash myself. There is another dark bruise on my arm showing the shape of his fingers and blood coming from my elbow where I knocked it against the door. I don't like him watching me. I am very thirsty so I drink some of the water as I wash and it feels good to be clean after all the walking and the heat of the truck. I rinse the blood off my arms and do my best to get the stain out of my dress. When I have finished the man takes me back to the room. I am afraid he will break my arm like a twig if I do not go with him. There is no one else nearby except the soldiers working on the trucks, who look at me with hungry dog eyes and laugh.

The officer is signing his name on papers. I wait. My eyes are fixed on the crocodile; it is carved in light wood, which has been stained dark, then the teeth have been chiselled out so that they show as white indents. The upper jaw is lifted and the teeth are rows of daggers. The crocodile's eyes are black and shiny and stare at me intently along the narrow snout.

The officer pushes his chair back with a screech, rises to his feet, steps to the door and locks it. He is moving towards me and I can hear his breathing and smell the sweat and dust on his body. He is not much taller than I am but the muscles in his arm below the short sleeves of his shirt are thick and sinewy. I stand up as tall as I can and look straight at him. The pupils of his eyes are deep brown and the whites stand out in the dark face like the teeth of the crocodile. I hold up my hands to keep him away but he seizes them and pushes them behind me forcing me back against the wall. I feel the blood rush into my head and I start to fall. The crocodile has wrapped itself round my abdomen and I cannot breathe. I open my mouth to scream but no sound comes out. The body presses into mine and fumbles with clothes. The crocodile is tightening its grip on my stomach and opening its jaws. I try to wriggle sideways but it thrusts into me harder. The pain is worse than anything I have ever felt. The mouth is over mine and blackness is coming into my head.

When I am able to see again he has moved away from me and is doing up his belt. I pull my dress down and lean back against the wall to stop myself falling. There is a burning feeling between my legs and I feel dazed and confused.

He unlocks the door and shouts.

'Ahmed!'

The thin man comes back again and seizes me by the hand. This time I want to go with him. I want to do anything that will take me away from the short man. I follow him out of the room and across the compound to a long brick hut under the thorn trees.

I am in such pain that I find it difficult to walk. Ahmed forces me towards the hut and pushes me through the metal door. I hear it shut behind me and the wooden door frame shakes as the padlock is clicked into place. Inside it is very dark but a faint patch of moonlight comes through the tiny barred window and as my eyes adjust I can make out mattresses laid on the concrete floor. There is a jerry can full of water; the top has been sawn off so that it can be used as a bowl. There is a battered enamel cup beside it and an old towel hanging on a nail above. I take a drink and then my legs go limp, my body crumples and I fall onto the nearest mattress. I feel shocked and frightened. I want Ma but I do not know where she is or what has happened to her. Will I ever see my family again? All around me are the unfamiliar noises of soldiers chatting and laughing, truck engines spluttering and dying, softer women's voices nearby, and the smell of a fire smoking. I dare not cry out in case they hear me and hit me again. The tears squeeze out under my eyelids and soak the dirty mattress. I curl into a ball trying to find a comfortable place where the pain between my legs and inside me will stop but there is nowhere I can go for comfort.

I sleep for a long time and wake to see a beam of sunlight filtering through the window. Someone is lying on the mattress next to mine. It is Deborah! I try to wake her but she is deeply asleep, her breath coming in shuddering gasps. I lie on my back and gaze at the roof of the hut. It has wooden rafters covered with corrugated iron sheets which are beginning to creak as the heat of the day builds. The metal door has a small barred window at the top with a rusted shutter closed across it. There are ten more mattresses in the room beyond the ones that Deborah and I are on. They are crammed together with scarcely room to stand between them. There is no sign of any other occupants but there is a smell of stale sweat and handmade soap.

The shaft of sunlight shifts and narrows as the sun moves overhead. I sleep again and wake to find Deborah's bloodshot eyes looking at me. One cheek is swollen and her lip has been cut.

'They hit you?' I ask. She nods.

'Ma? Is she...?'

'They shot her in the back; she was on the ground but I could see her chest moving then two soldiers grabbed me. What have they done to you?'

'The short man hurt me.' I indicate the place with my hands. 'And my arm is bruised from where the soldier hit it against the window bar. Where are the others?'

'They shot Peter in the leg when he tried to protect Ma. Rachel and Joel were standing by the truck but when I looked back after Ma fell they were gone. Oh Maria, I wonder if they managed to escape? If they could get to Nimule and alert our uncle....' We hold hands tightly for a moment. Then Deborah gets up and walks awkwardly to the water pot, stumbling over the mattresses. She takes off her clothes, rinses them out, hangs them on a nail to dry and wraps herself in her scarf.

'Maria, have you washed? You must keep clean.' I go over to the pot and she helps me and then we sit close together on the mattress.

'What are they going to do with us?' I ask.

'I think they want us to be "wives".'

'Does that mean they will hurt us?'

'Maria, it hurts when you are forced to do it but it is pleasurable when it is done in marriage and to bring children into the world.'

'Was it like that with you and Seme?'

'Seme is a good man and a gentle man.'

'Why do they want us to be wives? They have not paid the bride price.'

'Maria, these men want to hurt and destroy us, we are part of the battle now. We must pray that our uncle will find us.' We hold each other's hands again for comfort. 'You must try to please the short man, Maria. He is very powerful.'

The padlock is undone and the door opens slightly. A

woman with a narrow brown face hands a cup of porridge through the door. Deborah thanks her and she turns and spits at us. Then the door is locked again.

She is from the Nuer tribe,' says Deborah. 'They are fighting with the government now, against our forces.'

We share the porridge and then sit with our arms encircling each other trying to work out what we should do. I want to run away but she says it is impossible.

'The compound is enclosed with a wire fence and the only way out is through the office we came in by. There are soldiers on guard and they would see us straight away. We must do nothing to make them notice us until we can make a plan.'

I screw up my eyes and try to think but all I can see is the head of the crocodile and its huge teeth. It is getting bigger until it is larger than a real beast and coming towards me and then I am in its mouth and the jaw is closing. I scream and sob and Deborah holds me tightly with my head pressed into her stomach so that my tears are stifled by her dress and soft belly.

'Shhshh,' she says. 'Don't make a noise. We must not make them angry.' I am shivering in spite of the heat inside the hut. She fetches me a drink and I take gulps of it and wipe my eyes.

'I thought the crocodile would eat me.'

'What crocodile?' she asks and I tell her about the fat man's cane.

'They are all animals. You must try to please them until we find a way to escape or our uncle comes.'

There is nothing to do and we cannot leave the tukul. We put our damp clothes back on and talk about our grandparents, and visiting our ancestral lands in Bor, and the cattle with their long horns and soft smooth coats, and how our father had saved up to buy and rear cattle for a bride price for Deborah, Rachel and me to make good marriages. What will happen to us now, I wonder?

As the light starts to fade the door is unlocked again and a soldier points his gun into the corner.

'Sabbun,' he says, indicating the soap and we scramble to our feet, and follow him to a water tank. After we have used the latrine and cleaned ourselves he locks me in again but indicates for Deborah to walk towards the rows of huts where the soldiers are. I hear the soft pad of her bare feet as she goes with him across the compound. She does not return till morning. I cannot sleep and sit all night waiting for her. My chest is burning and my wounds are stinging. I feel angry that the Lord Jesus has not rescued us as Ma promised he would. I tell him that I am frightened and in pain but he does not come. Deborah returns after many hours and is too exhausted to speak. I take her a cup of water as she lies down on the mattress. She sleeps deeply for a while but then disturbs. She sits up and looks straight ahead.

'You cannot touch me. I am Dinka,' she says but when I look into her eyes she is fast asleep. She lies down again and tears stream down her face. I bend over her and call her name softly.

'Deborah, don't cry.' She starts to shout and cry out for Seme. I lie next to her and she goes to sleep again. When she wakes we sit close together and talk quietly. She tells me that there are several men who "share" her and take it in turns to lie with her.

'Does it hurt every time?' I ask.

'It is not as bad as the first time. There are some girls in another hut. It is their tribal custom to be cut and they are in very great pain. It is worse for them.'

Ma and Baba are Christians and do not follow the custom of cutting but my friend Nyanga's family do and she told me how happy her family were when she was cut and how proud of her, but she said it was a terrible pain for several days and she was not allowed to move while her aunties wrapped her in ground up leaves to heal the cut.

'Will I be taken to the soldiers with you and the other girls?'

The soldiers call the man with the cane "Colonel". He is an important man in charge of many soldiers. I heard them say he is at the barracks in Nimule. When he comes back you will be taken to him. You must try to please him,' says my sister. 'Perhaps he will tell you where Ma and our brothers and sister are if you are good with him.'

'How can I please him when he is doing terrible things?'

'You must think of Ma and Baba and our grandparents and ancestors and all that make us strong;' says Deborah, 'all the people who have come from our grandparents, and how our women are tall because we drink cow's milk.'

Each evening Deborah is taken away and returns tired and pale; her lovely dark skin is losing its lustre and her hair, usually tightly coiled is becoming matted. Each morning we are brought a bowl of porridge by one of the Nuer woman and each evening we are taken out to wash but the rest of the time we are locked in the hut. We hear the

Nuer women talking and the crackle of the fire; occasionally smoke and cooking smells blow into the tukul.

'Those women cook for the soldiers,' Deborah tells me. 'They are paid for their work.'

That night when the door is unlocked and Deborah is collected, I too am escorted across the compound. I stumble and look down at my feet and then I remember that I am Dinka and I hold my head up. A golden glow in the sky beyond the line of military vehicles shows where the sun has set and a small line of clouds overhead are tinged with orange. The moon is rising and a faint crescent is visible against the darkening sky. The crickets are beginning to sing and I feel the softness of the African night. A brief moment of life and then I am taken to a large concrete hut. I enter a room that is richly decorated with a patterned rug on the floor. The colonel is sitting on a sofa wearing a white tunic with a bronze sash. He has a long sinuous pipe in his hand, one end is in his mouth and the other is attached to an ornate brass column rising from a coloured glass bowl filled with water. I once saw a pipe like this when I walked with my cousin Emmanuel in Nimule; it is a nargile. There is a little fire at the top where special leaves are burned and then you breathe the smoke into your lungs to make you calm. As the colonel blows the smoke out, it rises in swirling clouds to the roof and writhes down again. The crocodile cane is propped against the padded arm; the teeth are visible through the swirling mists and its dark eyes are staring straight at me.

'Dakulu,' he says and beckons me into the room. I raise my head, walk carefully towards him and kneel. The colonel smiles and unties his sash. He picks me up and pushes me back into the sofa, pressing his body on top of mine and as the mist swirls over my head I remember Deborah's words and think of our family in Torit and in Nimule, of the long horned cattle that give us strength, and their milk that makes Dinka women tall. I think of my father fighting with the SPLA forces. If our land and animals are taken from us we will fight. We are strong and fearless.

The colonel keeps me for several hours and I try to please him. Another officer comes in for a while and they smoke together and talk. Then the colonel offers me and he quickly and roughly takes me and then goes. I am shamed but I cannot stop what they are doing to me. When the colonel is tired he summons Ahmed to take me back to the hut. I sit and weep until Deborah returns. I have tried to do what she said and please the man but it does not feel a good thing. I tell her what happened.

'You did well,' she says.

'I feel bad deep inside me,' I tell her.

'What they are doing is not right,' says Deborah. 'They will be punished one day but we are too weak to fight them. We must be practical and do what we can to survive.' I know she is right but I cannot accept what is happening so easily. When Deborah is gone I cry and shout into the mattress and beg Lord Jesus to help us.

A few days later five more girls are brought in; Dinkas from a village near ours who ran away when the government forces swept through their lands. They were separated from their families and have been wandering through the bush until they were picked up by soldiers on the edge of this camp. They are thin and hungry and when the porridge is brought in there is very little left for Deborah and me.

The days and nights run together and we are small dust clouds that swirl across the compound now that the rains are due, pushed to and fro with no direction until they finally collapse. We are "wives" by night and locked in by day. We do not see the sun except for brief trips to the latrine and water tank at dawn and dusk. We have lost track of the passage of time except for the delivery of a bowl of porridge and occasional greens. When the rains start we listen to the staccato noise on the roof and overnight the dusty compound becomes a slippery maze of shallow puddles and deep ruts where the truck wheels have slipped and spun. Grass has regrown at the perimeter of the compound and we hear the bleating and scuffling of goats as they try to reach it through the wire fence.

I am lucky because I only have to be a "wife" to the colonel. Deborah and the other girls have to go with many soldiers each night.

'They force us to be "wives" so that we will have children who are like them but we are still Dinka deep inside ourselves,' she says.

We never see the soldiers pray, dance or sing worship songs. Deborah insists that we say our prayers each night and thank the Lord Jesus that we are spared each morning. Six more girls are brought in the next night and there are not enough mattresses. Deborah asks for mattresses when the Nuer cook brings the porridge next morning but she shouts at us.

'No more mattresses. Soon you go to Juba.'

My heart jolts and my stomach tightens; I look at Deborah.

'How will Ma and Peter and Uncle Amos find us?'

'They will keep looking until they do find us,' she assures me but her fists are clenched against the folds of her dress so I know she is anxious too. Ahmed does not collect us to be "wives" the next night; instead the door is unlocked before dawn and we are taken to the latrine while it is dark. Then soldiers push us at gun point to the office where a line of women and girls stand against the back wall. Soldiers with guns are watching us so we dare not speak. Most of the girls are Dinka, as tall and dark as Deborah and me, some with the traditional tribal markings on their foreheads. Others are smaller with a reddish tint to their skin – Azandes from the west – all of us in ragged dresses and bare feet.

The colonel comes out of the office and stands filling the doorway, his huge belly thrust out, watching one of the soldiers check us off on a list. Then he nods and we are led through the office and out to a waiting truck. It is bigger than the one Peter bought, with a battered cab, metal sides and a wooden floor with a canvas awning stretched over metal poles. We are herded into the back and there is hardly room to breathe. The floor is covered with millet seed, pounded to dust by our feet. There must be twenty or thirty girls standing, bodies pressed together, before one of the soldiers slams the back and shoots the bolts. The truck starts with a cough and a jolt and bumps across the dirt roadside onto the pock-marked tarmac. We bounce and sway trying not to fall on each other. Millet dust from the floor and the awning clogs our eyes and noses. Those who can reach hold onto the metal posts of the awning. Deborah and I cling to each other leaning slightly inwards so that we are balanced on four legs rather than two but a sideways jolt nearly topples us. It is unbearably hot even though the sun is not yet up. We travel for several hours with no water, the rising sun striking the awning and our hands slipping on the metal poles as they become soaked in sweat. Those who have breath to spare talk.

'Where are you from?' we ask each other.

'How did you get here?'

'Do you know what happened to the rest of your family?'

The two girls nearest to me, Julia and Rosa, are slightly smaller than I am. They come from a village further north. The government forces came onto their land, setting fire to the tukuls and killing the men and women. They captured the young girls and made them walk for days through the bush. They were brought to the compound where we have been but they were in a much larger hut with many other girls. They too have been "wives" to the soldiers at night.

The truck stops in the middle of the bush and we are let out, watched by the three men who have been travelling in the cab. They are not in army uniforms but carry guns and their sharp eyes watch us constantly. We bend and stretch our cramped limbs and pick our feet up carefully as we move through the dry scrub, watching out for snakes. The browns and ochres of the bush are bright on our eyes after so many days indoors. Some of the girls have diarrhoea and we try to keep away from where they have squatted but the men threaten us with their guns to keep us together. One girl breaks out of the group and runs off like a gazelle into the bush. I have never seen anyone run as fast as she does and we all watch, and will her to have strength and speed. There is a rattle of shots and the girl falls to the ground, her dress splattered with blood and her neck twisted and broken. We are shocked, some of the girls weeping, others silent with immobile faces. Deborah, Julia, Rosa and I huddle together and cover our faces with our hands.

The guards shout. 'Back in the truck!'

We stumble forwards and climb as quickly as we can back onto the foul-smelling truck. None of us dares to speak or move and we stand close together as the truck lurches and jolts north up the road to Juba. Every muscle in my body cries out to go back towards Nimule, my family and my home; but we have no choice; whatever our childish dreams and hopes a future we never imagined lies ahead for each one of us.

8 *ABDA* - SLAVE

I was taken in the May raid. My mother was killed in the raid and my brother and sister were also taken. I don't know where they are.[8]

The truck reaches the outskirts of Juba when the sun is high in the sky. We try to move round so that everyone can get some air but we are tightly packed and girls in the middle of the truck are fainting. There is a low rumble and shake that causes us to bump against each other. Deborah and I are near the back about two rows in from the awning flaps. I catch a glimpse of the Juba Bridge over the Nile; metal beams crisscross to form the sides and the

---

[8] *This Immoral Trade: Slavery in the 21ˢᵗ Century* by Baroness Cox with Lydia Tanner and Mal Egner, 2013

metal plates that we ride on are ridged and ill-fitting where truck tyres have warped them. Girls are crushed, and cry out as the truck bumps and sways, but the men in the cab raise their guns and shout at us to be quiet. We cower against each other but I peep through a gap to watch densely packed grass-roofed tukuls lining the road behind us, with glimpses of the blue-grey waters of the Bahr el Jebel visible between them. A group of children are throwing sticks at a mango tree to get the fruit. Brick buildings line the street on the other side of the bridge, and open-fronted shops with concrete walls and flat tin roofs display fruit and clothing, laid out on benches at the roadside. Overloaded bicycles – some with eight full jerry cans balanced on them, others piled high with bamboo sticking out into the oncoming traffic – fill the road. The truck swings wide to overtake them. The air inside is already rank with the smell of sweat-soaked bodies and millet but diesel fumes, overripe pineapple, brick dust and rotting vegetables add their odours. The truck turns and lurches erratically over uneven ground with a rattle of small stones catching in the wheels. We tip down a slight slope and come to a stop on a stony area between two small shops. I hear a greeting.

'Salaam taki.'

'Salaam taki kamaan.' "*Peace to you.*" they wish each

other but their hearts are full of violence. There is a brief discussion and then the back of the truck is let down and we are told to follow a man in a dark jellaba. He leads us down a narrow alleyway between the shops and we trail after him, a long line of drooping figures. At the end there is a small dusty courtyard with a latrine and we huddle into this square space between the buildings. Girls start to use the latrine but before many have had time to relieve themselves we are on the move again, filing down another long alley to a bigger square and into a hall with a tin roof and open sides. Metal benches line each wall and we sit down gratefully, the proximity of our bodies holding up those who are too weak to support themselves.

Two girls our own age in dirty yellow jellabas bring pancakes and a can of water and those who are well enough to do so eat and drink. Then we are left sitting as the sun moves across the sky, casting squares of light onto one tear-stained face after another. The guards at the doorway ignore us unless we move, and then they wave their guns and shout at us in Arabic.

Deborah and I perch together on the metal bench, its heat scorching our buttocks through our dresses. Some of the girls talk but are immediately silenced by the gunmen. The sun beats down on the tin roof and the air gets hotter. A man in a white jellaba strides into the room adjusting the embroidered fez on his oiled hair as the guards raise their guns in salute.

'Allahu Akbar!' he shouts and raises a hand. Then he gestures for us all to kneel. As we do so he says again:

'Allahu Akbar!' Some of the girls murmur this familiar phrase with him.

'Say it. Think of the Lord Jesus,' Deborah murmurs.

'Allahu Akbar!' he says again and one of the guards fires his gun in the air.'

'Allahu Akbar,' we repeat, "*God is great*," pressing our foreheads into the floor.

Then the men make us stand by the metal benches. Double doors are opened and people enter and move along each side looking us up and down. A man in a brown jellaba with a large black book under his arm asks:

'These are all Muslim girls?'

'Yes, good Muslim girls,' replies the man in the embroidered fez.

I stand still with my eyes down watching the brightly coloured slippers of the men and women as they walk along the row towards me and smelling the different oils in their hair and beards. A woman with deep-set eyes points a finger at Rosa and makes her squat down, and then gestures for her to raise her arms above her head; she peers into Rosa's mouth and commands her to turn. The gold bracelets on the woman's arm collide with each other making the soft tinkling sound of shells falling on a rock. She inspects Rosa's shoulders and lifts her dress to look at her buttocks; then she nods at the guard, who has been watching closely. He prods Rosa out into the centre of the room. A lengthy discussion takes place with the man in the fez. Money changes hands, she clamps her hand firmly round Rosa's arm, her bracelets jangling as they become entangled, and leads her towards the exit. Julia darts across the room to kneel in the path of the woman.

'Take me too,' she pleads. 'We are sisters, we will work hard; we are good girls.' But the woman brushes her aside and Julia collapses sobbing on the floor as her sister is led away. Tears are rolling down Rosa's face neck as she follows the woman.

The guard prods Julia with a gun but she does not move. He hits her across the back and then kicks her until she drags herself on all fours to the gap in the line where she and Rosa had stood together. The man with the black book under one arm comes towards me. I look down at his brown leather brogues.

'How old?' he asks.

'I have seen eleven rains.'

He looks me up and down and then lifts my arms and inspects them. He asks me to stretch out first one leg and then the other. One of the guards has come over and is standing near.

'Open,' he commands, gesturing to my mouth and I open my jaw while he peers in and inspects my teeth. Then I have to turn and run on the spot. I imagine I am running away but I am just pounding the cracked floor with my bare feet.

The man with the gun forces me out of the line, a negotiation takes place and the man with the black book hands over several paper notes. I peer up at him; he has deep-set eyes under dark brows and deep furrows that plough downwards to his long thin nose. His cheeks are fleshy and broad and his mouth curves in a smile. The contrast between the fierceness of the upper part of his face and his fleshy smile is strange. The spine of the book he holds bulges over loose papers tucked inside. He flicks several pages over and writes down a number. Then he tucks it under his arm, gives a brief bow, palms pressed together, to the man in the embroidered fez and walks rapidly to the exit. I hesitate and look back at Deborah, whose eyes are wide and anxious. The guard jabs his gun into my side and pushes me towards the man with the black book. For the first time for many weeks I am neither locked up nor guarded and I look about for an opportunity to run to safety but as we set off across the square a young man joins us. He is lithe and athletic, with the same deep-set eyes as the older man, but his mouth is narrow and cruel.

'Salaam, abda,' he says with a smile and grabs my wrist.

'No, I am not a slave,' I cry and twist away from him. He tightens his hand on my wrist and grips my shoulder, digging his nails into my flesh. If I had an opportunity to escape it is gone and I follow the man in the brown jellaba, trying to keep pace with the younger man as he drags me along.

We walk in the afternoon sun, crossing many streets running parallel with each other. Tin-roofed buildings give way to tiled ones and then to buildings grander than I have ever seen before. We cross large areas of grass and wide streets where the fumes of army vehicles, trucks and cars catch at my throat and clog my nostrils. We reach a street where the buildings are surrounded by high walls behind which mango trees and banana palms cast their shade onto the roadside. We turn between two curved walls and stop in front of high metal gates. A wiry little man runs out and opens the gates, padlocking them again behind us. Two large dogs chained to the railings are barking and jumping up with saliva foaming out of their mouths.

My new master turns and faces me.

'This is your home now. Your name is Mirah.' This sounds like the Arabic word for "supply".

'Maria,' I correct him. He draws black brows together over the hooded eyes and the vertical furrows that link his brow and nose deepen. The younger man digs his hands into my shoulders until I am kneeling.

'Maria is not a good name for you.' the older man decrees. 'Mohammed, take Mirah to Atifa for a wash and clean dress.'

I am dragged through a low doorway at the side of the courtyard and along a dark passage, to a rectangular open space bounded on one side by small concrete huts with narrow metal doors and on the other by a high wall punctured by small elongated windows and a narrow wooden door. A woman comes out of the door; one shoulder is hunched awkwardly and one of her fingers is missing.

'This is Mirah, Atifa,' says Mohammed. 'My father orders she is to be washed and dressed.'

'Yes, master.' He walks away, locking the door to the passageway behind him.

Atifa takes me to a pump in the centre of the courtyard and tells me to remove my dress and wash. She tosses it into an unlit brazier in the corner of the courtyard and hands me a cotton shift with long sleeves similar to the one she is wearing.

'You must cover your hair,' she says, 'and never allow your ankles or your wrists to be seen.' She takes me to one of the huts; inside there is just enough room to lie down on the thin cotton cloth placed on the mud floor. She hands me a pancake and a sweet potato and leaves closing the door behind her with a rattle of metal against concrete. I sit down on the faded cloth, my back against the wall, and gaze at the barred window, high up in the wall opposite and at the pink flowers climbing over the tiled roof beyond. So much has happened and I am lost and disorientated. I know that my family will try to find me but how will they know where I am? Images flash through my mind, of my mother laying on the ground in agony, my brother doubled over with a gun pointed at his head. Evil spirits are flying about me; I feel their dark wings brush my hair and I hear Deborah's voice crying out to me. Where is Deborah now? Is she in this city? I see the face of Julia, beaten for trying to go with her sister. The evil spirits are laughing and mocking me. I want to cry but I dare not make a noise and the tears stay locked inside. As dusk falls I lie down on the hard floor with the cloth wrapped around me but I do not sleep. The demons are pinching my arms and legs and I cannot shake them off. They hold my hands and try to punch me but I resist. I do not know what to do. I have no-one to turn to but I remember Ma's prayers so I say, 'Our Father in heaven, praise to your name, your kingdom come...' and when I have said the whole prayer I start back at the beginning and say it over and over again until I sleep.

I wake with the smell of fried banana in my nostrils. I have been dreaming of Ma cooking our breakfast. As I become fully awake it is still dark and the scent of sweet banana and oil is replaced by strange smells, the reek of damp earth as water drips onto mud, and a faint perfume from the flowers tumbling down the walls. My limbs are heavy and I get to my feet feeling the areas that hurt most but apart from scratches and blisters I seem to be unharmed. A sudden blast of music makes me jump and a man's voice singing, 'Allahu Akhbar,' just as the dark begins to lift.

There is a rattle at the door and Atifa puts her head into the small space.

'You must pray five times a day; the master requires it,' she instructs me.

I had forgotten – I am supposed to be a Muslim now. I kneel with Atifa and a male servant and press my forehead to the hard mud floor but inside I am saying my own prayers and I vow that each time I am called to prayer I will kneel and pray to the Lord Jesus.

'Now wash,' says Atifa. 'You must wash before prayer tomorrow.'

'Yes, madaam,' I murmur. She hands me a small roll and a mug of tea.

'This is Solomon,' she says, pointing to the male servant. 'Mirah came yesterday while you were writing for the master,' she explains. Solomon is younger than Atifa. His piercing brown eyes look straight into mine. His hair is short and covered with a plain skull cap.

'Salaam, Mirah. I am master Ibrahim's secretary. Atifa is

the cook and housekeeper. You must do everything she says.'

'Yes, sir.'

I eat my roll and sip my tea while Atifa arranges some vegetables on a tiled shelf that runs along one side of the courtyard.

'Come,' she says and goes to the narrow door in the wall of the house.

I follow her along a corridor. Ahead of us is a hall with a tiled floor and walls covered with pictures of plants, trees and animals, embroidered in fine threads. Atifa opens a wooden door and we climb narrow stairs into a large room with two pairs of tall windows overlooking the street. Atifa explains that my work each day is to clean the wooden shutters, carved in intricate patterns of leaves and flowers, and clear any glass or china, wipe the tables and plump up the silk cushions scattered across the sofas and armchairs. I am to sweep the tiled floor and brush the elaborately patterned rug. Similar duties are explained for the many rooms of the house: clean the shining white baths, sinks and toilets, make the beds and pull up the beautiful soft covers embroidered with flowers and birds, sweep the passageways and stairs, dust the pictures and vases with care – if any are broken the mistress will beat me, Atifa warns.

'You do these duties each day and then once a week there will be other duties, which I will explain later.'

'Yes, madaam,' I nod.

'In the afternoon you look after the mistress's children when they finish their lessons, give them their tea and get them ready for bed. I will bring their food and explain everything to you then.'

I keep my head lowered and my eyes down but panic is rising inside me at the number of new things I must learn, and concern at how I deal with the children. I am used to looking after my young brothers. I make games for them in the dust of our compound or find sticks and stones for toys but how will I play with children in this clean shining house. There are many children in our village, and the grandmothers to tell stories, put herbal dressings on cut knees and cuddle babies. How will one girl look after two children alone every day?

'The boys are seven and five,' adds Atifa. 'You will need to be firm with them.'

'Yes, madaam'.

This was my work for the next four years. I cleaned and

dusted and swept from the first light of dawn till midday. Then I played games with the children in their beautiful nursery full of wooden toys or in the walled garden with its short prickly grass and trimmed clumps of bougainvillea. After dusk I would return to the courtyard and sit by the pump with Solomon and Atifa eating whatever food was left over from the family meals and listening to them talk while Atifa showed me how to prepare food for the next day. They talked about the family.

'The master is fair,' Atifa informs me. 'If you work hard he will be just but the mistress will find fault, and if the master is away in Khartoum with his other wife and children then she will find an excuse to beat you.'

I nod but inside I can feel my stomach knotted with fear.

'Mistress Kharimah is shrewd and gives the master sound advice with the business,' adds Solomon. 'But she does not like the master to go to Khartoum.'

Each evening I am sent to my hut. The demons come to trouble me and I want to be with Atifa and Solomon. I hear their voices as they talk quietly over the rest of the evening's chores. While Solomon cleans the brass and Atifa prepares the next day's dishes I piece together their stories from their quiet chatter. Atifa is a Bor Dinka from north of Juba. She was woken in the night to find her tukul on fire and ran with her three children into the bush. She was picked up by the mujahedeen, brigands on horseback, and taken through the scrub to join hundreds of other women and girls sold in the market in Khartoum. She has not seen her children since that day. Solomon is a Muslim from Khartoum but spoke against the government's suppression of the southern Sudanese. He was imprisoned and then sold.

I am constantly watching for opportunities to escape but we are locked into the courtyard except when working in the house. The mistress has many visitors for whom I must fetch trays loaded with pots of strong coffee in tiny cups, and malban – Turkish delight – that Atifa makes. There is a watchman at the front who unlocks the gates for each visitor and closes them again immediately. Two guard dogs roam the front and sides of the house. Only in the back garden are we unwatched and my time there with the children is the best part of the day but the walls are too high and smooth to climb and the bougainvillea branches too insubstantial to provide a foothold. One afternoon Farook, the eldest boy, shows me a length of strong rope and an old blanket he has found.

'Look, Mirah, we could get some wood to make a tent and play Bedouin.' My heart leaps – I could throw the rope into one of the jacaranda trees and haul myself over the wall. Farook tries to move the rope but it is frayed and rotten and disintegrates in his hands.

That night I lie awake wondering what would have happened if I had climbed the wall. Would the demons get me as I jumped? Who would help me? Here I am fed and have shelter from the sun. I am better off staying here. But the desire to be free rises inside me as I glimpse the turbulent waters of the Bahr el Jebel from the upper windows of the house. I ignore these feelings and concentrate on pleasing my captors but one day the flood waters overtop the banks of my control.

The master is away in Khartoum and the mistress has two visitors. They arrive, covered head-to-toe in black, with only their eyes visible. In the mistress's apartment they remove their hijabs to reveal brightly coloured silks and cottons. They perch on the edge of the sofas, gaudy birds pecking at the delicacies Atifa has provided. I am sent for more coffee and when I return the mistress is talking about her brother in London.

'Well, Kharimah,' says one of them, 'if you have connections in London why don't you join your brother? Things are getting worse here.' The mistress sees me at the door and glares at me as I put the tray on the low table in front of her.

'I will pour, Mirah, you can go.' When her guests have gone she calls me to her private parlour.

'How dare you listen to my private conversation?' she screams. 'You sly girl!'

'I'm sorry, madaam, I did not mean to listen; I brought the coffee you asked for.'

She picks up the small dagger on the table in front of her. I raise my arms to cover my face as she runs at me and jabs the knife into my under arms, where the long sleeves have slipped back.

'Never...' Jab. 'Ever...' Jab. 'Listen to my private conversations...' Jab. 'You must knock when you enter the room!' She screams. 'You foolish abda!'

She sinks onto her chair and I flee the room with blood pouring down my arms and find Atifa in the courtyard. She runs water over my wounds under the pump, puts ointment on them and bandages them with clean rags.

'I warned you what she is like when the master is away. What did you do?'

'Nothing, just took the coffee in. She has never wanted

me to knock before.'

'Now you must if you want to survive. These cuts will heal but there will be scars. Now lie down and I will look after the children this afternoon.'

When I lie down my limbs start to tremble. The demons hovering above swoop down and are sitting on my stomach. They want me to do bad things. I press clenched fists into my mouth to stop myself crying out. Where is my mother? Where is my sister? Why doesn't my uncle rescue me? The demons tell me to set myself free.

That night when the watchman comes for his supper I wait behind the door, slip past and run down the alleyway towards the front courtyard. I wait cautiously, checking where the dogs are. Footsteps pound behind me and Solomon grabs my bandaged arm.

'No, little one, that is not the way. The dogs will kill you.' He gently leads me back to the courtyard. I start to struggle and fight but he talks gently to me.

'Do not listen to the demons, Mirah. They will destroy you. Pray to God for help and wait until the omens are clear.'

I am wary with the mistress after that and learn to read her mood. She speaks harshly and occasionally hits me but she never again attacks me as viciously.

I listen to conversations whenever I can without attracting attention. The master has business meetings and I am summoned to bring coffee and refreshments I hear discussions about the importance of establishing a new caliphate in Sudan with allies in Libya, Tunisia and Egypt. Master Ibrahim refers to a neighbour, called Osama bin Laden, as a great thinker. Conversations became most animated when the subject of western influence comes up.

'We must avoid these degenerate westerners taking over the south and corrupting our women,' Master Ibrahim states and there is general agreement that enforcing Sharia law on southern peoples is the only way to make progress. It makes me burn inside to hear my people spoken of in that way but I have to pretend not to hear.

Even the children mock me.

'You are from the monkeys in the jungle,' says Farook one day. 'Monkey, monkey, monkey,' he jumps about. His younger brother imitates him.

Anger rises in me and the demons fly into my head and speak to me that the proud Dinka people should not be treated in this way but I ignore them and wait patiently, praying in my head until the children tire of their game.

I wake one morning to see blood stains on the cloth. Have the demons taken my blood in the night? I hear Atifa moving about and I wrap myself in a thin towel and rush out to show her what has happened. To my amazement she laughs.

'Welcome to womanhood, little one.' Since the day I tried to run both Solomon and Atifa have called me "little one" although I am taller than Solomon, who is not a Dinka, and nearly as tall as Atifa.

'Did your mother never explain?' she asks. Then I remember Deborah preparing for marriage because she had reached womanhood.

'The demons are eating my stomach,' I tell Atifa.

'That is a good sign that you will be fertile,' is her response but she gives me some rags to keep myself clean.

'And that dress is short for you. I will ask the mistress for a new one.'

I dream of my cousins in Nimule and long to see them again. I think of Emmanuel and how we would lead the singing and dancing, he drumming for the boys and me setting the steps for the girls. An additional cause of distress is the way the master's business friends treat me. Master Ibrahim himself is always courteous but distant, occasionally correcting me if something is not as he wishes but as I grow more womanly some of his visitors no longer regard me as just a serving girl. There is one man in particular who I dread finding in the main room. He usually makes an excuse to leave shortly after I take the coffee cups away and tries to catch me in the corridor on the way back to the courtyard. I push him away and speak sharply to him but each time his attentions became more urgent. Atifa comes into the corridor one day just as I am moving rapidly with his footsteps behind me. She looks at both of us and that evening I catch the edges of an urgent whispered conversation between her and Solomon.

A few days later I am summoned to Master Ibrahim.

'You are a good worker, Mirah, and conduct yourself well.'

'Yes, master.'

'I have many business affairs and my wife must accompany me. You are to be her personal maid, look after her clothes, help her to dress and of course continue to look after Farook and Kalim. A new servant will take over your household duties.'

'Yes, sir.'

In some ways this is a welcome change. I no longer take coffee to the meetings and so am less subject to unwelcome attentions but in every other respect life is more difficult. Mistress Kharimah is unpredictable and impatient. Some days she is as noble, generous and charming as her name suggests but more frequently she is discontented and prone to outbursts of temper. Her main interests are her clothes, her jewels and her friends. She seems to love her children but her interest is spasmodic where the younger two are concerned. Her elder son, Muhammed, who brought me to the house, is her pride and delight. Whenever he comes to see her I must bring his favourite cakes and drinks. In spite of her butterfly nature Kharimah has a sharp intellect and very little of what is going on in the household escapes her. Her angry tirades are usually over petty matters to do with her wardrobe or her friends but occasionally it is a business matter that absorbs her energies

'Ibrahim thinks that peace will be good for business,' she announces one morning, 'but it will not. As soon as peace is declared the west will intervene and flood our markets with their goods. I have told him this many times.'

In spite of her position as a good Muslim woman she takes

a strong interest in the western world. This is fuelled by regular letters from her brother in London. She and her closest friends pass magazines round and the political discussions in English are frequently on her lips. In public she supports her husband's cause of Islamising the southern peoples and building trade links in a Muslim super Caliphate but in private her opinions are surprisingly far from the prevailing views in Juba.

During the fourth rains since my capture my position in the household changes again. Solomon is accompanying Ibrahim to Khartoum more frequently and I take over his brass cleaning duties. The children have a longer school day and in the afternoon my time is taken up with the mistress, assisting her to arrange her many chests of clothes and boxes of jewels, mending her scarves and adjusting or making new clothes to her design. These often incorporate western influences drawn from the magazines she reads. I enjoy those quiet hours sitting in a small room adjacent to her private sitting room with a window looking out onto the pinks and purples of the bougainvillea as it billows over the paths and walls of the garden, more vibrant and sensuous than the silks I am working on. It delights my mistress to lead the local fashions and as I gradually become skilled in sewing and embroidery she is able to follow her instincts. I learn to dress her hair in the latest style but she boxes my ears if I am slow in understanding what she desires.

Solomon's trips to Khartoum with the master give him new insights into the actions of the government. He has been in the master's service for ten years now and his dark curly hair is tinged with white. Atifa too is showing her age and is plumper and slower than when I first came to the rear courtyard of Beit Ibrahim.

We sometimes quiz Solomon on why he does not take advantage of his increased opportunities to assure his own freedom but he always gives the same answer.

'The time is not right.' The reasons change as the political situation in Khartoum unravels.

'There is a rebellion in Darfur, many people are being killed and taken captive, and it is not safe to leave.'

Atifa agrees. 'We are well enough off here, the master is kind and fair and we are well-fed and safe, many slaves are in a far worse position and if we were recaptured it would not go well for us.'

Solomon is adamant that peace will come, that the Khartoum government cannot hold the south and that the negotiations that have been ongoing since the start of the second civil war in 1986 will one day take effect.

I have grown to love and respect Solomon but his counsel is hard to follow. I want to see my family. I yearn for life beyond the walls of the compound. I beg Atifa to take me to the market with her but she insists that it is not a safe place for a young girl and the master would not allow it. There are dangers for me inside the house.

Muhammed, who has ignored me for many years, seems suddenly to see me as I reach my seventeenth rains. His eye lingers on me when I pass and he often stops me to converse.

'Is it my favourite today, Mirah?' he asks as I bring the tray to his mother's room. 'Ah, you have something in your basket for me, Mirah?'

I answer politely and move to the next task. He waits for me in the long corridor between the kitchen and the stairs. I ask Atifa for advice.

'We cannot do anything,' she says. 'The mistress and master would never allow any complaint and it would get you into more trouble.' She adds, 'This is common in many households; I hear the girls talk in the market. You must be watchful and try not to be on your own when he is here.'

Relief comes from an unexpected quarter. The

atmosphere at Beit Ibrahim has become increasingly tense. Visitors are fewer; it seems the ladies of Khartoum do not wish to leave the relative safety of their houses. Only the mistress of the neighbouring mansion still visits regularly and urges:

'Don't wait for Ibrahim, Kharimah, make arrangements for you and your little boys to go.'

I overhear heated discussions between master and mistress. I have to sign my name to a paper that the mistress puts in front of me. One evening she is hysterical.

'They will attack us!' she screams. 'They have many guns and aircraft. They will bomb us! They will kill our boys and ruin our business!' I run to the courtyard terrified, but Solomon urges calm.

'They will not bomb Sudan,' he says. 'The Americans have many other concerns.'

But he is wrong. A few days later Khartoum is bombed and my mistress persuades the master that it is time to take their younger sons to her brother in London; and I must go with them.

9 DAYDREAMS AND NIGHT TERRORS

An increasing number of merchants grown rich on the African and/or West Indian trades moved out to country houses as the eighteenth century moved on.[9]

It is a fine clear Sunday in early May and we are on the Isle of Sheppey. There is a neck of land at the far end where salt marsh and beach fade into sea and the hills of the North Downs delineate the edge of the Kent coast where it meets the Swale estuary. The horizon rolls around us pearly grey and serene in the early morning light; the boundary between ocean and sky invisible except for slight striations between shades of grey. This illusion of soft gradation is punctuated by the silhouettes of container ships leaving Tilbury, their hulls riding high in the water and the building blocks of their empty containers piercing the skyline.

---

[9] *Slavery Obscured The Social History of the Slave Trade in Bristol*, Madge Dresser, 2001

Oystercatchers feed on the shoreline; conceited diners strutting about in their black and white plumage, delicately inserting their long beaks into the mud. Above them gulls are mewing; their cries long and plaintive. The air is fresh and carries the scent of early blossom mixed with the salty tang of seaweed left behind by the retreating tide. We had planned to paddle out to the Second World War Mounsell forts that straddle the water on their quadruped legs nine kilometres out but, though the sea is calm, there are sudden gusts of wind and it is too dangerous to take our small kayaks out into the shipping lanes of the English Channel. We need perfect conditions – in particular good visibility – so the forts will have to wait for another day. There is a debate about what to do instead but we have settled on paddling up the Swale estuary to the Shipwright's Arms on the marshes outside Faversham. Simon, who works in the Sheppey cluster of prisons, assures us that it has good food and is full of character. It is a challenging expedition for kayakers because Sheppey has a double tide and complex currents at the mouth of the Swale. Going out we will have the long shore current with us but we must allow time and energy for getting back.

'Right, that's decided then,' says Simon. 'Let's get launched.'

'We'll take one boat between two,' suggests Ben, and I am relieved. Launching from Warden Bay is a challenge because the sand rapidly gives way to mud and with the weight of the canoe it is easy to get stuck.

'Come on, Jane, let's get cracking.' Pete seizes one end of my kayak and we set off down the beach, followed by Ben and Simon with a second canoe. The mud flats are deserted; we left London as soon as it was light and it is only eight now; not even a dog walker has ventured out yet. The sun is lighting up the shallow pools on the mud flats with liquid gold. Shells crunch beneath us and small spouts of water shoot up as razor-shell clams dig down rapidly to avoid our pounding feet. We place two boats at the water's edge, swing our arms to relieve the pressure and return for the other two. Then we do a thorough check of safety equipment, water, flares, goggles, paddle, sun cream, hat, phone and camera in a waterproof bag.

'Ready?' asks Simon.

'Hang on, just need to get my camera bag clipped on.' says Pete. We set off paddling gently to begin with, keeping an eye out for the soft clay boulders that tumble off the Warden Bay cliffs and, more dangerous, the chunks of concrete, remnants of World War Two radar defences that descend with them.

'Flotsam ahead!' shouts Ben and we paddle slowly as a large piece of driftwood – perhaps a plank washed off one of the container ships – floats by. It is dark grey from prolonged exposure to sea and sun and studded with rusty nails that could damage our fragile craft. We turn to starboard and paddle parallel to the coast, moving rapidly as the current picks us up and washes us down past the chalets along the seafront and the concrete bulk of the sea wall. Even out at sea the sounds of pinball machines and video games are strident and a faint odour of jellied eels and chips wafts past us on the breeze. On the edge of the marsh a concrete watch tower stands guard, its sides gashed by narrow slits where soldiers once thrust their guns out to defend this strategic entrance to the River Medway. The white ridge of the Shellness spit curves enticingly inward and for a moment I long to stop and sunbathe on the crest of its perfectly concave bank of shells but we turn and head across the fast flowing current of the Swale making for the Oare marshes on the other side of the channel.

'Ware seals!' shouts Simon. I follow his gesturing arm and see what seem to be black buoys bobbing on the water until their heads turn and their eyes look straight into ours. They are curious, bobbing up and down as we ship our paddles and drift past. Six pairs of eyes regard us, docile but intense, sloping shoulders rising above the water, grey and glistening. Their heads disappear, their backs arch and they dive. The surface of the water is as if they had never been there.

'There's a colony of them on the sandbank across there.' Simon gestures towards a low bank of silvery sand. 'I used to watch them with binoculars from the Elmley side.'

The water is getting choppy as we cross the main current of the Swale where it meets the incoming tide. The waves cream and foam against the sides of the kayak, slapping the fibreglass as I angle the boat to get across the current. The wind pushes through my hair with icy fingers and I shiver in spite of the warm of the sun on my legs. The gulls wheel and shriek, diving down to take something from the surface of the water and then rising up again, their wings straining against the gusts of wind. I scan the water ahead for hazards, striving to stay alert, to paddle straight and to keep the boat balanced. Then we are into calmer water and my mind starts to freewheel and process the events of the previous weeks. Hearing Maria's story has been horrifying. Maria's family were caught in the struggle between tribes and cultures. It is difficult to contemplate the trauma she must have suffered watching her village torched, her neighbours bombed, fleeing her home and then being torn from her family. She speaks of her time as a servant slave in tones of calm acceptance but it is upsetting that such abuse is happening in so many parts of the world.

Many of the women I work with are too young and traumatised to be able to tell their story fully. I admire Maria's courage but find her unswerving belief that she will find her family and her trust in the Lord Jesus baffling; yet it seems to have given her the determination and sense of self to face the dark tragedy of her childhood and build a new life for herself.

'Jane! Halloooo!' Simon is calling.

'Jane, we need to keep left and stay together here or we will miss the creek.' Pete has come alongside and together we move towards the other two kayaks. We paddle into the creek, haul our kayaks out onto the bank, do a quick change behind a bush and leave our wetsuits drying in the wind.

It is good to sit in the cosy warmth of the pub. Four or five logs of wood are well alight in the open brazier and the damp patches where salt spray has crept down my neck are steaming gently dry. I have a glass of lager in one hand and a fork in the other ready to make a start on the substantial beef and ale pie that has been placed in front of me. The sun is shining through the panes of the casement windows making patterns of squares across the smoke-blackened timbers that support the roof beams. Between each vertical the walls are filled with rows of books so that sailors forced to wait here while bad weather clears can read in the low-ceilinged comfort of this ancient inn. For a while we eat and drink and allow our muscles to relax. The wind gusts and drops making the rigging of the boats in the marina screech and tap as it fills and then releases them.

'Still blowing a bit,' comments Pete.

'Weather forecast said it will drop after two,' says Simon. 'We can wait till then and still have plenty of time to get back round the coast.' He gathers up the glasses and goes to the bar.

'You were daydreaming out there,' says Pete.

'I was thinking about someone I met recently, a South Sudanese. One of the most courageous people I know.'

'Why?'

'She fled when her village was bombed by the Sudan Armed Forces and then was separated from her family, abused and trafficked to the UK, probably at the end of the nineties when the US bombed Khartoum but her dates are very vague. She has managed to make a success of her life in spite of appalling hardship. She seems to have clung on to her beliefs and retained a strong sense of identity in spite of trauma, which is unusual. I'm hoping to produce a booklet about her for the Trust's anniversary. I've been contacting the Red Cross and some of the agencies we work with to try to trace her family.'

'What's happening in South Sudan now?'

'It's a bit grim. There's still sporadic "cattle raiding," their euphemism for tribal fighting. The roads are dire, no repairs have been made for years and the potholes are so deep they swallow whole lorries.'

'Who's in charge?' asks Ben.

'No-one really. There are the vestiges of colonial administration with a regional governor in each province but until a national government is agreed there is no real power and the conflict between the Nuer former vice president and the Dinka president has not been resolved.'

'Is it safe to go there?' asks Pete.

'Definitely not, but I am usually under the protection of UN forces.'

Simon has appeared with two full glasses.

'Here's to your travels, Jane! Rather you than me.'

Pete raises his glass and we clink. They are good mates and I have sometimes wondered if Pete could be something more but his dream for the future involves a country cottage near the sea and a teaching post in a rural school. I am sure he will find someone to enjoy that life but I know it is not for me. He is a good friend.

Our return is easier going. The wind drops and the sun is warm on our backs. The tide is out and wading birds are digging in the mud for the shells and worms that live below the tide line. My thoughts turn to the work in Bristol. The Trust Board has given the go-ahead to open negotiations with the Hamiltons to lease the house. It will be for a peppercorn rent but we still need to find the funds to renovate the building. I know Andy will have a tough conversation with David about how much Hamilton funds can contribute towards the renovation costs. If we can turn the large rooms on the ground floor into office space we can rent desks out to small voluntary organisations and start-up firms and generate income to run the building. My hands clench on the paddle and a knot of anxiety is forming in my shoulders and neck. I hope Andy and the trustees have thought this through properly. There is going to be a huge amount of work to do to renovate and adapt this sad old house. And then how are we going to fill it? We will need referrals of clients from Bristol as well as London.

'Hey, Jane, hurry up! Fish and chip shop is open.' Ben is shouting to me and I realise that the other three are well ahead, level with Leysdown now. I shake the anxious thoughts away and put all my energy into paddling. We pull the kayaks up on the beach. While Pete and Ben go off to get supper, Simon and I perch on a breakwater and watch the sun sinking into a low line of cloud. The sea is lapping softly on the soft mud at our feet and there is a faint popping noise as sea creatures below the surface find their evening meal and expel excess water.

'Beautiful spot.' says Simon, gazing across the bay to the red brown cliffs.

'Yes, it's been a great day,' I agree. 'Shame we've got to work tomorrow.'

'Yeah, this place makes you want to spend the rest of your life as a beach bum!'

'No good in winter, though,' I remind him. 'Too chilly!'

'Too bad you're so practical, Jane,' he teases. Pete and Ben arrive and we eat fresh battered fish in our fingers, lingering over a can of beer each as the red light of the setting sun gilds the soft clouds on the horizon in pastel pinks and oranges. It's been a beautiful day; shame I have to go to Bristol tomorrow.

……………………………….

The embankments of the M4 motorway are white with May blossom and as we approach Bristol we see the whole of the city laid out before us, tower blocks and spires in the foreground and far away the modern docks at Portishead. Somewhere in the woods on the north side is Avon View House, and the visit Andy and I are making there today could change the future of the Olaudah Trust.

'What's your impression of David Hamilton?' asks Andy.

'Intelligent, controlled, used to assessing situations quickly, respected by his employees,' I tell him. 'His wife is as sharp as he is; a family lawyer, I think. She's Ugandan; they married when he was working in East Africa. I get the feeling she's embarrassed in some way about the house.'

'Because it was built with money from slavery?'

'I doubt it.' I remembered the evening by the Nile, and the bishop apologising for his ancestors. 'Her grandfather was a chieftain, may have dealt in slaves himself!'

Andy snorts and continues: 'and the mother? Mrs. Hamilton senior?'

'She's quite exotic, has a strong accent, which I cannot place. She was happy at Avon View House when she was bringing up her family. She says she doesn't want to see it left empty. None of them want to sell.'

Andy flicks the indicator and turns onto the M32. Safely inserted into the flow of traffic he glances across at me.

'Why is that?'

'None of them need to. David and Glycella have plenty of money. David's sister, Isabelle, is also comfortably off. But there is something else, I'm sure. Whenever Geoffrey's name is mentioned David and Glycella shut down and there is pain in the elder Mrs. Hamilton's eyes. I don't think Geoffrey knows that they have offered the house to us.'

'What do we know about Geoffrey?'

'As I said in the report to the trustees, he was convicted of fraud five years ago and sentenced to two years in prison.'

'You've checked with Companies House?'

'Yes, their records confirm the court case and the outcome.'

'And since then? Search for his name and see what comes up.' We are winding our way through the centre of Bristol now and it takes me a while to get anything up at all.

'I'm getting a gardening writer and a doctor but nothing else.'

'Try the name of the house as well.'

'Nothing... I'll search on the court case and see if I can find anything from that... Yes, here we are, dated May 2010, that's the date of the trial. It says "Mr. Geoffrey Hamilton, who owns Avon View House in Leigh Woods, where he has been living with his wife and two children, may be forced to sell in order to pay the fine imposed by the court at yesterday's hearing." Here's another one:

"Geoffrey Hamilton, convicted of fraud at yesterday's hearing, has resigned as director of Hamilton Investments. Inside sources say his older brother, David, may return from overseas to take control of the company."

'Older brother?' comments Andy, 'wonder why the younger was running the family company.'

We are turning into the drive of Avon View House and there is no time for further questions. Andy pulls up opposite the massive granite porch that slices across the front of the house and runs his fingers through the trickle of water that drops from the ledge into the pool below.

'Serious money!' he comments quietly, eyes scanning the gleaming white walls and manicured garden.

Glycella opens the door and greets us warmly with that slight hauteur that seems to say "Keep your distance until I know you." Andy's natural ebullience is stifled by her poise and after a subdued 'Good morning,' he follows her into the lounge. His untidy frame looks out of place on the leather sofas, and his large hand is cupped carefully around his cup and saucer. I have politely refused the offer of coffee and asked for a glass of water. David arrives.

'Good morning. How was your journey?' He shakes our hands.

'Good, thank you.' We have the usual conversation about traffic conditions and then David leans towards Andy and says:

'I expect you want to see the house before we discuss the details.'

'Yes, that would be helpful,' agrees Andy. Glycella excuses

herself; she has a case to prepare.

'I hope you don't mind, Jane,' says David, 'My mother would like to speak with you; she is in the summer house. Would you stay with her while I show Andy around?'

'Yes, of course,' I say, inwardly disappointed; I was looking forward to watching Andy's reaction to Avon View House but David obviously wants him to himself.

Anka Hamilton is seated in a large wicker armchair with a richly patterned blanket over her knees. I am invited to occupy the basket chair next to her. Her back is straight and her mouth set in a tense line, though her eyes are kind.

'What a beautiful day,' she says. We gaze at the vivid green of the sloping lawns and I wonder why she has brought me here. The midday sun is throwing the white walls of Avon View House and the Coach House into dazzling relief, casting dancing shadows on the grass and bringing a translucent blush to the blossom on the fruit trees.

'I enjoy sitting here,' she continues, surveying the elongated windows of the gazebo. 'It is between two worlds; the old house and my new life at the Coach House.'

'You miss the old house, Mrs. Hamilton?'

'Yes, I do. I thought I would end my days there but it was not to be.' I decide to take a risk. I sense that Mrs. Hamilton senior has not asked for me in order to make small talk. Andy and I need to know the background to this family's financial affairs and she may hold the key.

'Because of what Geoffrey did?' I ask. She turns her head to face me; the grey eyes are dark in the shadow of the summer house and the smooth serenity of her face is creased with a frown.

'Geoffrey was a delightful boy, full of fun, quick and alert,' she says. 'He was often in trouble but he soon charmed us all again. David was more serious, responsible, quiet, but did not have that immediate rapport with people that Geoffrey had. Isabelle and Geoffrey took after Gerrard – gregarious, sociable. David was a loving child but reserved and clever, he went to university and then to a job with an international bank, working and living in London. Geoffrey went straight into Hamiltons as an office junior and worked his way up. He was popular with the staff and Gerrard was delighted to have one of the children working with him, particularly after Isabelle married so young and moved away. When Geoffrey and Estelle married they moved in with us, as we had done with Gerrard's parents. Around the same time David was posted abroad, met Glycella and made a new life for himself in Nairobi. It all seemed so natural but I think we allowed Geoffrey too much responsibility too early and we did not realise how ambitious he and Estelle were. This does not justify what he did, of course, it was quite wrong and has harmed many people but I think he reached a position where he was too isolated. By then Gerrard had retired and Geoffrey gained a respect that he had not really earned because he was so like Gerrard. We realised too late that he lacked that inner moral strength that is essential in running a financial business.'

I am sitting straight in my chair, watching her face and trying not to interrupt this flow of confidences but many questions are going through my mind. Have David and Glycella asked her to explain? Has she sensed that Andy and I have been making our own enquiries? Of course they must know that we will run due diligence checks. Why has she taken the responsibility to tell Geoffrey's story? I need to say something respectful. How would I feel if I had a family business?

'The reputation of the company must be very important to you?' I say. She nods and some of the tension in her face eases.

'Gerrard and I built up the business together from the small local insurance firm to the international company it is today. We are all shareholders. Geoffrey betrayed the family as well as the business.' It is painful to see the eyes of this proud matriarch mist over with emotion. 'You have read the trial reports?'

'Yes, Mrs. Hamilton, as soon as we were informed. I had to include a summary in my report to the trustees.'

'Geoffrey paid a heavy fine in order to reduce the prison sentence. He had to sell the house and resign from his position in the firm.' Her voice chokes with emotion and I instinctively reach out and cover the gnarled hands folded in her lap with my own. To my surprise she does not rebuff me but closes her hand on mine. We sit in silence for a moment and then she continues.

'It has been very difficult for David and Glycella. They left a successful life in Nairobi, uprooted the boys from their school and moved here. David managed to get their money out of Kenya and with the help of a loan from his firm he and Glycella bought out Geoffrey's share of Avon View House. But they could not bear living there so they built the new house. Glycella was able to get a good job and her income helped while David rebuilt trust in the firm.' I remembered Glycella's anxiety as they were showing me round the house and the alacrity with which she led us back through the shrubbery to her own home. How difficult to be uprooted from a good life to deal with the mess left by a brother-in-law.

'David has done an excellent job and Hamilton Insurance is doing well again,' she says, 'but it has left us all with the feeling that while we do not want the house to go out of the family none of us can live there at the moment.'

'It is a beautiful place, Mrs. Hamilton, and I am sure if the trustees decide to go ahead we can bring it back to life again.'

'And I must look forward not backwards,' she says. 'That blackbird is getting soaked trying to have a bath in Glycella's waterfall!' We laugh together and I release her hand and sit back in my chair again. I think we are both relieved: Mrs. Hamilton to have shared the story of Avon View House, and I to understand some of the emotions I sensed at our first meeting. I believe we can draw up a plan that will be good for the Trust and for the family too. For them it will be reparation for the damage Geoffrey has done and maybe for past involvement in the slave trade.

I relay a summary of my conversation with Mrs. Hamilton senior to Andy in the car as we drive away and then ask him what he thinks of the old house.

'Well, Jane is it larger than I thought. It would be a big project for the Trust. We will have to find partners to help use and pay for the space and set up a local board to oversee it.'

'Can we fund the renovation and the running costs?' I ask.

'We can apply to grant-making bodies for the renovation and we need other organisations to rent rooms and provide us with an income to run the place.'

'What about the office in London?'

'Not sure yet.' He shakes his head. 'I'll have to look at the figures.

He drops me off outside the Record Office.

The B Bond warehouse is calmer today with only a handful of people in the entrance hall. I join the queue for lunch and take a table in the window looking out over what my phone tells me is the "New Cut".

'Miss Taverner, may I join you?' I look up to see the narrow features of Rory Odhiambo staring down at me.

'Oh, err, yes, of course.' There really is no way out of this. He places his tray on the table and sits in the chair opposite me.

'You know Bristol well?' he asks.

'No. This is only my second visit.'

'So what do you think of the city?'

'Well, I'm finding it rather confusing. Most of the centre seems to be water.'

'Yes, the Floating Harbour.'

'Why is it "floating"?' I ask. He laughs.

'The Avon has a large tidal range and a narrow channel. Originally boats sailed right into the heart of the city on the high tide but when the sea went out they tipped over and the cargo was damaged. Many plans were made to remedy the situation but nothing happened until Ferdinand Jessop came up with a bold plan to reroute the Avon and block its original channel to make a huge lake, "The Floating Harbour". We are at the western end of it here.'

'Oh, I see, so where is the river?'

He chuckles and points a finger through the window. 'That is the new course of the Avon, you can see the mud banks where the tide has gone out.'

'The New Cut!'

'Yes.' He beams at me as if I were a star pupil and his grin is infectious; we laugh together.

'May I get you a coffee?' He is so amiable compared with his behavior at our first meeting that I feel caught off balance. I am usually a good judge of character but at the moment I cannot reconcile the hollow-faced terse man I met last time with the ease he shows today.

'A lemonade, please.' I look out of the window at the weeds growing along the edge of the New Cut, the dark shiny banks and the trickle of muddy water in the bottom. Bristol is an intriguing city, vibrant and sophisticated in its human landscape, and wild and savage in its physical environment. I wonder if its inhabitants share some of the same characteristics – the poise and generosity of Glycella, David and Anka Hamilton and the greed and carelessness of Geoffrey and his wife. Is Rory Odhiambo equally quixotic? It certainly seems so from the two encounters I have had so far. He returns with lemonade and a coke.

'We have a new project starting in Bristol so I am going to be here quite a bit. What other sites should I see?' I ask him.

'You must drive up to Clifton Down to the view of the gorge and the suspension bridge.'

'I stopped on Clifton Down on my way to an appointment the other day and peered into the gorge. Impressive!'

'And then there is Queen Square and the inner harbour – the original part of the docks.'

'I haven't found that area yet.'

'Let me know next time you are coming to Bristol and I will take you on a walk through the city centre.' I look at him wondering if he is serious or trying to mock me. His brown eyes are steady and his mouth is curved in a smile.

'I'll do that. Thank you.'

'Good.' He shifts his chair back and takes the plates to the counter. I do the same with the glasses and follow him across the entrance hall and down the corridor to his office.

. . . .

'Rory Odhiambo is an odd man,' I comment to Andy as he picks me up. 'The first time I met him I found him very rude and suspicious. Today he could not have been more helpful over the permissions we need for the displays.'

'It's your natural charm and empathy, Jane,' says Andy, 'It seems to have worked a treat on Mrs. Hamilton senior.'

'She had made up her mind to explain,' I tell him. 'It was difficult for her but I think she wanted everything out in the open. She seemed very aloof at first but I like and admire her.'

'Yes,' he agrees, 'quite a lady!' He drops me at Mrs. Jackson's as he has to drive back to London tonight while I am staying on. Mrs. Jackson seems delighted to have my company regularly but I find the constraints of the house rules testing. There is never anywhere to sit and work quietly without having a cup of tea and a piece of cake and a requirement to chat with other guests. I spend most of my time in a coffee shop in Bedminster when I am catching up on emails. Once the renovation of the house is underway I hope I can find a quiet corner to use as an office.

Mrs. Jackson is apologetic when I arrive.

'I'm very sorry, dear, I've had to put you in the room at the back.'

'That's no problem.'

'I've put new curtains in so the lights won't bother you.'

The red and gold curtains are thick, but I am intrigued and later that evening when it is dark I pull them aside and look out of the window. Mrs. Jackson's has been extended beyond the rear of the house next door and overlooks it. A bright light is visible behind opaque white blinds; nothing that is likely to bother me once I am asleep. I am far more troubled by noise and disturb in the night when a siren wails; I get up for a drink of water. I can see my way to the wash basin well enough without turning the light on and when I pull aside the curtains the light is still burning brightly next door. Perhaps they were disturbed as well.

I go back to bed but my sleep is troubled by a dream about an Arab dhow on the White Nile; it is sailing downstream heavily loaded with sacks of dried leaves. Water washes over the deck as it turns north towards Gordon's Hill overlooking Nimule. The sun is setting and a light on the mast is visible through the sail. As the light fades and the boat tips, people start to come up on deck; they see me on the shore and start to wave. I wave back but they shout and cry. Are they calling for help? I wake up sweating and anxious with the room still in darkness. I keep getting these night terrors, usually it is a recurrence of the giant rising from the White Nile that I had in Nimule. When will it stop? I go to the sink to wash my face and see the grey light of morning filtering under the curtains. I draw them back. The light is still on next door and dark silhouettes are moving across the blind. What are they doing at this time of morning? A cold fear seizes hold of my stomach. Who is there? I watch from behind the curtain. There are three or four of them moving across the window sometimes all together, sometimes one at a time. I see the sacks of dried leaves in my dream and realise that the light behind the sail cloth and the light behind the blind have the same intensity. What is the dream telling me? Or is it just my own anxiety getting hold of me?

I give up trying to sleep and go along to the shower. As I eat my breakfast Mrs. Jackson comes over; she is inclined to fuss over me and I break into her questions with one of my own.

'That house next door – there were some men arrested from there weren't there? What happened to them?'

'Oh, they went to prison for drug smuggling, got three

years each they did, and so I should think!'

'So who is there now?'

'Nobody, dear; there's a man comes in once a week on a Friday afternoon. I see him by the dustbins sometimes.' Other guests enter and she bustles away to get their breakfast, her primrose yellow dress covered by a bright pink apron dotted with tiny purple flowers. I finish my scrambled egg thoughtfully, my mind full of reports we have received from the Metropolitan Police on forced labour on marijuana farms.

If I hurry, I can call in at the nearest police station before my meeting and still catch the midday train to London. I have another session with Maria this afternoon; I want to find out how she freed herself when she arrived in the UK and how she ended up at Lucille's.

10 FREE!

So maybe my years as a slave were finally, finally over. Maybe I was truly free after all.[10]

I have not been outside Master Ibrahim's house for five years. Solomon and Atifa were always nearby but as Kharimah's maid I spent many hours alone sewing and mending in the small room next to hers. Now I am on an aeroplane sitting next to her and the boys. They are excited and chattering; all I can think about is that I am leaving my country and my family. I am terrified that the spirits that keep this tunnel full of people in the air may forget to fly. As we land I can feel them pressing on my ears and I nearly cry out. They are hurting my head and I

---

[10] *Slave* by Mende Nazir and Damien Lewis 2004

177

cannot hear properly.

I hold the children's bags and follow the mistress. If I lose sight of her I will be taken by the demons. I remember the English I learned as a child but the demons are muddling my thoughts and I cannot understand what people say.

Kharimah's brother, Abdul, drives us to a place called "Slough" where he lives with his family. Their home is not the grand palace the mistress has been describing to the boys but a narrow brick house in a row of identical doors and windows. I am shown the kitchen, which is inside the house and has a large sink where the water comes out of a pipe and many cupboards. I sleep in a small room off the kitchen. Life goes on much as it did in Juba except that there are no other servants for a household of ten people. Sewing, cleaning, and cooking for so many means that I do not sleep until far into the night. It is very cold. I have only the cotton shift that I wore in Juba, a thin pair of shoes the mistress gave me and a blanket. I hope it will soon get warmer but instead the sun disappears for many days and it is darker and colder as each day passes.

For the first few weeks there are many visitors – relatives

greeting Kharimah and exclaiming over the boys. Then Abdul returns to his work at the airport and his wife to her job in a factory nearby. Life is dull for the mistress and the little masters. Soon she is talking of their return to Juba and I am pleased that we will leave this cold dark country. Then I overhear her talking with her brother one evening:

'You will be stopped. They will not allow you to take her on the plane without proper papers.'

'What else can I do?' the mistress replies.

'Leave her here, you can find another maid in Juba.' That night I cannot sleep because of cold that goes deep into my bones. I shake and pray to the Lord Jesus that I will not be left in this terrible land but they depart for Juba without me.

I clean and cook. I do not sleep at night because the demons that live in the water pipes make strange noises and I am afraid they will come out to get me. The food is different and there are witchcraft spells on it so I do not eat much. Kharimah's brother and his wife speak to me in English but I do not understand. I pray to the Lord Jesus each day that I will see my family again and that he will keep them safe but I feel very weak and wonder if I will survive in this cold land.

English phrases I learned in school in Torit gradually come back to me. I am given cast-off clothes. The days grow a little warmer and I feel less desperate. I do not think the mistress explained about me. I begin to realise that Abdul and his wife do not watch me as the mistress did. Doors are left unlocked. I am encouraged to "get some fresh air". There is a gate at the end of the garden opening onto a narrow path behind the houses. I begin to walk there each day. But if anyone tried to speak with me I run back inside. I hide things in the gap under a cupboard – food, clothes, a torch, soap and a toothbrush. Soon I have a pile of items and an old cloth to tie them in. I pray each day for Jesus to help and guide me.

Abdul and his wife usually leave the house at different times but one day they leave early and together. I tidy the house and then tie up my bundle. I walk out through the back gate and along the path until I come to a road with many cars. I do not know which way to go so I walk towards the sun and southern Sudan. I know I cannot get back on my own but I walk in the direction of the aeroplanes landing over me. Maybe I will find a way if Abdul does not see me. I pray and put my feet down one after the other. I am carrying my bundle beside me – too scared to put it on my head. People in cars shout at me if it swings out into the road. I turn into a quieter street and keep walking until I come to a park. I hide in the bushes behind the building on one side of the park and stay there until the sun sets. Then I eat some of the food in my bundle, stretch myself out on my cloth and sleep for a while. I walk again. The planes flying overhead seem nearer. Two women come up to me and shove my bundle into my leg and say something I do not understand.

'Airport?' I ask them.

'What you want to go there for?' one of them says. 'You looking for work?' The other girl moves round so that they are on either side of me.

'Go Sudan,' I tell them. They laugh and call two men over.

'Hey, Carlos, you should 'ear this! She's walking to the airport to get to Sudan!' The man called Carlos comes up close to me.

'Hey, darlin', how ya doing? You got money and papers?'

I have nothing but my bundle with clothes and food. 'You come with us, we'll fix you up.' The girls link arms with me and walk me to a room at the back of a shop. I sit between them on a sofa covered with a filthy cloth. Carlos and the other man perch on a desk.

'So, darlin', what's yer name?' Carlos says. I hesitate. For many years I have been "Mirah" but that is not my name.

'Maria,' I say.
'An' where you from, Maria?' says Carlos.

'Slough.' I wave a hand in the direction of the house I have left.

'You want to go to the airport but you got no papers?' I nod. 'We can fix that for you, can't we, girls?' They smile at me but I cannot smile back. I feel numb inside. I have not sat close to anyone for many years; it does not feel right. One girl still has her arm linked in mine and Carlos's long legs are stretched out across the door.

'Here's what we do,' he says. 'We got this shop, see? We make deliveries to some of the customers. We pay you to do the deliveries. All local, you can walk it easy. We get you proper documents and you pay for them out of what you earn. OK?' I nod again. His accent is different and I do not catch everything.

'You understand?' asks Carlos and I shake my head.

'Look!' He grabs a bag of white crystals from the desk behind him. 'Sugar!' he says.

'Sukkur?'

'Yeh. You take this to houses I show you. I pay you. OK?' It sounds straight forward. I nod.

'I get papers, for Sudan?'

'Yes, that's right, for the airport. You sleep here. Tomorrow you take the sugar.' They leave, locking the door behind them. I am too tired to worry any more. There is a small basin in the corner of the room and I drink from the tap. I take the cloth off the sofa and lay it on the floor with my own cloth over me and my bundle under my head. I will get money and the papers for the airport. Then I will be able to fly back to Sudan and find my family.

I wake after sunrise and tidy the room. I shake the cover

out of the narrow slot of a window and collect some of the dirt off the floor and throw it out. The window is too small for me to climb out. I am there all day and have no food. I begin to worry that I have done the wrong thing but as the sun is setting Carlos appears. He has a bag over his shoulder and a piece of paper in his hand.

'Maria, how yer doing?' he says as he comes into the room. He tries to put an arm over my shoulder but I wriggle away. He laughs and says something I cannot understand. He shows me roads drawn on the piece of paper. I have to go to the houses marked in red and deliver the packets he has in the bag. I must collect an envelope and bring it back to him at the shop.

For the next few evenings I deliver my parcels, hand the envelopes to Carlos and receive a few coins from him, which he says are English pounds. After five days he brings me a small book.

'Here, Maria. This is your passport. Here's your picture and your address at the shop. Your age is twenty two, yes?' I nod, although I know I am younger than that.

'You owe me a thousand pounds now. You pay me by working. I take your money from now on. You stay here till it's paid, then I give the passport to you.' He is paying me three pounds a night. It will take me many years to pay him what I owe but cannot think of another way. He locks me in each night to "keep me safe" but I know it is to make sure I pay for the passport.

After a few days Carlos asks me to deliver to more houses. Some of them are far away and I have to go by bus. He comes with me the first time then I have to go on my own. He keeps increasing the number of houses until I am working late into the evening. When I need money for food I ask him. I also have to pay my bus fares. Very soon I need most of the money I earn. I try to pay him five pounds a week. It is going to take a long time to pay the thousand pounds.

I am very tired. I feel confused. I pray and tell Lord Jesus that I am sorry. I am in worse trouble than before. Solomon was right; it is difficult to escape. The demons in the water are making my stomach hurt and pinching my legs when I sleep. I never speak to anyone except Carlos and a brief 'Good evening' when I deliver the packets and collect the envelopes. I miss the busyness of Master Ibrahim's family, even though they treated me cruelly, and I long for the advice of Atifa and Solomon.

One night it is as warm as southern Sudan and I sleep with the window open. I can hear the chatter of people in the shop and smell the oil from the chip shop across the road. I am woken before dawn by banging and shouting in the shop. I stand up, wrap my cloth around me and wait. The noise becomes louder. I can hear Carlos shouting and then a muffled thud and the steadier tones of another man giving instructions. I dress quickly and wrap everything I have in my cloth.

There is a splintering sound, the lock on the door crashes to the floor, the door swings open and two men in dark uniforms burst in. I back against the wall holding my bundle tightly to my chest. I am so frightened I dare not move. One of the men raises a gun and yells.

'Hands on head!' I do not understand. He gestures and shouts again. I drop my bundle and put my hands on my head and watch the other man search the room. They find traces of sugar on the floor where I was sleeping. They put metal bracelets on my wrists, take me out to a car and tell me to sit in the back with a woman in the same uniform. The car smells of mud and sweat. There is a voice talking in the front but I cannot see anyone so it must be a spirit. Carlos has gone and I am afraid in case the man with the gun comes. More men in black uniforms are running down the street. I press myself into the corner of the car and try to stop my body trembling.

Another woman in uniform gets into the front of the car. We wait in silence until a man joins us and starts the car. The curtains at the houses are closed; everyone is asleep.

We pull up and the woman beside me gets out and says 'Come on' and jerks her head for me to follow her into the building. She takes me to a small room with bars in the window and tells me to sit down on a long padded seat. She locks the door on her way out. I stay there all day. They bring me food and water. Then a woman and a man come in and ask me questions.

'Do you have any identity, passport, papers?' they ask.

I shake my head. 'Carlos has,' I say.

The woman starts asking questions.

'What is your name? How old are you? Where are you from? How long have you been delivering crack?'

I answered as carefully as I can. I have not heard the white sugar called "crack" before. She goes away for a while and then returns with a piece of paper with writing on.

'Maria, I would like you to read this. If you are happy please sign your name here.' It is in English characters. I have learned some words from reading road signs and shop windows but I cannot read her writing. I was taught to sign my name in English in Torit so I sign where she points.

The next few weeks are confusing. I am moved from one place to another and each time there are forms to be filled in. Twice I am taken to a room they call "Court". There are people with strange curly hats covering their heads. I think they are witch doctors because people respect and fear them. Finally I am taken to a place called "Send Gaol". Here there is another set of forms to fill in and they take my clothes and give me new ones. I share a small room with a girl called Jade, and we are locked in together at night.

'What you in for then?' she asks.

'For sugar,' I tell her.

'Oh, another druggy! Well you keep to your own side of the room and I'll keep to mine.'

For weeks we live in the room together but with an invisible barrier between us. She knows many of the other girls and sometimes they push against me in the corridor.

'Hey Maria, got any "sugar" for us?' they ask. I am afraid to go out of the cell because they laugh and jostle me.

When we are locked in Jade avoids looking at me and never speaks unless she feels I have crossed into her side of the room. I wait until she is asleep at night before I say my prayers.

I am told to clean the corridors while Jade works in the laundry. She complains about long hours and too much work but to me life is easier than usual. I clean for a few hours and then I can rest. In the afternoon we go outside for an hour. Many girls complain that there is not enough food but three meals a day is more than I have ever had.

A few weeks later I am sent to English classes. I am pleased because I have tried so hard to learn. After ten weeks I get a certificate to show that I have done well. I keep working hard until I have four certificates and the tutor is congratulates me. One morning she comes over to the desk where I am working and says,

'Maria, I enjoyed your last piece of work. You have a good imagination.'

'I did not make it up, Miss Hanley; that is how I lived before I came to the UK.'

'I see,' she says and pauses, looking at me carefully. 'It was well described.'

A few days later she calls me over to her desk.

'Maria, you are doing so well I would like you to do an extra essay.'

'Yes, I will do it.' I am pleased that she is praising me.

'I want you to write a description of what happened when you left Juba to come to the UK. You can write a bit at a time during the class. I will give you a special notebook, which you can hand to me at the end of each class.'

For the next few weeks I sit at a desk in the corner and write all I can remember about life in Juba and the months in Slough. Each week she corrects my work and I try hard not to make the same mistake again.

One day there is a prison officer waiting for me as I leave my class.

'Maria Kuol, you are wanted in the chaplain's office. Come with me.' I fear that I am in trouble. The officer knocks on the door.

'Come in,' says a voice so soft I can hardly hear. The officer opens the door and stands aside for me to enter a room crowded with books and armchairs. There is a bunch of blue flowers on the window sill. They remind me of the jacaranda flowers that bloom on trees in Sudan.

'Maria, come and sit down.' The chaplain has a small

slight figure and light reddish brown hair caught in a clip at the nape of her neck. Her eyes are blue and intense. She wears a flared skirt and high-necked blouse with a white pastor's band across her throat.

'How are you?'

'I am well,' I answer.

'And you come from Sudan, which part?'

'From Torit, ma'am.'

'You can call me Susan, the Reverend Susan Howith.' She extends a hand so I hold mine out as I have seen other people do and she shakes it up and down.

'Tell me about yourself, Maria. You worked for a family in Juba before you came here?'

'Yes, I cleaned their house and prepared food and looked after the children.'

'Did they pay you for this?'

'No, ma'am.'

'Did you like the work?'

'The cleaning and cooking, yes. I did not like looking after the boys because they hated me.'

'Maybe they did not hate you. Young children can be very mischievous sometimes?'

'They said I was a monkey and the mistress said I was lazy.'

'The "mistress" is their mother?'

'Yes.'

'How did you get to the UK?'

'The mistress brought me with her when she visited her brother but when she returned to Juba she left me behind. One day I ran away.'

'And then what happened?'

'I didn't know what to do. I needed someone to help me get back to Sudan. A man called Carlos offered me work for money. I didn't know he was doing wrong things. I am sorry that I did wrong, Ma'am.' I do not dare to call her Susan, it seems disrespectful.

She asks me questions about Carlos, where I slept and what I did each day, and I answer as clearly as I can. I explain that I was unwell and frightened and did not understand what I was doing.

She stands up and makes us both a cup of tea from a kettle

in the corner of her room. There are little cakes with icing on.

'Tell me about your family,' she says. 'When did you last see them?' So I tell her how we had to flee because of the bombing, and about the soldiers taking us and being made to be a "wife". I tell her I pray to Jesus every day that I will see them again.

'How did you learn about Jesus, Maria?' Reverend Susan asks.

'My mother and father told me stories about Jesus. I went to St Andrew's church in Torit and sometimes to the New Jerusalem church in Nimule.'

'And were your mistress and her family Christians?'

'No!' I am shocked. 'They are from north Sudan. They make me say Muslim prayers but when I hear the call to prayer I pray to Jesus.'

'I run a group every Wednesday afternoon for people who follow Jesus; would you like to come, Maria?'

'I would like to.' She reaches into a drawer and hands me something in a box.

'This is for you, Maria.' It has the words "Holy Bible" on

the front of it. I have heard my mother speak of such a book but I had never seen one before this moment.

At about this time I start to learn hairdressing. I cut hair the western way for some ladies but for others I comb and twist their hair the southern Sudan way, dividing it into rows or squares.

One day one of the prison officers comes into the class while I am washing a girl's hair and tells me that the governor wants to see me.

'What you done, Maria?' the girl asks. 'I bin here five years and I never seen the gov'nor.'

I dry my hands, take off my apron and follow the officer. We go through part of the prison I have never been in before and wait outside a shiny wooden door until someone comes out. Then the officer says,

'Maria Kuol, sir.' And we enter.

I am terrified. I do not know what I have done. I am looking at a man who is shorter than I am. He has dark penetrating eyes, and a fleshy mouth. His jacket is stretched across powerful shoulders, and he has a brown and orange striped tie.

'Sit down, Maria. How long have you been here?' I sit

trembling on a wooden chair with a padded seat in front of a massive dark table.

'Four years, sir, I came here in May 1999.'

'And you have a conviction for drug trafficking and forged papers?'

'Yes, sir.' I look down at my hands. My fingers are twisting over each other in my lap but I cannot feel them – it is as if they do not belong to me. The shame of what I have done sweeps over me. I can smell again that strange smell when a police officer tipped out one of the bags I thought was sugar.

'The chaplain and your tutor have advised me that you have been a victim of trafficking.' I do not understand what he means and look up at his face.

'You were brought to the UK against your will.'

'Yes, sir.'

'There has been a miscarriage of justice.' I cannot understand these words. 'You must prepare for your release.' He looks at me sternly.

'Yes, sir.'

'Continue with your studies so that you are ready to find

proper work.'

'Yes, sir.' The officer escorts me back to my cell. As we pass through the long passageways my thoughts are in turmoil. "Release" means getting free. My tutor says that the tests I am doing will allow me to be a hairdresser. Where will I go? What will I do? I feel confused and anxious.

Many people help me; I have an interview with a careers adviser; another lady shows me how to apply for something called "benefit", which she says will give me money for food and a bed. I am taken out of the prison for a day to see a lawyer who will help me apply for a legal passport. The chaplain finds me a place to stay. She tells me that someone will meet me when I am released and help me get to London where I am to work. It takes many weeks. Everyone is kind but it is bewildering; so much is new to me. In January 2003 I walk out of the prison and am put into a car with a lady from the Salvation Army and taken to the station to catch a train to London.

The same lady takes me to her church. I have supper with her once a week and I can ask for help at any time. This is the most difficult time of all. There are so many things to think about, finding a place to sleep, getting food, opening a bank account, starting work. I would not have been able to manage without her help. Her name is Sara, and her husband's name is Jon. They have been a mother and father to me. I want to share this story because life is so difficult for people who are taken from their country. I work hard and earn money. I have my own flat. Now that I am the manager I am saving for the airfare to go to South Sudan. I have survived. I am free!

11 RORY

By felon hands, by one relentless stroke,

See the fond links of feeling nature broke,

The fibres twisting round a parent's heart,

Torn from their grasp and bleeding as they part..[11]

Sitting in the window of the cafe in the M Shed Museum in Bristol is not the peaceful place I had hoped for. On the table next to me there are four families with young children, and there is a constant clatter as spoons are dropped, bibs misplaced and toys lost. Now a bundle wrapped in a blanket is being taken to have a nappy changed and I'm trying to ignore them. I turn towards the window and watch the gulls wheeling over the harbour; their cries are briefly audible but drowned out by a crescendo of wails. Someone's favourite cake has fallen

---

[11] *Slavery* a poem by Hannah More , 1788

icing side down on the floor. Parental order is restored but while their attention is engaged with the cake a small boy is crawling under the tables towards me. I ignore his heavy breathing as he chugs past my chair and I watch the gulls. My view is impeded by the four disused cranes derelict on the wharf. Their height is immense, dwarfing the three story bulk of the museum. Steel giants - arms raised, heads bowed, limbs locked to the quayside - relics of the 1950s glory days of the Floating Harbour when big machines replaced manual labour before finally giving way to computer-driven containerisation at Portishead. I wait anxiously for Rory to appear, half hoping that something will delay him and he'll be forced to cancel.

I don't know what prompted me to make such a rash call. I suppose I was daunted by the thought of several days of meetings with a weekend in between and frustrated by all that I had to leave undone in London. I spent many hours last week helping Nina to keep on track with her programme. I have downloaded the last part of Maria's story from my tablet. I'm shocked by how hard it has been for Maria to rebuild her life – she should never have ended up in prison. I want to help develop better systems, not be trapped in meetings; yet here I am stuck in Bristol for a meeting at Avon View House and then a session with the voluntary sector to find charities who might be interested in renting space. It has been arduous and dispiriting. I have a day's sea kayaking in the Severn to look forward to tomorrow, booked through the local club. What mad impulse led me to take up Rory Odhiambo's offer of a walk through central Bristol? I made the call yesterday morning and it was every bit as awkward as I might have anticipated.

'Hallo, Rory, Jane Taverner here.'

'Good morning, Miss Taverner, how can I help you?'
Sugar, that sounds formal.

'I'm sorry to bother you. Last time we met you mentioned a historic trail and I wondered where I could find out about it?'

'It starts from the M Shed at the top end of the Floating Harbour. Are you planning to go today?'

'No, I'm staying over for a few days. I've nothing planned for Saturday and I thought I might follow the trail you mentioned.' There was a brief pause at the other end, then a slight cough.

'I'm free on Saturday morning; I could take you round? I know the route well.'

'Well, if you can spare the time...'

'I have to drop my son off at his chess club, can we say ten thirty?'

Oh no, he's married, I should have realised – but he doesn't wear a ring.

'Will your wife come?' I ask. I need to get out of this somehow.

'I'm a widower.'

Oh! That's sad; he's not much older than I am.

'Oh, I'm so sorry, I didn't realise.'

'I can drop Camarg off and meet you at the M Shed. I'll have to collect him by one but that should give us plenty of time.'

'Well, if you're sure...'

'There is a cafe on the ground floor museum, I'll see you there.'

'Thank you. Bye.'

I'm embarrassed that I contacted him. I'm rarely needy for company but the prospect of a day on my own in a strange city seemed depressing. Now I've let myself in for a morning with a maudlin widower. At least he has to collect his son or I might have landed myself with him for the whole day.

'Sorry,' says a voice in my right ear as a man stoops to scoop up the roving crawler from under my table. 'He's into everything at the moment.'

'No problem.' I smile and remove one end of the scarf I'd draped over the back of my chair from the baby's sticky grasp and wipe it on a paper napkin, leaving a faint residue of white fluff on the gold, red and ochre hues of the cotton. As I look up Rory comes through the door from the museum. I hurriedly wipe the stickiness off my hand and rise to shake his.

'I'm sorry,' he says, 'I didn't think it would be so busy. Let me grab a coffee. Can I get you another?'

'No, I'm fine, thank you. I don't drink coffee.'

By the time Rory returns the families have gathered up their offspring, loaded them into various folding contraptions and are walking them along the quayside.

'Sorry to be late; Camarg didn't tell me his club fees were due.'

'How old is Camarg?'

'He's twelve.' I expect him to tell me more about his child, most people do but he stares at his coffee cup and stirs it thoughtfully.'

'It is very kind of you to show me around.'

'It's no problem. You're here for several days?'

'Yes, until Tuesday. I have appointments and it didn't seem worth driving back to London so I've booked onto a sea kayaking course on the Severn tomorrow.'

'Kayaking?'

Yes, most weekends I go out to Kent or Essex, somewhere on the Thames with my local club. Do you have a hobby?'

'I play in a band.'

'What sort of a band?' I'm surprised; he seems such a sombre character.

'Jazz mostly, a bit of Mardi Gras and hip hop, popular songs played with a jazz rhythm if we are doing a dance.' His face creases in a smile and his eyes light up. 'I do gigs most Friday evenings and some Saturdays, if I can find someone to keep an eye on Camarg.' He drains his coffee. There is an intense sadness in his eyes as he stares down into the cup, as if trying to read a better future in the coffee grounds. Then his head comes up again and he grins.

'Shall we get going?' he says.

'Yes, what's the plan?'

'We'll mooch along the waterfront to the Redcliffe caves and then over the bridge to Queen's Square but first there are one or two things to show you here.' I gather up my scarf and bag and follow him upstairs to a cylindrical enclosure within the museum. The inside walls tell the story of slaves bought and sold. We stare in silence at the evidence of a brutal trade – iron shackles, an iron collar and chain, invoices detailing slaves bought and sold three hundred years ago.

'There were a few brave people, even in Bristol, who campaigned for abolition,' he says and crosses to where a glass cabinet holds a miscellany of objects.

'I recognise that,' I say, pointing to a small disc showing a figure kneeling on one knee, chains dangling from his upheld arms. 'It's the Josiah Wedgewood design used in the campaign against slavery.'

There is a small wooden boat further along in the cabinet, the upper deck removed to reveal lower decks, where black stick bodies are crammed together. I gaze into the wooden ship, small as a child's toy, drawn into the misery of that voyage across the Atlantic, shackled together for weeks; no mattresses, no slop buckets, just a channel running down the centre of the deck. As I peer through the glass it seems as if one of the figures lifts himself up on one hand. The face is as narrow as Rory's but younger and a lighter brown. He waves at me and his eyes are huge and pleading.

'Jane, come and see the other side of the trade.' Rory breaks in on my reverie and I follow him across the display hall to a gilt-framed oil painting. It shows a wide street, running beside a narrow waterway. Men in long frock coats, white leggings and tricorne hats are in earnest discussion in the foreground. Ladies in long dresses with feathers in their hats stroll along looking in the shop windows.

I ponder the inequalities between those who walked the Bristol streets in previous centuries, their comfort built on plantations and the trade in slaves and those whose forced labour created their wealth. Britain led the world in banning slavery in the past and I am glad that we have taken the lead once again in passing a bill to control modern trafficking.

We leave the M Shed Museum and walk past the cranes towards the bridge. A line of low red cliffs is visible a few metres in from the water's edge, with a row of terraced houses above.

'There are rumours that slaves were confined in Redcliffe caves, and under St Mary Redcliffe church,' says Rory. 'There's no evidence but St Mary's rang the church bells in celebration when Wilberforce's Abolition Bill was defeated in 1791!' He laughs drily.

'I suppose Bristol was against abolition.'

'Completely divided – merchants argued that they were giving people jobs and looking after them but others were committed abolitionists. Hannah Moore wrote a famous poem about the cruelty of slavery in breaking up families.'

'That is the worst part: one of my clients has not seen her family for over twenty years and has no idea whether they are alive or not.'

We sit on the benches in the centre of Queen Square. It's a windy day and clouds alternately block and reveal the sun, highlighting in turn the dark red brick and stone quoins of the English Heritage office, and the whitened stones of the 'American Consulate', so the blue heritage sign proclaims.

'This was the site of the first riots,' says Rory. 'Bristol can erupt when you least expect it. There was an outcry when the shopping mall was named "Merchants Quarter" and it had to be renamed Cabot Circus, after the early explorer.'

'You've lived here all your life?' I ask him.

'No, I came three years ago from London. I worked as a foreign correspondent, but I had to change career when Grace died.'

'What happened?'

'She had cancer. She was beautiful and brave and bright, a social worker and a fantastic mum. We thought she had made a good recovery but then they found secondaries and she went very quickly.'

'I'm sorry; it must have been difficult with your son to think of as well.'

'I carried on and Grace's mother looked after Camarg but it became too stressful. It was no good for Camarg; I'd have very little notice of a posting and he'd come home from school and find me gone. He was unsettled and Ma was concerned. In the end I retrained and got the job here. I enjoy the research but I miss London.' His eyes have that hooded, sad look again. I can see how deeply he is affected by talking about his wife, and the life he had. He unfurls his long legs from beneath him and springs up from the bench; a few pigeons scatter in disgust.

'We'll walk into the old part of the centre,' he says, 'along King Street and the Corn Exchange.' We wander through the busy streets, narrow and crowded in this part of Bristol. Some buildings have stucco figures illustrating port activities, the arms of the Merchant Venturers, the bust of America with a head dress of tobacco leaves. Rory pauses in front of an imposing Victorian building with pairs of classical columns on either side of many windows.

'This was one of the big local banks,' he says. 'The wealth of Bristol came from the reparation payments when slaves were freed, which enabled the merchants to move out into grander properties on the outskirts of Bristol. '

'You mean the money they were paid for releasing slaves?'

'Yes. This statue is Edward Colston; his money came from the sugar trade.' We stop in front of a bronze statue of a bewigged gentleman, one hand resting on his cane, head dropped forward, the other hand cupped beneath it, impressive waves of hair falling either side of his face; he looks wise and benign.

'Look,' Rory breaks in on my musing, 'I have to collect Camarg in a few minutes. Will you join us for lunch? I promised him a snack at the Mud Dock. He loves the bicycle shop underneath!' He pauses expectantly as I hesitate. I don't like children but Camarg sounds old enough not to cover me with stickiness and I'm intrigued at the thought of eating somewhere called the Mud Dock.

'Yes, I'd love to.'

So he leaves me sitting by the strange rabbit ear funnels of the Pero Bridge to look back on what has been a surprisingly agreeable morning. The sunshine slants in under trees lining the street making dappled patterns on the cobbled pavement. I watch people passing on the bridge, and water taxis slicing their way through the choppy waters of the harbour. Then I start to get impatient. Rory is longer than the few minutes he promised. How long will they be? Why am I sitting here waiting to have lunch with an adolescent youth and his father? The answer surprises me – because he is good company, because he understands many of the issues that interest me, because I'm intrigued by the contrast between the narrow confines of his work and the wide range of his interests.

'Here we are, sorry for the delay; I thought you might've given up on us. Camarg, say "hallo" to Miss Taverner.'

'I'm Jane,' I laugh and extend a hand to the quiet, sensitive looking boy. I'm disconcerted; the face I'm looking at is the same as the boy who waved at me from the slave ship in the museum. He shakes firmly with a quick, shy smile. He has his father's dark eyes and narrow nose but his face is wider and slightly paler, framed by wiry corkscrews of hair.

It's a short walk from Princes Street to the Mud Dock, which is a two-story warehouse opposite the Redcliffe Caves, part of Bristol's industrial past recycled as a chic cafe. We climb exterior metal steps, which open into a wooden floored space filled with windows looking out onto the harbour and a curved deck area with tables and umbrellas.

'Inside or out?' asks Rory. I opt for inside as the wind is picking up and we settle at one of the mismatched tables underneath an old bicycle hung from the roof.

'Did you have a good morning?' I ask Camarg. He answers politely and quietly but his eyes light up with enthusiasm as he starts to describe the details of his chess games.

'Hang about, old chap, let's order some lunch,' breaks in his father and Camarg grins and opts for a burger and chips. They seem to have a good relationship but there's a slightly lost air about both of them.

'What brings you to Bristol this time?' asks Rory once we have ordered. He seems more relaxed over the meal table, less inclined to lose himself in factual details and stories.

'The Olaudah Trust has been offered a substantial property for use as a hostel for people who have been trafficked. It's a very generous gift but we have to renovate the property and make it pay.'

'Where is it?'

'Avon View House in Leigh Woods, the other side of the suspension bridge. It belongs to the Hamilton family.' Camarg, who has been consuming his burger with steady efficiency, looks up suddenly, bun held awkwardly in one hand and dripping tomato juice onto his plate. I catch his eye and his skin darkens slightly, then his eyelids drop and he appears to give his full concentration to mopping up the tomato juice with the bun. But there was a flash of recognition in those dark eyes and I wonder how he knows Avon View House.'

'I remember; Matt Williamson helped you with information for the display panels.'

'Yes, the difficulty is going to be finding anyone who

wants to rent that far out of central Bristol.'

'I may be able to help; can I put the word about through the band?'

'Yes, of course.' I look at him enquiringly.

'We play gigs at community venues around west Bristol and the Ashton area; we might be able to link you up with some of the community organisations in the area.'

'Thank you. We'll get payments for each client once we get referrals but we need rents as well to fund such a large building.' I can feel my stomach knotting up with anxiety. I've broken the light-hearted mood.

'Time for a pudding,' says Rory. 'The cakes are good here.'

'Chocolate layer cake, please,' says Camarg. His father laughs and looks across to me. His eyes sparkle with amusement and the long line of his mouth is creased in a grin. He looks boyish and relaxed.

'Can we tempt you with lemon drizzle cake or walnut and coffee – my favourite?' I had decided not to have a pudding but his laugh is infectious and Camarg is watching, eager to see which I choose.

'Well, I'll take Camarg's recommendation and have the chocolate cake.'

'I'm slighted!' says Rory and leaves Camarg and I giggling as he goes to the small corner bar to order.

'Tell me about the bike,' I ask the boy and he launches into a description of its gears and racer handlebars, how he needs a special piece so that he can do stunts with the other boys.'

'I hope you wear a safety helmet.' My remark inspires a further explanation of helmet straps and knee pads, his face animated with enthusiasm for his hobby. I recognise his passion for special equipment in my own delight in new kayaking gadgets.

'Now Camarg,' chides Rory when he returns, 'I've already bored Jane this morning with my stories of the slave trade!'

'Did you take her to the caves, Dad?'

'Yes, we looked at the model slave boat in the M Shed and then walked along the harbour to Queen Square and Corn Market.'

'Cool, did you show her the sugar loaf house, Dad?'

'No, we didn't get that far.'

'All the houses in Bristol seem to be built of sugar, even Avon View House!' I respond. Camarg's face stiffens again. The camaraderie over the chocolate cake has dissipated, to be replaced by a fidgeting unease.

'Can I go to the shop now?' he asks.

'OK then, have you got your money from Nan?'

'Yes, in my trouser pocket.' He slithers out from the table and disappears through the door.

'Good cake,' I comment as I scoop up the last few crumbs of chocolate, 'and a charming boy,' I add as Camarg closes the door onto the stairs.'

'Yes, it's worked out, moving here.'

'You took a risk, and sacrificed your own interests.'

'Well it's not been so bad. I've made good friends and the main thing is for Camarg to be happy.' Rory finishes his own cake and then adds, 'He was at first but he's been more difficult recently. He's moved up to a good secondary school this year and become very moody.' I look at him inquiringly. 'You saw how he was just now, one minute chatting happily and the next he's off.'

'He just wants to get on with his bike stuff,' I say.

'No, it's more than that, the last parents evening was odd. He used to get good marks, particularly in English but now the school says he's not keeping up. It doesn't make sense.'

'Maybe he's just growing up.'

'He's certainly doing that, but he's got in with an odd crowd as well. He no longer plays with the local kids but goes off with some boys from north Bristol on his bike. His eyes are troubled and a deep cleft has appeared between his brows.

'Look, it'll be alright,' I tell him. 'You couldn't have done anything else; it'll work out, it's just a phase.'

'You're probably right,' he says. 'Look, I'm going to have to go soon. I've got a gig tonight and I must organise some supper before Camarg goes to my neighbour.'

'Thank you for the walk, and for lunch. It's been fun.'

'You're welcome. When are you next in Bristol? I'll arrange a babysitter for Camarg and we can go for a proper meal somewhere.'

'I'd like that,' I say. Apart from a few teenage crushes this will be the first time I've agreed to a second date.

....

It's several weeks before I'm back, for a meeting with David Hamilton and the architect planning the renovation of Avon View House. As David leaves there is an incident that confirms his fears about security. Three lads in their early teens cycle up the drive and start practicing bike stunts on the front lawn. When we confront them I recognise one of them as Camarg, and David recognises another – Robert Hamilton, his brother Geoffrey's son. I have the embarrassing task of phoning Rory to tell him that Camarg has been trespassing. He sounds shocked and comes immediately to collect him. David's phone call is less satisfactory; I hear a torrent of angry words and when David explains that legal access to the house has passed to the Olaudah Trust the irate tones rise to screaming pitch. David gives the woman the option of coming to collect Robert or having the police involved. She arrives in a small convertible, tearing down the muddy drive at speed and swerving to a halt in front of the house. Small and wiry she grabs Robert by the shoulder and thrusts him into the car.

'You'll be hearing from my solicitor,' she shouts back at David and with a jerk of the steering wheel and roar of the engine she disappears back down the drive in a cloud of dust, gravel flying up from the wheels.

Rory arriving in his battered Volkswagen, avoids a collision at the gate by millimetres and pulls up beside us.

I've been asking the other boy's name; he is Paul White, in the same class as Camarg. Rory walks towards us, his triangle of beard jutting out and his dark eyes stern.

'Right, lads,' he says. 'Hop in the car and you can tell me all about it on the way home. Let's get you out of these people's way.' He turns to David with a slight incline of his tall frame as if he was about to bow.

'Mr. Hamilton, I apologise for this embarrassment. I'll make sure it doesn't happen again.' He grimaces at me as he gets into the driver's seat and drives sedately back down the drive. I see Camarg talking as they drive past and there is the suspicion of moisture at the corner of his eye.

'I think we can leave that one with the father,' laughs David. 'I apologise for my ex-sister-in-law's behavior; relationships with Estelle have been strained since Geoffrey's prosecution. She didn't want to let go of the house and insists, in spite of legal advice to the contrary, that it'll pass to Robert.'

'Well, at least we've solved the mystery of the boys on bikes,' I say. 'Hopefully there won't be any more of them.'

'Not once we get a new fence up,' David agreed. 'Are you going to be alright here? I've known Tom, the security guard for years.'

'I'll lock the door of the flat in case there are any more marauders,' I laugh.

'Well don't hesitate to call if you need anything. Goodnight.'

The flat is comfortable, though basic. There is a kettle, microwave, fridge and television in the larger room with a couple of armchairs and a desk. The window looks out across the woods to the Avon Gorge and on this summer evening the view is breathtaking. One end of the Clifton

Suspension Bridge is visible and the setting sun is catching the crags on the far side of the gorge. The bedroom overlooks the front of the house and is quite dark due to the overhanging trees. It will be better when the garden has been cleared. The walls are cooling as the sun goes down and I can hear the creak of roof timbers and a scurrying noise in the pitched roof of the bedroom. I add Pest Control Officer to my "to do" list, lock the door and turn the television on for company. The phone rings as I wait for the microwave to heat my supper. It's Rory.

'Jane, I'm sorry. It seems that the three of them have been truanting from school to go to the house and practise stunts on their bikes. Camarg and Paul have been grounded for a month. Their bikes are locked in Paul's father's shed. I'm ringing to ask if you would join me for supper tomorrow night. Camarg is at his grandmother's in London for the weekend so I'm free to take you wherever you fancy. It's the least I can do.' I'm amused by his contrite tones. I was planning to drive straight home after checking on the fence contractor tomorrow but I've no plans for the weekend. I could stay another night.

'Thank you,' I say, 'I don't need to get back till Sunday.'

'We could go to one of the restaurants in the centre or the Pump House at the lower end of the harbour.'

'The Pump House?'

'It's a gourmet pub.'

'Sounds good to me.'

'I'll book a table, is six o'clock too early?'

'No, that's fine; I'll be finished by five.'

'I'll pick you up at 5.30 then. Bye Jane.'

'Bye Rory.'

....

It's just on half past five on Friday evening. Thankfully I've a spare top with me. I'm showered and ready to go as I hear Rory's car rattle up the drive. I run down and open one side of the double front door. He's brought a bunch of roses – orange, yellow and white, and hand written notes from Camarg and Paul apologising for their behavior.

'How've they reacted?' I ask.

'Contrite and promising to work hard to catch up at school,' he replies. 'I think Camarg is relieved. Robert is an older boy and constantly in trouble.'

As I take him up to the flat to put the roses in water I show him the plans for the house and how it is being divided into rooms for our clients upstairs and office and meeting space downstairs.

'There's quite an atmosphere to this place,' he comments. 'Camarg has been telling me that Robert lived here as a child and his father still owns it. I corrected that information but then Camarg started talking about looking through the windows and seeing people dancing. He can be quite imaginative sometimes.' As we drive into central Bristol I tell him about the Hamilton's long association with the house and Anka's stories of parties and concerts when she first lived here.

The sun is still high in the sky when we park the car and there is a light breeze which sends little waves dancing into the golden light. Above the harbour sunlight is reflecting from the windows of the brightly painted houses. Kayaks and rowing skiffs have launched from the marina and are bobbing about as their occupants settle themselves into a comfortable position; it is a magical evening to be out on the water. We are early enough to find a seat outside, and sit protected from the breeze by a huge brick pillar, hot with the sun and encircled by pots of lavender, which shiver in the wind and scent the evening air.

We choose food and a bottle of wine and chat about the day. Then, warm and relaxed, we discuss the complex politics of central Africa. Rory is interested in my trips to South Sudan and well informed on the escalating tribal conflict, on the violence between Muslim and Christian tribes in Central Africa Republic and the systematic rape of women in eastern Congo.

'What are you hoping to achieve when you go to South Sudan?' he asks.

'Try to reduce trafficking through making children and parents more aware of their rights and setting up a number they can call.'

'I think you'll have your work cut out, Jane. Slavery has been endemic in central Africa for centuries, way back before the Europeans or the Arabs came. Look at ancient Egypt. The pyramids were built with slave labour from Nubia.'

'Yes, but if people are made aware of their rights and that there is a law against slavery they will be able to help their children to be more aware, to know where to go to report traffickers feeding the European and Middle Eastern markets.'

'It's not just external traders. It was natural for nomadic cattle herders to cross into each other's territory and take captive what they needed to survive, animals, child soldiers, young brides. You're working against ancient and deeply entrenched patterns. The answer is to settle people and introduce crop growing so that the politics of the empty belly and the big Chief no longer rule.'

'There are organisations waiting to do that but it's not safe. Until rule of law is established it won't be possible to develop the agriculture. We have to put a stop to the supply of child soldiers.'

'Well that won't happen through legislation. People are rooted in a different culture; the witch doctor has as powerful an influence as the chief because the spirit world is a reality to them.' We toss the issues to and fro and I'm impressed by his knowledge and interest.

'How do you know so much about the Nilotic tribes?' I ask him.

'My father is Kenyan, a Luo, so I've always been interested although I was brought up in the UK.'

'Don't you miss the travel of your old job and the challenge of it all?' He hesitates for a moment and then looks me straight in the eyes and I see again that dark brooding pain and anger that was my impression of him the first time we met.

'Yes, I do, of course I do. But Camarg is all that I have left of Grace. He matters to me more than my work. When he's older I may be able to get back to it. I do a bit of writing for the local papers, mainly on the archives but sometimes a freelance piece.'

A ferry boat comes alongside the Pump House wharf and the boat-hand throws a looped rope accurately over the mooring post. It drops into place and as he pulls it tight an idea snakes into my mind and slots over Rory's comment with equal precision. Maria... the story... the anniversary...

'Rory, there is a woman I've been working with, who was trafficked from South Sudan in the 1990s and has been telling me her story. It's very powerful and I'm looking for someone who could take the recorded notes and make it into a booklet for the Trust's anniversary. Would you be interested?'

'I'll take a look – what form is it in at the moment?'

'It's her first-hand account, recorded onto my tablet plus some essays that she wrote in English classes. It's compelling but disorganised. Would you be able to take it on as a project and make a story of it in time for the Trust's anniversary in November?'

'I don't see why not. Have you photos as well?'

'No, I was thinking that I could take some when I go to South Sudan in October.' And so it's agreed that Rory will write up Maria's story.

We spend the rest of the evening discussing how it should be done to make the most impact. Rory's face is alight with excitement. No wonder he seems so sad when he is at work. He is far more creative and innovative than his present job allows.

Eventually with the sun long gone and the evening air chill we walk along the harbour side. As we cross a bridge over an inlet off the main harbour he turns towards me and takes my hand.

'Jane, it's been a great evening. You have re-energised me. Thank you.'

'Thank you, Rory, I've really enjoyed it, and please thank Camarg and Paul for the notes and the flowers; I appreciate the effort.' Rory chuckles and then places a hand on my shoulder and pulls me into the side of the bridge so that someone can pass. I can feel his strong narrow hands through my shirt. A gust of wind makes the bridge shake and we laugh. I look up and in the midst of mirth see the intensity in his eyes. Deep inside me there is an answering response. Our eyes lock together and somehow we are kissing. I can feel the drumbeat of his heart. I taste the sunlight of Africa on his lips. Our worlds are colliding and all that we have discussed, the searching for answers is drawn into this one moment. When we break off he seems as stunned as I am.

'Jane, I'm sorry, I didn't mean to...'

'That's ok,' I murmur and to my surprise, it is.

We wander back along the harbour hand in hand and sit on one of the benches at the Pump House, now closed.

'Tell me more about Grace,' I ask him. 'How did you meet?' If we're going to get involved with each other I need to know about his wife.

'Her family were from Barbados originally; her grandfather arrived after the war and gradually brought the rest of the family over. They settled in Brixton and then moved out to Tooting. I met Grace when we were at London School of Economics. Mom still lives in the family home in Tooting.

What about you? All those macho kayakers!'

'They're good friends, no more than that. My family live in Surrey and there was an expectation that I'd follow a profession and then produce grandchildren. One of my girlfriends has just started a family and tried to fix me up with someone but it was a disastrous evening!'

'I had no time to socialise when I was travelling, feeling guilty about Camarg and trying to spend every minute with him when I was in the UK. It's better here; the band rehearse at my place and there are neighbours who are happy to have Camarg when we have a gig.'

As we drive back to Avon View House I watch his hands on the steering wheel, strong musician's hands with tendons standing out from the dark flesh.

'What instrument do you play?

'Saxophone or guitar; it depends what we are doing; sometimes providing entertainment for a pub, or playing for a dance, occasionally a wedding, then Camarg comes along and helps us move all the equipment in.' He turns into the drive of Avon View House and pulls up carefully near the front steps.

'You're not staying here alone?'

'No, I'm in the flat at the top of the house and there's a security guard downstairs. The family live next door so I can pop through the shrubbery if I need help.' He looks concerned.

'I'm fine, there's a good lock on the door and David's known Tom, the guard for years.'

He seems about to protest further but Tom appears.

'Hi Tom, this is Rory. He's given me a lift.' Tom shakes hands but with a degree of suspicion.

Goodnight, Jane.' says Rory.

'Goodnight and thank you for a lovely evening.' The point of his beard brushes my neck as he kisses my cheek.

'Take care,' he says. There's a discreet cough behind us and Rory turns back to his car as I go into the house. I hear the splutter of the engine and the scrunch of the gravel as he turns back down the drive. I climb the main stairs aware of an eerie sense of past lives and the echo of waltz music and I remember Rory's comment about Camarg imagining seeing people dancing through the windows of the house. I'm thankful for Tom's presence in the office adjacent to the front door and scurry up the second flight of stairs.

What have I done? Rory is a lively and intelligent companion, and when relaxed a polite and attentive one. But I don't want to get involved. He loved Grace and there is Camarg – I have too many complications in my life already. He'll be a good person to work with on Maria's story but no more than that. I reach the top of the second flight of stairs, shut the door of the flat and bolt it securely……….I don't remember ever having such a good evening.

12 MARIA'S FAMILY

The history of the Sudanese church is a remarkable one, a wonderful reminder of the way God blesses his people even in the most difficult of circumstances. [12]

Jane has asked me to come to her office today to see Paul's anniversary display. It is the final one about trafficking and the work of the Olaudah Trust. Jane has them in three cylindrical boxes next to her desk.

'Let me see if I can get the right one,' she says and reads the labels on the side, then raises the lid of one and lifts out a black metal frame holding a roll of plastic strengthened by a metal bar with a hook. She and Ellie lift it out, slot the four sections together and then unroll the

---

[12] *Lost Boy No More* by Abraham Nhial and DiAnn Mills, 2004

thick plastic and hook it over the top of the pole they have just made. It springs up like a sail before the wind and there is my face covering half the display. It is huge, four or five times life size, my eyes staring straight ahead and a slight smile on my lips. Around my head are photos of the Nile and a village of grass-roofed tukuls.

Underneath the portrait huge letters state:

'Maria was captured by the Sudanese militia, sold into slavery in Juba and trafficked to the UK, where she was abandoned. She tried to find her way back to Sudan but with no passport or means of support ended up in prison. She was eventually released and has rebuilt her life as a hairdresser working and living in South London. She has become an ambassador for the Olaudah Trust to help others who have been enslaved.' Then there is a section about the work of the Trust.

'What do you think, Maria?' asks Jane. 'It's a powerful display, isn't it?'

'It's a strong image,' says Ellie. 'You look wistful, Maria.'

'I was thinking about my father and others who wanted to make a new Sudan where people could be free.'

'It captures that longing for a better future,' says Jane. 'Maria, are you happy?'

'It is good, I am happy.' It has been difficult to tell Jane what happened to me; sometimes it has brought back the nightmares of the crocodile, my village burning and losing my family, but if this panel helps to prevent other people from suffering then I am content. She and Ellie dismantle the frame and roll the plastic away into the box. Jane says:

'Maria, there is something else I wanted to see you about, let's go into Andy's office.'

We sit down in the armchairs by the window and she opens her laptop. Then she lifts her head; her brown eyes seem to penetrate into my heart.

'You remember a few weeks ago I said that Pamela, our colleague from Doves of Peace, would be meeting with the Bishop of Torit? We have received an email from the Bishop.' She turns the screen towards me and I lean over and peer at the black characters dancing across the page stamping out rhythms from an invisible drum. I cannot take in what they mean. Then Jane reads the characters out to me:

Dear Miss Jane,

Greetings to you in the name of Jesus. Pastor Pamela has spoken with me about the relatives of Maria Kuol.

There is a lady in this diocese, called Peninah, who lost a daughter called Maria in the fighting. There is also a sister here, Deborah. The brother is Pastor Peter, who leads the reconciliation team in Nimule. Both ladies are living with a relative, Amos Kuol, near the New Jerusalem church.

The mother has given me school records relating to Maria Kuol. Mr. Amos Kuol has confirmed that a child of that name stayed in his household until the age of eleven, when she was taken by the Sudan Armed Forces.

The mother can come to my office next Monday. May you call my number at six in the evening.

Write to me that you agree to the call and that Miss Kuol will be present.

May the Lord Jesus Christ bless you,

Bishop Michael Kawa, Torit Diocese

'Jesu Christo Rhodhua, they are safe!' It is as if a band that has been tightened about my abdomen for twenty-three years has been released. I have prayed so often and feared so much and now I do not know what to feel. Joy, relief, love, elation come tumbling out of me as uncontrolled as children spilling out of school.

'Maria, is that your family? Do you recognise the names?'

'Yes, that is Ma's name, and my brother Peter and sister Deborah. Uncle Amos is the one we stayed with in Nimule.' Alongside my thankfulness that Ma and Deborah and Peter have survived comes a numbing anxiety. He does not mention Aaron or Joel or Rachel? What about Baba? I look to Jane.

'What about the others, he does not write about the rest of my family?'

'No,' says Jane, 'perhaps they are not in Nimule.'

I cannot take it all in. I am paralysed by conflicting emotions of joy and fear. Jane runs her finger along the last line of letters but the words they convey do not register with me.

'The Bishop says we can call them on Monday. You want to do that, of course?'

'No!' The word bursts out of me before I can control it.

'Maria, do you understand? You can phone the Bishop's number and speak with your mother and your brother and sisters.'

'No, no, – I cannot do that.' I stand up and walk towards

the door.

'But Maria, why not? You wanted to trace them. I don't understand.' Jane moves towards me, and when I fold my arms, turns and walks to the window. I know she is irritated with me. She has worked hard to get in touch with Pamela and explain what happened to my family. But I cannot help it. My head is numb and my feelings are tattered banana leaves slapping about in a storm. Of course I am relieved that Ma, Deborah and Peter have survived. After all these years I will be able to speak with them again, but I am afraid. What will they say when they find out that I have slept as a "wife" with men that I was not married to? And that I pretended I was a Muslim. Will they think I have betrayed the beliefs my father and brother were fighting for and disgraced my family and community? Jane is watching a van unload in the street below, piling boxes and cartons on the pavement. She turns back to me.

'You have wanted to see your family for so many years, Maria. What is the problem with making this phone call?'

'In our culture if you are defiled you are scorned. They will not want to speak with me.'

'But Maria, they will not know anything about what happened, and after all these years surely they will want to hear that you are safe.'

'I have been with men I was not married to. I have been in prison. There will be shame.'

'None of those events were your fault. You do not need to tell them. All they will know is that you have a hairdressing business in London. They will be proud.'

I wrap my arms around myself and try to think clearly. I collapse into the chair and cover my head. I hear Jane leave the room closing the door gently and I rock to and fro trying to untangle the feelings that are rising within me. I have my hair done in small plaits and I grasp two and turn them over and over until my head hurts. Jane returns with a glass of water and places it gently on the table beside me.

'Maria, you do not have to call if you do not want to. If it is the idea of phoning that bothers you, we could write?' I shake my head and the tiny plaits swing vigorously. I hear Jane take a deep breath.

'Maria, close your eyes and imagine you are back in South Sudan when the soldiers caught you.' Her voice calms me and I clasp my hands in my lap and do as she suggests.

'What do you see?'

'I see my mother on the ground and Peter beside her.' I try to keep my hands still in my lap but they are twisting and writhing as I relive the memories I have shut out.

'And why are they there?'

'Ma screamed at the soldiers and Peter ran to protect her.'

'Why did she scream?'

'She was trying to stop them.'

'So she must have loved you very much to risk her life for you.' Her words pierce the maelstrom inside me.

'I wanted her so much but the soldiers closed shutters and hurt my arm. I could not see what happened.'

'But she lived, Maria; she is alive, and so are you. And she must love you very much.' Tears squeeze out of my eyes and stream down my face onto my hands. I weep for a long time, mopping my eyes with the tissues Jane hands me as she sits beside me until the tears stop flowing I take a sip of water and say,

'Shall I come here on Monday evening?'

'If it is six o'clock in Nimule it will be four in the afternoon here, there will be other people about. Would you prefer to make the call from your own home?'

'Yes, that would be better. You will be there?'

'Yes, if that is what you want. Give me your address and I will come at half past three. We can settle ourselves and be ready to make the call.'

'Thank you, Jane, thank you. You have helped me. I do not know what to say.' We embrace and say goodbye until Monday.

....

Even before I am fully awake I know from pain in my stomach that it is the day; the twenty eighth of June 2015 and I am going to speak with my family. Morning light is coming through the curtains but my phone shows it is only five; I have woken early and I am too alert to sleep again. I make a cup of tea and take it onto the tiny balcony at the end of my kitchen. The first rays of the sun are touching the trees in Burgess Park and the pigeons are flying down onto the path to check for scraps of food they missed last night. The main door of the block opens and my neighbour leaves for his shop in the Walworth Road, a bundle of brightly patterned tunics hanging over one arm. I shower and tidy my small flat; I polish the table and two wooden chairs in the living room and straighten the cushions on the armchairs. They have wide arms covered in bright flower patterns of oranges, reds and yellows which remind me of the chairs in the Bishop of Torit's house. It is still only seven. I sit down and open the Bible I was given in prison at Isaiah chapter 18. This is my favourite passage because it talks about my land, 'The land of whirring wings, beyond the rivers of Cush.' And my people, 'tall and smooth skinned, a people feared far and wide.' That is a good description of the Dinka people; we are tall and respected for our strength. I can hear the pigeons calling and the rumbling sound of traffic.

I work all morning and return home just after three. Jane arrives at a quarter to four apologising for being held up. We sit at the table with the phone between us and I watch the digital display change 15.55, 15.56... Our eyes meet. We wait. 15.57... I look down at my arm and finger the scar where the soldier hit me with his gun and slammed the shutter onto my arm as I heard my mother's screams. 15.58... Jane checks Bishop Michael's number. 15.59... She starts to dial. An unfamiliar tone shrills through the flat ricocheting off the walls. 16.00... Jane turns the speaker up so that we can both hear.

'Miss Jane? Greetings in the name of the Lord.'

'Greetings, Bishop Michael, this is Jane Taverner. Maria is here with me.'

'Good evening, Miss Jane, or – good afternoon for you in

London. I have Peninah Akol beside me. We have questions to ask for identity.'

'Yes of course, Bishop, here is Maria.' She passes the phone. 'They have to check you are the real Maria,' she mouths.

'Good afternoon, Bishop Michael. I am Maria.'

'Good afternoon, please tell me your birth name.'

'I was called Adut until I was baptised.' There is a discussion in Arabic in the background as Bishop Michael checks. I can hear my mother's voice.

'Yes, that is correct. And the name of your father?'

'Joseph Kuol Deng.' Again a sound of conferring.

'What were you doing on the evening before you fled from Torit?'

'I was playing by the river.' There is a shuffling noise and a new voice comes on the phone.

'Adut, Yin ca muoth.' I hear her voice again, soft and deep, a little cracked with age, or perhaps with the strain of the occasion.

'Ma? Ye kede?'

'My precious daughter, praise God that you are alive! I have prayed that I would hear your voice again. Tell me what has happened to you.'

'I am well, Ma, I have trained as a hairdresser and I run a salon here in London. The business is going well and I am the manager.'

'You have food, Maria?'

'Yes, plenty of food.'

'You have done well, Maria.'

'And you, Ma, how are you?'

'I am well. My back has pain but I can still walk a little. Your uncle is very good to us. Your brother and sister are here waiting to speak with you.'

'Maria, it is Deborah. I looked for you in Juba but no-one had ever heard of you. I did not know that you had gone to London.'

'What happened, Deborah? I missed you so much and I tried to follow everything you had said about praying to Jesus and remembering I was Dinka.'

'I was sent to a family in Juba as you were but when the peace discussions came my uncle was able to buy me back. I am with Seme now and we have five children.'

'Oh, that is good to hear, Deborah.'

Then Peter takes the phone.

'Maria, this is Peter, how good to hear your voice.'

'Peter, I am happy that you are safe.'

'We give thanks to God our father that you have survived, Maria, and that He has blessed you with this good position in London. I am a pastor now. I work for peace and reconciliation in Torit diocese.'

'And Baba, he is there with you?'

'No, Maria, Baba was killed in the fighting.' I feel an immense sadness. I knew so little of my father and now I will never know him except through the memories of others.

'And Aaron, Rachel and Joel?'

'Aaron has returned to our ancestral lands in Bor. Conditions are harsh but he has been able to build up the head of cattle, with my uncle's help. He has four boys and a girl to help him. Joel was a soldier but when peace came he left and went to Juba; we have not heard from him and we think he may have tried to reach Europe – that was always his dream. We have no news of Rachel since the day the soldiers captured us. We have prayed for both of you to return and the Lord has given you back to us.'

No news, my little sister who was only ten, where is she now?

'Maria, I will ask the bishop to send you a phone number where you can call and also send emails. Here is Ma. Goodbye my sister, God bless you.'

'My daughter, Peter will email our news and we can talk some time on the phone. I thank the Lord Jesus that we have found you.'

The bishop comes on the line.

'Maria Kuol, I will send Miss Jane the address for you to email your family.'

'Yes, thank you, bishop.'

'May God bless you for his precious name's sake.' responds the bishop and closes the connection. I sit back, unable to speak, my eyes clouded with tears. Jane has been out on the balcony and comes in with two glasses of water.

'Well...?' she asks.

'My Ma is well, but her back was damaged when they shot her so she cannot walk far. My brother Aaron has returned to Bor. I spoke with my brother, Peter, his leg was too weak for him to fight but he has trained as a pastor and works for the bishop and for peace.'

'He has done well!' Jane's face looks thoughtful but she does not say anything so I carry on:

'Yes. My sister, Deborah, was bought back by my uncle. She sounds strong. Joel is in Juba but my father is dead and Rachel has not been found. Jane holds out her arms and we hug. The tears are streaming from my eyes again.'

'I am sorry, Jane. I cry so much.'

'You have had so much to take in, and it is a mixture of good news and sad. '

'Yes, I am so happy to hear Ma's voice and to know that Deborah survived and that my brothers are well. But I am sad for Baba and Rachel. She had only seen nine rains; she was too young to be in the bush alone. There are so many questions still to ask. I do not know what happened to my uncle's family.'

'You can ask all these questions by email, Maria, and perhaps you will be able to phone your brother and speak to your Ma again soon. I have a question too; when I was in Nimule in February I met a tall man with a limp, who the bishop referred to as Pastor Peter. He is the peace and reconciliation officer for Torit. When you speak to them will you ask if he remembers me?'

……………………………………

I am sitting in the square outside the Olaudah Trust office enjoying feeling the sun on my skin. I miss the heat and golden light of the Sudan even after all these years in the UK. There are brightly coloured daisies and marigolds blooming in the flower beds and the birds are hopping around my feet waiting for some of the rice and beans I have for my lunch. I have asked one of the girls to take messages and book appointments while I am out and am waiting for Jane; she wants to discuss something and suggested we meet outside as it is such a fine day. I am reading the email that arrived from my mother, sent by Peter this morning; I was too excited to take in all she says when I opened it earlier.

> *My precious daughter, it is a miracle that you are safe and well. We have prayed for more than twenty years that you would be returned to us and now the Lord has answered our prayers.*
>
> *When peace was declared in 2005 Amos was able to travel to Juba and redeem Deborah. She*

told us that you had been taken by a businessman. Amos returned many times but no-one knew of you. We never thought that you would be taken to London. Praise the Lord that you have had schooling and now have your own business. We are very happy that you have done so well, my daughter.

There are many stories to share. I will tell you first what happened when you were captured; Joel and Rachel hid under the truck when the soldiers started shooting and then ran towards Nimule. Joel ran all the way to his uncle's house and Amos came straight to the barracks, paid money and took Peter and I, both very sick back to his house. Rachel did not run as fast as Joel and fell behind; she has not been heard of to this day. Peter recovered but walks with a limp and was not able to fight. Now he travels throughout Torit diocese talking to people about reconciliation and asking them to put down their weapons. He is married to Rebecca and they have a girl and a boy child. I help look after them while Peter makes visits and spends time in prayer. Deborah and Seme are here with me in your uncle's house. Amos and his wife are very generous; they have built concrete rooms for us in their compound so that Deborah and her children, and Peter's family have a room to sleep in. We are very crowded so Peter lives in the refugee camp. Deborah and Seme have four children now. They are lively and noisy and I love to watch them from my small room and tell them stories. Aaron and one of his boys bring an animal to us every few months so that we have meat to eat. We have fruit and vegetables from the markets in Uganda so we eat well but many of our people are suffering because the fighting has destroyed crops and cattle. There are many thousands in camps in Uganda and here in Nimule and we see the United Nations lorries bringing in supplies.

We were happy when South Sudan became independent in 2011 but sadly the fighting between our people and the Nuer rebels, led by Riek Machar, has brought more deaths and the plans for peace are delayed.

We are all so proud of you, my daughter. Please pray for us. In recent months there have been many outbreaks of fighting. Our bishops are calling for peace so that our country can be rebuilt. Bishop Michael is a good man and works hard to help people but he has no money except what is put in the collection in the church each week and it is very little.

Please write and tell us what happened to you. Do you have your own room and food to eat? We long to hear what you are doing. Peter is writing this for me and sends all his love as we all do.

With God's blessing and all our prayers,

Your loving mother

I rest my phone in my lap and hot tears drop onto it. I wipe them off hastily and put it safely in my bag. I was afraid that my family would not want me because of what happened but instead they are proud. They need my help. I will send the money I was saving for an airfare to them and will trust the Lord that I can reach them one day. I have a little spare each month after paying my rent and electricity.

Jane arrives on her phone as usual with her lunchbox in the other hand and struggles to open the metal gate. There are papers protruding from the big leather bag she always carries. I jump up to help her but she has finished the call and dealt with the rusted gate before I reach her. We embrace. She has phoned me many times to check that I have recovered from the shock of finding out about my family and I have been learning more about all she does. She is hard working and does not think of herself enough.

'Maria, thanks for popping over. I've something to show you and I thought it would be easier to meet out here. How are you?'

'I'm fine, Jane, Jon and Sara are praying for my family, and so are many other people. I've had a letter from my mother and I'll write back to her this evening. How is life for you?' Jane has taken out a sandwich and munches thoughtfully.

'It's good but very busy. There are so many things to sort out with the project in Bristol. We have to have a bat survey before we can start the work and the drive needs new gravel laid so that we can get lorries in.' I do not know what a "bat survey" is but I can see that it is troubling Jane.

'Rory, from the Record Office, is being very helpful; he has local contacts.' After a slight pause she adds, 'He invited me to go for a walk round Bristol with his son,

Camarg.'

'Just the man and his son?'

'His wife died some years ago and he and Camarg are alone.'

'You went with him?'

'Yes; I thought it would be good to explore a bit more of Bristol.'

'He is a good man?'

'I didn't think so to begin with; he was rude the first time I met him. The second time he was more friendly; that's when he suggested he should take me round the centre when I was next in Bristol. I had several meetings across a weekend so I gave him a call on the way down.'

There is something slightly defiant about Jane's tone of voice. She is usually so strong and confident but she seems unsure of herself. I've never heard her mention her private life before; she is always thinking about her work. Her eyes are soft and deep, and the brown curls that frame her face lift slightly in the wind.

'You like him?' I ask her.

'He is kind but firm with his son, and interesting to talk

to, compassionate. I had a meal out with him last week.'

'That is good news, Jane. You work too hard, you need to relax. When do you see him again?'

'I haven't made any arrangements. I'm on a course in London next week and then it is Nina's court hearing and I'm kayaking at the weekends. I shan't go to Bristol for a month.'

I empty out the last few pieces of rice and beans onto the ground. The pigeons, who have been strutting about in anticipation come waddling towards us and eagerly peck at the grains caught in the dust. I glance across at her troubled face.

'You must feed on whatever happiness is offered in life, Jane; it may not be there tomorrow!' I say as we look down at the birds. She laughs and crumbles the last of her sandwich. Sparrows fly in and snatch up the tiny crumbs. I think there must be good spirits watching over her. She starts to pull papers from her bag.

'I've had a strange email,' Jane says, handing it to me. 'From someone called Manny Deng. I've printed it off for you to read.'

13 July 2015

'Dear Olaudah Trust,

I am a South Sudanese living and working in Baltimore city in the United States of America.

Many years ago, when I was a young boy, I ran away from Nuer forces who massacred my people in the town of Bor in South Sudan. I fled into the bush and walked for hundreds of miles, with other boys in a similar position, through many dangers, finally reaching the refugee camp at Kakuma in northern Kenya. After a while I was granted a place on a United Nations programme to take three thousand and eight hundred boys to the US to be educated. I am now a qualified lawyer.

A year ago I managed to trace my family in South Sudan and have been talking regularly to my aunt, Anna, wife of Deng Garang, of Nimule. In our last conversation he mentioned that a childhood friend, who has been lost for many years, Maria Kuol, was living in the UK.

I have been trying to trace Maria through the Salvation Army and they have suggested I contact your organisation.

Please help me to find Maria.

With sincere thanks,

Manny

Emmanuel Deng, Baltimore Harbour Law Firm

My hands are trembling so much that Jane has to hold the paper steady.

'Do you know him?' she asks.

'It is Emmanuel.'

'The one you used to dance with?' I nod as the tears come flooding out and deep wrenching sobs rise up from my stomach. Jane puts her arm around me and holds me tight.

'He is alive,' I whisper over and over again. She sits silently beside me, holding me until I am calm again.

'Would you like to come to the office and send a reply?'

'I do not know what to say.'

'We can do it together, just let him know you're here.'

14ᵗʰ July 2015

Dear Emmanuel

I am Maria Kuol, daughter of your Aunt Anna's friend, Peninah. Your email came to Jane Taverner at the Olaudah Trust.

I am in London, the manager of a hairdressing shop. I have recently found my family in South Sudan; Jane helped me. They live in Nimule.

I am happy that you are alive and going well.

Please reply to the email address below, which comes to my phone. I would like to hear your news.

With best wishes

Your friend Maria

13 JANE AND RORY

An Act to make provision about slavery, servitude and forced or compulsory labour and about human trafficking, including provision for the protection of victims;[13]

Fi and I are meeting at a small Nepalese curry place in Southwark just south of the river before she goes on holiday to Thailand in a couple of days.

'Jane, you've been a difficult girl to track down recently!'

'Sorry! I've been away in Bristol, or kayaking in Kent, and busy supporting a new client.'

'We'll have a good catch up. I asked Mr. Chettri for the table in the window.'

'Great, I love that view of the Shard. Drink?'

---

[13] *Modern Slavery Act 2015*
http://www.legislation.gov.uk/ukpga/2015/30/contents/enacted

'Chardonnay for me, please.' We order and settle into a corner table with a view across the City skyline.'

'So what've I been missing in London?' I ask Fi.

'Not a lot, it's been a mixed bag weather-wise. Quiet at work. Anna and I met at Greenwich a few Saturdays ago and showed Poppy the meridian. She's toddling now.'

'I hope she appreciated walking in two hemispheres at once! How is Anna, I haven't seen her since March?'

'She's fine, back at work and Poppy goes to nursery three days a week. They seem happy but she looks worn out - all that juggling of child care and work schedules. Now tell me about you.' The waiter arrives and we order, which gives me time to collect my thoughts.

'Well, kayaking was great; we had mostly fair weather and found some good pubs on the rainy days.'

'Was it the usual crowd?'

'Yes, we all get on well.'

'You look better and I hope you've come back less intense about work.'

'Well I wouldn't say that, it's been a bit crazy.' I tell her about the renovation on Avon View House, the challenges of supporting Nina, and the additional task I have given myself of collecting Maria's story.

'Maria sounds impressive.'

'She is. Quietly spoken and dignified. She's made a life for herself in spite of the trauma. She never lost hope of seeing her family and now we've been able to put her in touch with her mother and remaining siblings.'

'Fantastic story!'

'I have a journalist friend who is working on it and we hope to get it published for the Trust's twenty-fifth anniversary in November. It'll be timely with the passing of the Modern Slavery Act.'

'Who's the journalist, anyone I know?'

'I shouldn't think so. He's an archivist in the Bristol Records Office but he used to be a freelance correspondent covering Africa and the Middle East.'

'Whooa, a new man in your life, Jane. What's his name?'

'Rory Odhiambo, and he's not a new man, just someone who is helping me on the Avon View House project.'

'What's he like?'

'Early forties, widowed with a twelve year old son.'

'No, I mean his character?'

'He seemed rude the first time I met him. The second time we had lunch in the cafe and he was more friendly. We've been out a couple of times for a pub meal.'

'And..?'

'I don't know, Fi, he's an odd man. Very reserved and sad, but when he's off duty good company, fun, well informed.'

'Jane! Here, have some wine and tell me more.' She tops up my glass and calls the waiter to ask for another bottle.

'No, Fi, it's not like that,' I tell her. 'He misses his wife and the most important thing in his life now is his son, Camarg.'

'And yet he's taken you out a few times and helped you with the house project.' Fi is pushing me too much.

'He's just a colleague. Now tell me about your itinerary for Thailand.' We chat about holiday plans for the rest of the evening and then walk back along the South. It is always good to see Fi; she and Anna are my closest friends, but her questions about Rory have unsettled me. He is part of Bristol; hearing myself speak to Fi about him has brought him into my London life. I'm not sure I'm ready for that.

....

In spite of the late night I'm in work early. I need Ellie to start looking into the cheap flight options for the conference in Juba in October. The government and the rebels signed a power sharing agreement in August that will reinstall Riek Machar, the rebel leader, as vice president, and divide government jobs between Dinka, Nuer and smaller tribes but there is no indication the rebels will keep their side of the bargain. A failure to restore peace could jeopardise my trip. I must leave that to Ellie and get on with recruiting a manager for Avon View House; someone with an understanding of the work we do. This afternoon I'm meeting Maria to go through the proofs of her story.

I scan rapidly through the backlog of emails that have accumulated while I was away for the one I need - from Rory with the draft attached. I haven't seen him since we met at the Pump House two weeks ago. We've been exchanging emails about how to present Maria's story so that it makes an impact at the anniversary event – nothing personal. This one says:

Hi Jane

Here is the first draft. It would be good to meet with Maria so that I can bring the story right up to date. Will she be willing to do that do you think?

I have also indicated places where it would be useful to have some photographic material. Will you be able to get some images on your trip in October?

Camarg and I are in Tooting from 5th August visiting his grandmother. I have tickets for an Evening of Swing at the Royal Albert Hall on Tuesday 11th August, can you join me? It's classic Jazz – Louis Armstrong, Glenn Miller, Cole Porter, and Duke Ellington. I'm holding a table at the Elgar Bar if you can get off work in time for supper.

Regards

Rory

How strange, after the conversation with Fi last night, that he's going to be in London.

I print out two copies of the draft, call Maria and arrange to meet her in the coffee shop across the square.

'Rory wants to know if you are happy to meet and tell him what happened once you were free.' I've covered up the last paragraph of the email with my hand but Maria picks it up and reads the whole note slowly.

'Mr. Odhiambo is a thoughtful man,' she says and looks at me. Her gaze is direct and enquiring. She has changed since she found her family. The longing and desolation in her eyes has been replaced by joy and assurance, and the strength and determination that enabled her to survive has become more apparent. I do not have faith in Jesus as she does but I can see that the fulfilment of her anguished prayers has been important to her. Hope and optimism have replaced the quiet endurance that was her main characteristic when I first met her.

'Yes,' I respond. She still has the email in her hand. South Sudanese do not distinguish between surface thoughts and the depths of the subconscious; the material and the spirit world are one to them; I know she has read the last line and sees right into my dilemma.

'He has asked me to go to a concert with him,' I admit.

'You will go?'

'I don't know.'

'If you don't you will never know how your story might end,' she says quietly. I look at the manuscript on the table in front of us. Perhaps there is a narrative to my life too, a tale less extraordinary but worth telling. Whatever else he may be Rory is not shallow; shall I risk taking the next step?

'Perhaps you're right, Maria,' I say, 'I'll accept.' Our eyes meet and we smile; co-conspirators in the story of each other's lives. 'Maria, there's something I hope you'll say "Yes" to.' I continue. Her eyes remain fixed on mine but the eyebrows arch and gently curved lines form in the ebony forehead. 'We're going to be looking for a manager for Avon View House. I hope you will apply.' She gasps and the curves are replaced by two deep chasms between her brows.

'I cannot, I would not know...'

'We're looking for people with an understanding of slavery and trafficking, familiar with the Upper Nile regions, experienced in management and child protection. You would have to apply online but someone could help you, not from the Trust of course, but one of your church friends perhaps. I can send you the information?'

'I will pray, and talk with Jon and Sara; it is a serious matter.'

'Good. Right, let's go through the manuscript.' We read over each line and amend it until she is comfortable with what is written.

....

The Royal Albert Hall is a staggeringly impressive building; why have I never been here before? Part of me wants to disapprove of its imperial opulence but I love the richness of the red and gold decor and the ostentation of its columns and loggia boxes.

Rory seems quite at home.

'I used to come here regularly for the Thursday night jazz evenings,' he tells me as we wait for our food. He seems jaunty this evening, as if the buzz of the capital has rejuvenated him. His eyes crinkle at the edges and the deep creases on either side of his mouth are lifted in boyish delight as he describes some of the evenings he spent here.

'What happened to the dour archivist from the Record Office?' I ask him as we cut into grilled swordfish steaks.

'Dour?' His look of genuine consternation is comical, the thin face puckered and the goatee beard dropping as his mouth opens in surprise, fork half lifted to his lips.

'I thought you were the most peculiar man I'd ever met. You kept looking at me as though I was something unpleasant that had crawled in from the river.'

'Well, you took me by surprise. I was expecting some dough-faced charity worker, vague and unappealing and instead you rattled out a list of requirements and jerked those dark curls and...' For once Rory seems at a loss for words.

'Why did you keep staring at me? I was totally unnerved!'

'I wasn't staring, I was captivated. Have I made up for it since?'

'You have been bafflingly charming and I have had to totally revise my first impression of you!' He throws his head back and laughs and people around us look on in amusement at his full-throated chuckle. One of them raises a glass and comes over to say 'hallo'.

'Jane, Oscar, we used to jam together.' We shake hands and he and Rory reminisce for a few moments before Oscar returns to his table.

'Sorry, Jane, it's good to see old friends again. He was a big support when Grace was ill.' His words slip through my ribs and jab at my heart but I have to get used to the fact that he has been married before.

'Is it hard to come back here without her?'

'She only came once or twice; classical music was more her

thing. We sometimes went to a prom together but it was difficult when Camarg was a baby and she became ill soon after that.'

'What would she feel about you bringing me here?'

'We agreed that if anything happened to either of us the other one should be free to move on but I had not given it a thought till you walked into the office. I never felt able to leave Camarg until I moved to the archive job and joined the band.' I think of Poppy and wonder how it would affect them if something happened to Anna's husband. Would she want to go out in the evening and leave a bereaved child with someone else?

'How old was Camarg when Grace died?'

'He was just eight, old enough to understand and young enough to feel insecure.'

'Other family?'

'My mum died years ago and Dad went back to Kenya. I have cousins in London but no-one else close except Mom, Grace's mother. And you?'

'Mum and Dad live in Surrey and my brother is in Twickenham and works in the City. We're very different. He has two children and a big house and garden.' I smile wryly and Rory places his knife and fork carefully together on his plate and comments.

'Sounds nice but boring.'

'Yes. I was supposed to follow the family pattern and become a lawyer but I read Social Science and Criminology instead.'

'Not much money in that, but much more of a life! Talking about interesting lives,' he continues, 'Maria's story, is she OK with the draft?'

'Yes, bit overwhelmed, I think, but determined to help others and happy for us to use her story to explain the Trust's work.'

'It could be more than just a pamphlet, Jane.'

'Oh?' He glances at his watch. 'Look, we'd better settle up here and find our seats and then I'll explain an idea I've had.'

We still have ten minutes before the concert starts and there is a hubbub as people enter the auditorium from all sides, greet friends and settle themselves. On stage music stands are adjusted and the piano given a final polish.

'So, explain your idea,' I urge him.

'At the moment, Maria's story is an account that is shocking and disturbing and outside most people's experience.'

'So?'

'I could put it in context, fill in a little more background, illustrate what happens to children who are without the protection of their families, make it into a book rather than just a pamphlet. Have you got notes of your work that I could build something from?'

'Well, a lot of it is confidential of course, but I keep an audio diary of sorts. I'd need to edit it before you have a look at it!'

'And I thought I'd found a way to expose your guilty secrets!' We are laughing as the lights go down and the band files onto the stage and tunes up. I mull over what he has said. The thought of sharing my notes and audio diary makes me feel vulnerable. It's not easy to hand over areas of your life that are painful and I'm impressed once more by Maria's determination to share her story and to endure having her anguish revealed.

The opening bars of a Louis Armstrong song soar across the open centre of the concert hall where hundreds are swaying to the shifting beat. Rory listens intently, his long limbs relaxed and moving slightly to the rhythm. My fingers start to twitch and I remember playing the piano in my teens and loving Scott Joplin. This is more developed, smoother but equally engaging; the intensity of listening with such a large body of people absorbs me. 'Sing, sing, sing, sing, everybody start to sing;' the Louis Prima song gets everybody's foot tapping. As the music pulses upwards I gaze at the slender colonnades high above, where those unable to get seats crane their ears and eyes as they lean over the railings and peer down into the auditorium below.

'What is this thing called love?' croons the singer. I glance across at Rory and he raises an eyebrow, I can feel the heat of his knee next to mine. 'Is there anybody who can solve this mystery?' Not me! I wonder where this is taking me? There are many sides to Rory - maybe it will be fun to try to find them all.

In the interval we order wine, and continue the previous conversation.

'I'm going kayaking in Pembrokeshire next week until after the Bank Holiday, I could sort through my audio diary before I go,' I say and his face lights up.

'I'll draft a story outline while you're away and buy you dinner when you get back,' he offers. 'It would have to be in Bristol because of Camarg.'

'I'll be in Bristol frequently in September. The renovation of Avon View House is starting, and we're interviewing for a manager. I'm back to Juba in October so I need to get everything sorted before I go.'

'September.' He says, lifting his glass and draining it; and we return to the auditorium.

Clapping, cheering and listening to encores until no more can be extracted from the band we roll out, swept along by excited crowds into the dark, warm night. Rory insists on accompanying me back to Bethnal Green and we walk across Hyde Park to Marble Arch. When the underground train arrives it is full and we're forced to squeeze together in the packed carriage. Rory puts his arms around me to steady us both and I can feel his beard tickling my forehead.

'Jane, will you come to lunch with Camarg and Mom tomorrow? She hopes to meet you. She is an incredible person, and a superb cook!'

'I would love to meet her.' I reply; this relationship is unexpected and complicated but as I relax against his steadying presence I'm glad we are together.

14 A WARM BREEZE

No one shall be held in slavery or servitude; slavery and the slave trade shall be prohibited in all their forms. [14]

The September breeze is blowing through the open windows soft and mild but the nights are becoming colder and the leaves on the sycamore trees along the drive have turned russet and gold, their veined leaves outlined against the dark needles of the Scots pines. Squirrels are active in the old oak tree by the gate, gathering their winter hoard and burying it in the lawn, patting each acorn into the soil with steady purpose, confident that when winter comes they will have good supplies. They scamper into the undergrowth, chasing each other up the trees and rampaging across the roof until the thinning sunlight fades.

The sturdy rafters creak, bracing themselves for the

[14] *Universal Declaration of Human Rights, Article 4*
http://www.humanrights.com/what-are-human-rights/violations-of-human-rights/slavery-and-torture.html)

onslaught of winter, and the house settles into the damp soil waiting for the cold to wreak further deterioration.

One morning a procession of white vans and trucks makes its way up the drive and round the side of the building, creating new ruts in the muddy gravel. Their occupants climb out and unload leaving a trail of sand, sawdust and cement up the rear steps, along the service corridor and up the back stairs to the first floor. A returning tide of fallen plaster, rotted wood, rusted metal, and brick rubble flows back to the skips lined up against the side wall.

In the attics abandoned treasures are cleared and carted away. Access hatches are opened and for several days strong, young workmen and women tramp across the rooves, replacing tiles, mending broken gutters and chasing startled squirrels from their winter hideaways. The leaking downpipe is replaced and a power hose applied to the brickwork, removing the dark tear stain. Broken windows are mended and frames and external doorways painted. The fresh white paint against the scoured brickwork gives the house a fresh, dapper appearance.

The young woman with dark curly hair is resident in the attic flat and appears downstairs in the morning to direct people to their appropriate locations or take them to task when they depart from the brief.

'Morning Miss Taverner, two rolls of cable. OK to put them in the hall?'

'Definitely not. The floor of the entrance hall must not be marked. All deliveries to the store room by the rear door.'

'Right you are.'

The sound of building, hammering and sawing rise to a crescendo as cables are fed through the rafters, new ring mains inserted and channels carved into the walls for extra plugs and light fittings. In the stairwell an earnest young man concentrates on installing the wireless server box and liaising with the electricians on where to place the connections.

'Excuse me.' He is interrupted in his work. 'You cannot have your equipment there; that is where the disabled lift is going. Have you looked at the plans?'

'Sorry, miss. Where do you want it?' She opens up a tablet, presses the screen a few times and shows him.

'Please make sure you follow instructions.'

'Yes, Miss Taverner.' But she has already moved on to the kitchen where Agnes, leaving her usual work for David and Glycella's household, serves mugs of tea or coffee three times a day. Between Agnes's supply of beverages and Jane's vigilance the renovation work is in safe hands.

Walls are demolished; rotted storage areas removed and antiquated equipment disconnected in the poky confusion of small rooms and passageways behind the dining room. One cupboard is taken over for the new eco-boiler that will power the entire house with the help of solar panels on the inward facing eaves; and there is an audible sigh as the original gas pipe is sealed off. The kitchen, a spacious but dilapidated room, is completely cleared and, with a clang and clatter, shiny brushed chrome units are brought in, an industrial dishwasher installed and a double oven connected to the rerouted gas main. Several small rooms are opened out into a utility room equipped with three washing machines and an industrial size tumble dryer. The heart of the house experiences major surgery as the clogged pipes of the original heating circuit are removed and new plumbing installed, sending controlled waves of hot and cold water through the building, and filling new radiators and taps with reviving warmth. The house runs to a new rhythm, purring like a contented cat as timbers dry out, walls lose their moisture and damp air is forced to flee.

Carpenters and decorators start on the refurbishment of the main rooms. The lounge retains its Victorian picture rail and elaborate skirting but is painted a uniform cream, the Victorian plaster work picked out in pale green and the central chandelier replaced by a projector. The tiled floor of the hall is cleaned until it shines and a large mat placed in the porch to protect from careless footprints. The heavy front door, with its gothic bolts and bars is replaced by double glass panels, which open automatically for wheelchair access, and one side of the porch steps is covered by a sturdy ramp.

Upstairs bathrooms are ripped out and refitted with sleek white units and the larger bedrooms divided into single or double rooms to accommodate male clients on one side of the main stairs and females on the other. New light fixtures are installed in dark corners, chasing away the ghosts that once inhabited the corridors. The white vans wind their way down the drive for the last time.

The next morning David Hamilton, who had once run in sock-padded feet along the corridors, comes up the porch steps with Andy Kernow, followed by Jane and Ellie. They set up the boardroom with a table, three chairs facing the door and a single chair facing the French windows. Ellie supervises the initial screening of six candidates and then ushers them in turn to the single chair. Finally, the three interviewers sit round the table facing each other.

'Well only three of them meet the essential criteria,' comments Andy.

'Yes, I think we can rule out the first two as lacking experience,' says David, 'and the last one fared poorly in both the test exercises so I don't think he would be suitable, which leaves Maria, Candia and Stewart. What do you think, Jane?'

'Yes, I agree we can't appoint those three.' comments Jane. 'I thought Candia spoke well during the interview but in the case study exercise she didn't understand all the implications of the client's condition and that will be important in helping people to settle in.'

'I agree,' says Andy, 'our clients are fragile. They need to be supported in the right way from the start. Stewart's background in social work and a wide range of experience is helpful; he knows the local agencies.'

'I thought he was a bit misogynistic,' says David. 'He was denigrating women trapped into the sex industry.'

'I think he'd just had one or two difficult cases,' says Jane. 'I was more worried about the way he wanted to follow the "pathway" that he's developed in his current post. We need someone who can be flexible and respond to each client appropriately.'

'What about Maria?' asks Andy.

'She is fairly new to management but has voluntary experience with difficult young people,' says Jane. 'I suggested she apply because she has an understanding of our clients but her only qualifications are in hair dressing.'

'She did well on the spreadsheet test,' says Andy, 'but her English let her down on the case studies and she seemed tentative at the start of the interview.'

'I think she was extremely nervous,' says David. 'Did you see how her hands were twisting in her lap? But once she started speaking I really liked the way she explained how she would respond as new clients came in. She seems to have a very caring personality.'

'Yes, and dignity,' says Andy. 'I think she would be quite inspiring with more confidence and experience.'

'How big a problem is the English?' asks David, turning to Jane. 'You have worked with her.'

'She's been talking with some of my clients and has an immediate connection with them over the trauma of flight and how slavery affects self-esteem but I think she'll struggle with more formal situations.'

'Well, it's the first time I've met her,' says Andy, 'but I was impressed by the way she spoke about supporting the clients.'

Ellie enters and hands a paper to David.

'Thanks, Ellie,' he says. 'These are the test scores, as we already know, three of them had below average scores on the tests. Candia has the highest score on the spreadsheet but did very poorly on one of the case studies, but that gives her a good score overall. Maria and Stewart are close with Stewart doing slightly better on the case studies and Maria on the spreadsheet.'

'But we have reservations about Stewart's attitude to clients. I think we can work with Maria to improve her English but it is more difficult to change fundamental attitudes.'

'Totally agree,' says David. 'I think she has leadership potential, which would be developed through this post. Jane?'

'I'm concerned about her emotional strength given what she's been through. I think we'd need to make sure she had good supervision particularly during the move from London.'

'Well if you two are happy to look to that, I think we've made our decision,' says David.

They rise and move to the kitchen for a cup of tea. The soft cream walls of the spacious room embrace the silence as the door closes behind them and the air stills. The house absorbs their decision into its bricks and mortar; a new sort of family, born of mutual support and joint endeavour to rebuild damaged lives. Avon View House has survived another revolution of the economic cycle, established on the wealth generated through slavery, it will become home to victims of modern trafficking.

One morning several days later a large truck, loaded with equipment, negotiates the curve of the drive with care. All that day the house trembles as chainsaws take down rotted trees and a rotating drum chews them into bark chippings, which are spread on the forgotten flower beds. When all the mess and debris has been cleared a tipper truck arrives from the local quarry, upends its load of gravel, which a team of volunteers spread and rake smooth. They return to clear flower borders, trim shrubs and lay a new vegetable plot. Finally, the animated chatter, the snip and slash of secateurs and the scrabble of rakes, hoes and spades retreats and the house is left once more in peace.

The ridge tiles of the roof protrude above the trimmed trees. The porch has regained its welcoming appearance now that a fresh sea of gravel laps at its steps. Raked earth covers the beds and borders ready for winter frosts to clean and break up. As the setting sun casts a soft glow over the rear lawns the freshly painted white trellis of the verandah spreads along the back wall in a huge smile and the newly cleaned windows of the rooms above catch the pink and violet light in the western sky and wink. Darkness envelops the house, the downbeat to activity that will rise and swell over the following weeks reaching a climax on the last Saturday in November.

15 DIFFICULT DECISIONS

Since the outbreak of the South Sudan crisis in December 2013, the human rights situation of the population has sharply and dramatically deteriorated.[15]

'Jane, I need to see you,' says Andy as I enter the office.

'Yes, of course,' I say but inwardly groan. I fly to South Sudan next week and I am driving to Bristol this evening to check on the refurbishment. Oh well, I had better go and see what Andy wants.

As I enter he hands me a single sheet from the top of a stack of papers.

'Well done, Jane, we have been awarded a Big Lottery grant of fifty thousand for further work on Avon View House. If you look at the section I've ringed, their decision

---

[15] United Nations Human Rights Council A/HRC/31/CRP.6 10 March 2016

was strongly influenced by the case studies of Nina and Maria.'

'So we can go ahead with making the west wing into office space?'

'Yes, and fully refurbish the attic flats.'

'That's fantastic. Maria can live on site and we'll have somewhere for Paul or me to stay when we are working in Bristol. No more Mrs. Jackson!' We laugh then he continues, 'Jane, this does have other implications; it means that we will be closing this office and moving the Olaudah Trust to Avon View House. I've spoken to Ellie and Paul already. Paul will continue to work in London but bring clients who need residential support to Bristol. Ellie is starting a family: the baby is due in January and she will then go to working part-time to assist Paul. They will both work from home and come to Bristol for staff meetings. One of the interns, Sophie, is staying on one day a week to assist Paul with the female clients. I want you to head up the work at Avon View House, with Maria reporting to you. We'll appoint a part-time admin assistant based in Bristol. If you wish, you may have one of the attic flats and Maria the other one, or if you prefer, you can find your own accommodation in Bristol.'

'All my work will move to Bristol?'

'Yes, is that a problem?'

'Well, I knew I would be spending more time on the project but I thought it would be split between Bristol and here.'

'The trustees have decided we cannot afford to keep both

offices on. I can give you the option of working from home some days if you want to keep your flat in London but Paul and Sophie will handle the London referrals.'

'Starting when?'

'The lease on this office comes up for renewal in January.'

'I need to think about it. It's a bit of a shock.'

'Yes of course. We'll have another chat next week. Take some time to look around while you're in Bristol.'

I blunder out of his office feeling dazed. I should've seen this coming but I've been too busy and settled in a routine of working alternately in Bristol and London. I love my flat in London and my weekends on the Kent coast. How dare Andy uproot me when I have so little time to enjoy it anyway? I put my coat on and go out into the street. The sky is overcast but the air is mild and I cross over and sit in the park. The leaves on the plane trees are turning yellow and the big chestnut in the centre is dropping conkers. I love to see them in their spiky padded shells – brown and glistening when they first appear, soon darkening once daylight gets in. Different seasons have different offerings; the marigolds and daisies of summer are gone, in a few weeks lights will be hung on the trees in preparation for Christmas, and the Olaudah Trust will host the mulled wine and mince pie party for local residents for the last time. How am I going to see Fi and Anna? What about Mum and Dad? Will it take them longer to get to the outskirts of Bristol instead of central London?

I struggle through the rest of the day distracted by thoughts of moving. I want to sit quietly in my flat and think about it all, perhaps go and see Anna or meet Fi but

I have to drive to Bristol. I finish late and there is torrential rain on the M4. I'm supposed to be meeting Rory and Camarg for supper but I'm running so late I'll have to cancel.

'Rory, I'm sorry, it's raining heavily. I don't think I'm going to be with you for at least another hour and a half. I'll go straight to Avon View House.' He sounds disappointed but pragmatic.

'Don't worry, I'll give Camarg something and you and I can eat later.'

When I finally arrive, it is gone half-past eight. Camarg has finished supper and biked round to a friend's house.

'He's promised to keep to the recognised cycle tracks and make sure his lights are working,' says his father ruefully. 'He gives me the route before he goes out and I sometimes check on him, but he and Paul have separated from Robert's influence and his school work is up to his usual standard.'

He brings me a glass of wine and I settle back into the baggy armchair in one corner of the sitting room and relax. It is a pleasant room with a bay window onto the street, high ceiling and square proportions. Rory's saxophone stands in one corner and Camarg's homework is laid out on the table in the window. A sofa occupies one wall, facing a small television in the opposite corner. I watch the silhouette of the sycamore tree on the other side of the street; bending under the weight of rain and alternatively blocking and revealing the street light as it sways in the wind. Rory clears Camarg's laptop and places plates of omelette and coleslaw on the table. I try not to eat greedily; I didn't have time for lunch.

'Has it been a tough day?' He is being so kind. The room is cosy and comfortable and as the tensions of the drive and the busy day start to lift off the suppressed ball of anger beneath is released. I tell Rory about the conversation with Andy and then hear myself storming, burdened with tears and tossed this way and that like the sycamore tree.

'He could've told me earlier,' I sob. 'I asked him whether he would do this ages ago when we first met the Hamiltons, and he was dismissive. I thought with the grant from the City Council we'd keep both offices on. We only pay a peppercorn rent in London. Why is it me that has to move, just because I don't have a family? My home and my friends are in London! I can't bear the thought of starting all over again.' I know I look a mess but I cannot stop myself from crying and protesting. Rory tops up my wine and then perches awkwardly on the arm of the sofa.

'Why is it so bad to come to Bristol?' he asks and I feel his arm about my shoulders.

'I don't want to move. I've never even had the chance to do my flat up.'

'You could find somewhere that's already done up,' he suggests.

'I want somewhere with character, not some modern apartment!' I jerk my head and the sudden movement makes him shift position. His arm tightens round my shoulders.

'Jane, I have been wanting... meaning to ask you...' His voice is deeper than usual and falters over the words. I feel him take a deep breath and start again. 'Will you marry me? I have been afraid to ask because it would involve such a change for you….. Now is the wrong time, I know, but could you share your life with me?' His sincerity pierces my weariness and anger. Images and a torrent of feelings flash through me. The fun of our walk through central Bristol, my admiration for his concern for Camarg, the intensity of the evening at the Pump House, the joy of the night at the concert. I remember his mother-in-law's warmth over lunch and her quiet aside to me in the kitchen about Rory's strength in steering a steady course through tough times. I saw the love between the three of them that has seen them through their grief.

'Oh, I'm not the marrying kind…' I say instinctively but suddenly everything slots into place; not moving on my own to an unfamiliar city but marrying Rory and building a home together; not isolated in an unfamiliar flat but sharing a new life. I turn to him:

'But… I might make an exception!'

He pulls me towards him and I cling to him as we kiss – no longer shocked by the depth of passion released but acknowledging the deep tie between us.

'What about Camarg? How will he feel?' I ask eventually.

'We can ask him when he gets back but I think from his comments when you came to lunch with Mom that he will approve.'

'What did he say?' I ask, intrigued.

'He just said that he thought Nan liked you, and she was always right! How do you feel about taking on a readymade family?'

'I like Camarg. His "sorry" letter stole my heart weeks

ago!' He chuckles and I add, 'Rory, I know Grace will always be an important part of your life and Camarg mustn't feel that he cannot talk about his mother. She has left you a wonderful legacy.' His eyes are moist; he says nothing but gently kisses the top of my head. As he does so the door bursts open and Camarg comes in.

'Dad, I taught Paul to do a double loop and we want to come to your gig on Friday. Can we?' He pauses and looks at me and then Rory.

'I've asked Jane to marry me, son, and she's agreed.'

'Cool!' he exclaims. 'Dad, can I have a coke?'

'I think we should have something to celebrate,' says his father. 'There's a bottle of champagne tucked away somewhere.'

'I'll get it.' Camarg darts into the kitchen and can be heard moving bottles. He returns in triumph and watches with satisfaction as Rory takes three champagne flutes out of a cupboard over the television, eases the wire and produces a satisfactory explosion that sends the cork ricocheting off the ceiling.

'Camarg, you're too young in normal circumstances but tonight you can join with us. To you, Jane.' We clink glasses, our full flutes against Camarg's half-full one. He is soon sent to bed and Rory and I finish the bottle, sitting close together on the sofa and talking late into the night.

………………………………..

I call my parents the following morning.

'Hi Mum, it's Jane.'

'Jane, are you alright?'

'I'm fine, Mum, sorry to ring so early. I'm engaged!'

'Engaged! Richard, Jane is engaged! Congratulations, my darling. Is it the one who took you to the concert? What was his name? Rory? When will we meet him?'

'Soon. I'm in Juba next week but we could come the weekend after.'

'Yes. Richard, they are coming on the seventeenth! Here; he wants to have a word.'

'Congratulations, Jane! Will we like him?'

'I hope so, Dad, you'll be able to judge for yourself the weekend after next.' He's gone and Mum is back planning the menu.

'Mum, he's a widower with a son, who will be with us.'

'Oh. Right. Sausages? Fish fingers?'

'Camarg is twelve; he'll be fine with whatever we're having but keep it simple.'

'Twelve... Good. Did you hear that Richard? A boy.'

'Mum, I've got to go. I've got a meeting. Speak soon.'

Poor Mum, she was shocked but she'll be fine when she meets them. I hope Rory can get Dad talking politics. I pick up my bag, heavy with all the papers I need and drive to the City Council offices.

I'm meeting Sally Walters about trafficking referrals. Rory says she has a reputation for being conscientious and detached. She's a small plump woman in her forties with long neatly trimmed blond hair.

'We have an Anti-Trafficking Partnership here in Bristol,' she informs me. 'The police, voluntary agencies and the Council work together so that we have a clear view of all cases.'

'The Olaudah Trust will be able to provide accommodation for eight women and five men.' I explain. 'We'll be referring clients from our London operation, but expect to hold places for local clients as well.'

'Your visit is well timed,' she replies. 'I've several young men and women we'll need to place soon and all the hostels in Bristol are operating at full capacity.'

'I'm afraid we won't be open until the beginning of December; we may be able to take one or two before then but it'll depend on our London intake. What is the story of these clients?'

'They came to us when the police raided a marijuana farm in South Bristol. They've been in specialist units for medical treatment and counselling since June and will soon be able to go into the community but with support.' Something clicks in my mind and I have to suppress a chuckle. How fitting if our first referrals to Avon View House are the result of the illicit activities next door to Mrs. Jackson's. We'll be able to help those ghostly figures I saw crossing the window in the middle of the night.

Thankful that the initiative I took in reporting to the police has had such a positive outcome I drive to Avon View House, picking up Maria from the station on the way.

'How are your family? What does Peter think of the situation in Juba?' I ask her. Her brother, Peter, remembers me and this has helped to bring her two worlds together.

'They are anxious about the outbreak of fighting. Peter says the tension between the Nuer and Dinka tribes is increasing. Inflation is very high. I am sending what I can to help.' I listen with dismay; such a sad change from the optimism when Independence was gained in 2011. Now the two years of fighting since November 2013 are undermining people's access to the basics of life.

'I'm so sorry, Maria, you must feel worried about them.'

'God will keep them safe,' she says. A few months ago, I would have ignored her blind hope but I am beginning to wonder about the God she believes in. Can her Lord Jesus help me build a good life in Bristol?

'Jane, you haven't told me how you are? Have you seen Rory?' I am touched by her concern.

'Rory asked me to marry him yesterday evening.'

'And you said "Yes"?'

'I did.'

'Oh, that is good news. I'm very happy for you, Jane. He is a good man.'

'Thank you, Maria.'

I show her round Avon View House and explain the systems we need to put in place for handling the bookings.

'This is the contract organisations renting office space must sign,' I tell her. We go through line by line and then she places a copy in the side compartment of her bag. She is wearing a black skirt and white shirt as usual but there is a splash of colour in the pink and lilac scarf she wears. She looks professional and competent.

I show her the one bedroom apartment I have been sleeping in, which will be hers and she seems delighted. We look briefly into the other attic rooms, where the paint is discoloured by age and there is a thick layer of dust.

'These will be refurbished soon.' I explain.

We move down to the bedrooms on the first floor. The smell of wet paint pervades everything. There is a box room, which is awaiting the arrival of two small armchairs and a desk.

'This will provide meeting or counselling space,' I tell her. 'You will be responsible for allocating the rooms and ensuring that each client follows the programme developed for them. Paul or I will explain how their funding works and you'll need to liaise with the City Council, London or Bristol, to make sure the money comes through.'

There is a light knock and the door is pushed further open.

'I hope I'm not too early,' says Glycella. She has come to meet Maria and will keep an eye on her until I have moved to Bristol. She looks immaculate and as usual makes me feel untidy and dishevelled although I'm dressed smartly for the meeting with Sally Walters. Maria doesn't seem to be so easily wilted and stands immediately holding out her hand. She is slightly taller than Glycella and they eye each other, backs ramrod straight and heads erect.

'Maria, I'm delighted to meet you, welcome to Avon View House. I hope you will be happy here.'

'Thank you,' Maria replies with dignity. 'I hope your family will be proud of what is achieved in this house.' Good girl, diplomatic answer.

We complete the tour with a review of the storage space while I explain to Maria that she will be responsible for ordering domestic supplies.

'Has anything been done about a catering manager?' asks Glycella.

'No, we're still working out what to do about that.'

'Do you have any catering experience, Maria?'

'Yes, I cooked for the household, eight people when I was in Slough. At Lucille's we serve coffee, tea and cakes. I'm used to ordering supplies and supervising the ones who serve.'

'Well, that might be very helpful in the short term while the numbers staying here build up. What do you think, Jane?'

'I'll have a word with Andy.' We are only employing Maria for thirty hours a week. We could increase her hours to full time and employ some additional daily help; she will send the additional wages to Nimule of course.

On the way back to the station Maria asks:

'Do you remember Manny, the one who emailed you to

find me?'

'Yes, I do, how is he?'

'He is well. He is making a visit to the UK at the end of November and will be here for the opening of the house. May he attend?' I digest this information with some surprise; I had no idea that Maria was in regular touch with him.

'Yes, of course. What has prompted him to come over here?' Maria's colour deepens and her hands lock in her lap.

'He helped me for the interview. He was going to visit his family in South Sudan but because of the fighting he cannot go and he would like to come here instead.'

'I look forward to meeting him, Maria.' So, this childhood friendship seems to have blossomed into an adult relationship.

'Thank you. He can stay at Mrs. Jackson's?'

'You'll need to book. I'll give you the number.'

As I drop Maria off at the station my phone rings.

'Hi Ellie.'

'Sorry to bother you, Jane, I know you're very busy but we've had a message from Pamela, you know, the Doves of Peace lady?'

'Yes? What has happened?'

'She says they're picking up reports that fighting is no longer confined to the oilfields in Unity State but is spreading south. Do you want me to cancel your tickets?'

'Is my conference still on?'

'Shall I check and ring you back?'

'Thank you, Ellie.'

I drive back to Avon View House trying to work out what to do for the best. The conference has been arranged by one of the big international charities working in South Sudan. If it is cancelled I will miss crucial opportunities to meet with people. On the other hand if other organisations are pulling out it becomes more dangerous to be a western face in Juba.

I consult with Rory when I meet him after work.

'Ellie has booked me on a flight on the evening of Saturday 3rd October; the conference runs Monday to Thursday, fifth to eighth. I meet with the South Sudan Women's Movement on Friday morning and fly home on the Friday afternoon. I'll be in government offices the whole time and they usually have a military guard. What do you think?'

'Let's have a look at what Reuters and the other news feeds are saying.' Rory looks at his phone.

'There's been fierce fighting in the north over the oils fields,' he says, 'but not in Juba, in fact President Kiir has reduced the military presence in Juba. Difficult to know whether that is a good or bad sign.' He carries on flicking through screens and scanning.

'Ah, this is why the small agencies are leaving; Sudan Tribune reports a murder and a series of robberies on small western agencies.' He turns to me. 'Of course I don't want you to go, Jane, but I know how difficult it is to set up appointments and this opportunity won't come again. I suggest you keep to the plan but take no risks.' My heart swells with love and respect. He knows the dangers, better than I do, yet he is willing to support me.

I put my arms around him. 'You would go?' He clasps me tightly.

'Yes, but I would make sure I was met at the airport and could get safely from the hotel to the conference venue. Have you booked your hotel?'

'Yes, Ellie booked me into one adjacent to the government offices.'

'So you can walk?'

'Yes'

'Go, then. I'll check with a contact in the UN security forces and see if there's anyone who can keep an eye on you.'

'Thank you.' We hold each other tightly.

'Stay safe, babe,' he says, 'and do your job.'

....

Sunday 4th October 5pm East African Time

Dear Rory,

I hope you received my text from Nairobi.

There were no problems with the journey; it's always miserable arriving at Nairobi airport in the early hours but my connection was on time and the hotel sent a taxi to collect me. Juba is tense but there are no obvious signs of unrest. The driver spoke a little English and says that the military presence is keeping the city quiet. There are a couple of guards outside the conference centre and a makeshift wooden guardroom at the corner of the street. The uniformed porter on the door of the hotel is carrying a gun. I'm not sure whether that makes me feel safer or not.

My room is fine with clean bedding and fresh towels but there is no plug in the sink and the water is tea coloured.

Love,

Jane

Sunday 4th October 4pm British Summer Time

Dearest Jane,

Good to know that you are safely at the hotel. I have checked Reuters and there are no reports of unrest at the moment.

I know you will be careful. Keep an eye on your baggage.

I love you.

Rory

Monday 5 October 9pm East African Time

Dear Rory,

Thank you for encouraging me to come; the conference is well worth it.

I had an interesting breakfast with Marianne, who works for a

Dutch agency supporting orphaned children.

This morning we heard the latest report from the United Nations. South Sudan's record on child protection is one of the worst in the world. A speaker from the Ministry of Gender, Child and Social Welfare explained that their main focus is to bring back children stranded in Khartoum and to set up three drop-off centres. This is a start but it does not seem much in view of the numbers of orphans.

I hope all is well with you and Camarg.

Love,

Jane

Monday 5th October 8.30 pm British Summer Time

Hi Janey,

I wish I could be there with you.

Now that the leaflet about Maria has gone to the printers I am starting to draft out how we might make a longer story. I hope you don't mind me going through your audio diary while you are away?

Sleep well, my darling. I love you

Rory

Tuesday 6th October 8pm East African Time

Hi Rory,

Of course, go ahead with the diary. I record it when I am stuck in traffic, or waiting for a meeting. There's quite a bit of background noise on some sections.

I haven't been sleeping too well since I arrived here. I have a recurring dream of a giant rising from the Nile and striding across the bush trailing weed and hampered by chains. I've not had bad nights for several months but it woke me last night and the night before. The locals here refer to the river spirits so perhaps I'm allowing their fears to influence me.

We had more discussion today about how to establish better child protection. I'm going to suggest to Andy that we raise funds for more centres for the huge numbers of children recruited as child soldiers and 'wives'.

I'm wondering how things are going at Avon View House and what you and Camarg are doing. I am missing you.

Love,

Jane

Tuesday 6th October 11pm British Summer Time

Hi Janey,

River spirits are very powerful and can cause infertility and madness. But it sounds as though your dream is something more archetypal than that. There is a spirit of Africa itself that comes out in the rhythm of the music and the exuberance of the people. My father calls it the 'jitu'. In Kenya it is the energy which powers the harambee movement but South Sudan is a new nation and maybe the 'jitu' is trapped by the past and wandering without purpose.

We popped into Avon View House this evening and everything is fine there. The attics are finished.

Camarg was commended by his teacher for his English essay.

I've spoken to a colleague who has the software to get your audio tapes transcribed and printed out. Are you OK with that?

I'm missing you and realising how lucky I am that you are willing to take Camarg and me on.

Thank you, my darling.

Rory

Wednesday 7th October 6pm East African Time

Hi Rory,

Wow, I had never thought of the dream like that. There is a determination here to make things better but so many views and no-one seems to know how to do it yet. And whatever is tried tribalism threatens to rise up and overwhelm it. I feel bad for professionals based here; they have worked so many times to build something and seen it torn down by fighting before it is complete.

Today has been focussed on protection of girls. Young teenagers are forced into marriage as compensation for inter-clan killings and then moved on to slavery or prostitution. Attitudes are twisted as a result of conflict for most of the last fifty years.

I've been meeting some of the women's movement; they hold the key to how we can protect these girls.

Yes, good idea to get the tapes transcribed.

Tell Camarg well done on his essay.

I love you

Janey

287

Wednesday 7ᵗʰ October 10.30pm British Summer Time

Janey, my darling,

There is concern in the media here about the announcement that the president is dividing South Sudan's ten states into twenty-eight. It may destabilise the country again. Just be careful what you say. I love you

Rory

Thursday 8 October 2pm East African Time

Dear Rory,

The president's announcement has been widely reported but it's not affecting the atmosphere here.

We split into groups this morning to discuss child protection in each country. For South Sudan so much depends on when a proper Government of national Unity will be formed.

See you Saturday morning.

I love you.

Janey

16 MARIA AND MANNY

The story of several thousand Sudanese children wandering through wilderness without parents, falling prey to bullets and wild animals and disease, would receive widespread news coverage ten years later....[16]

How will I recognise him? I am standing by the ticket barrier with Jane and Rory waiting for Manny to arrive at Temple Meads Station. He is part of my happiest memories. Whenever I heard him play the drum my feet fell naturally into the right steps. But what will he be like now? What has happened to him in twenty-five years?

Men in dark business suits race discreetly to get ahead as they come to the barrier, women in high heels with tight

16 *The Lost Boys of Sudan* by Mark Bixler, 2006

skirts, are trying to look elegant but really they are hurrying too. I can feel their tension tightening my own nerves and sinews.

'Relax, Maria,' says Rory. 'This isn't our train; the board will tell us when the London train is due.'

The rush of people slows and I look at the clock – another five minutes yet. Jane and Rory are talking quietly. They were worried about a visit to Jane's parents but it went well and she seems relaxed. They are good for each other. His face is full of sadness but when he is with Jane he laughs, and she seems to be able to slow down with him in a way that she never does at work.

'...train arriving on platform six is the fourteen forty service to Cardiff.'

'That's Manny's train,' says Rory.

We move closer to the barrier. A couple of young men with rucksacks push through, followed by an elderly couple with children swarming around them, then a tall lady with a dog. Perhaps he's missed the train?

A crowd of people arrive together and I can't see them all. We might miss him and he'll wander through this massive station thinking we have forgotten him. I can see a dark figure at the back of the crowd, his brown skin is wrinkled and his hair grey. Have Manny's troubles aged him so much? No; this man hefts a bag onto his shoulder and greets a woman waiting just beyond us. Two large ladies come through trailing wheeled suitcases. As they pass me a tall angular figure is revealed behind them. He is wearing a zipped jacket and carrying a holdall. His skin is as black as night and he scans the crowd at the barrier with a quick intense gaze. Deep in my heart there is a jolt of recognition. He puts his ticket into the barrier and comes through as I move forwards; and our eyes meet.

'Maria,' he says and takes both my hands.

'Manny, Manny – I never thought I would see you again.' He is taller than I am, lean and smartly dressed with an open-necked shirt under the leather jacket. He drops the holdall and we look at each other and then place our hands on each other's shoulders in the warm South Sudanese greeting our elders used at the New Jerusalem church. We are alive; we have survived; we have made a new life. He has done well it seems. His face is slightly lined but cheerful. The prominent cheeks that were a feature when he was a young teenager are rounded like plums and rise in his face as he smiles at me.

We let our hands drop and I turn; Jane and Rory are right behind us; there are beads of moisture at the corner of

Jane's eyes and Rory's are crinkled and warm.

'This is Manny.'

'We guessed that,' laughs Jane and takes his hand.

'Welcome, brother,' says Rory, and they shake vigorously.

'It is Jane who has helped me get in touch with my family,' I explain.

'And Rory is helping Maria to publish her story,' says Jane.

'I'm pleased to meet you,' says Manny. 'Many South Sudanese in the US have been writing their stories. They call us the "lost boys". Well done, Maria, for doing this also.' He looks at me with respect and I am proud that I have achieved something he recognises as important.

'Let's get out of this melee and find the car.' Rory picks up Manny's holdall and we follow him out of the station, weaving our way through the jostling crowds. He stows Manny's bag in the boot and offers him the front seat. Manny protests but we insist that he is the visitor and should enjoy the sights of Bristol. Rory takes us over the bridge and along the Welsh Back, past the restaurants and floating bars that line the upper end of the harbour. He turns past one side of Queen Square.

'This is our Georgian gem,' he explains, 'nothing to rival the Royal Crescent at Bath but the best that remains of the eighteenth century port.'

'Parts of Baltimore are similar,' comments Manny. 'We call them row houses.'

We cross the Avon and turn into Bedminster Road.

'The guesthouse isn't in the best part of Bristol,' apologises Jane, 'but it's clean, well run, and reasonably priced.'

'It's good,' says Manny. 'This will suit me well.'

As we pull into the car park at the rear a lady in a brightly flowered dress is seeing someone out.

'Be there in a moment!' she calls as Manny gets out and holds the door open for Jane and me. She comes across to us. She is what we call "a big mama" in my country.

'Mrs. Jackson, meet my friends, Rory and Maria,' says Jane, 'and one of your guests for the night, Manny, just arrived from the US.'

'Pleased, I'm sure,' murmurs Mrs. Jackson. 'Come this way, young man, and wipe your feet on the mat.'

Jane catches my eye. She has told me about Mrs. Jackson's house rules.

'We'll pick you up around seven, brother, and take you out for a meal,' says Rory.

'Thank you. I look forward to that.' Manny picks up his bag and follows Mrs. Jackson into the guest house, wiping his feet carefully as he goes.

....

Several hours later the four of us are sitting at a rough wooden table on the Grain Barge, a floating pub moored in the harbour. Rory is introducing Manny to the local cider and recommending the homemade pies.

'This is familiar,' Manny comments. 'In Baltimore we have a renovated harbour area and many restaurants where people like to relax after work.' We watch as several rowing eights negotiate the choppy waters, carefully avoiding the route taken by Bristol's blue and yellow water taxis.

'You live and work in Baltimore?' asks Jane.

'Yes, ma'am, I qualified in Washington, which is where I was taken when I first went to the US. I have been working for Harbour Attorneys for two years. I have a small apartment on the outskirts of Baltimore.'

I feel very shy of this smart American in his casual trousers and open necked shirt. He looks clean and well-fed, so different from the boy I remember, who looked after the village goats and came to visit his family in Nimule.

'Is your father well?' I dare to ask.

'He sounds well. I haven't seen him. I was hoping to go this week but there is too much fighting. Many people are fleeing over the border again. My brothers are in the Anzara refugee camp just outside Nimule. They get work when they can.'

'And your sisters and mother?'

'My older sister and her husband have returned to our tribal lands in Bor. We do not know where my Ma is, she and the little girls fled to Uganda but they are not in the refugee camps near Nimule. We do not know where they are.'

'I'm sorry. May God bless them.'

'And your family?'

'They are in Nimule. I speak to Ma every two weeks; Deborah and Peter are with her but my Baba was killed in the fighting. Aaron has taken his family back to Bor. Joel has come out of the army and gone to Juba to look for work. We do not know where Rachel is. She disappeared when I was taken.

'Sorry.' Says Manny.

'Ma writes that food is getting more expensive because of the fighting in Unity province over the oil.'

'Yes. My father too says inflation is high,' replies Manny.

'Three hundred percent over the last year,' agrees Jane. The pies arrive and for a while we are busy passing the vegetables and enjoying the gentle rocking motion as motor cruisers on the harbour sweep past sending ripples against the sides of the barge. The sun is setting behind a low bank of cloud and the harbour is bathed in golden light.

'Manny, tell us what happened to you. How did you reach the United States?' Jane has asked the question I dared not ask. Manny rests his fork against the side of his plate, finishes a mouthful of pie and looks up, staring beyond us out across the water.

'We were in the bush looking after the goats. We heard fighting and terrible screams; people started pouring out of the town and they told us to run for our lives so we

296

scattered into the bush. I was with Kuol and Ngang and we wandered for days too scared to go back to the town, living off fruit and insects and drinking from the streams. Then some older boys told us that everyone had been killed and we should go to Ethiopia, where we would get help and schooling so we joined with them and walked eastwards. More boys joined us and soon there was a long column walking to Ethiopia. It took us many weeks, some died. There were no streams and we were very thirsty. We heard lions in the bush at night. The older boys told us that we must keep walking and they kept us hopeful with songs about how we would get an education and train to be soldiers to defend our people.'

'Did you know what had happened to your parents?' I ask as Manny pauses for breath.

'No, I thought they must be dead. I didn't think anyone could survive that day of fighting and killing. I knew that we must look after ourselves. We reached Ethiopia, found a camp, Panyido, where we stayed for several years but then we were told we must leave the camp and go back to South Sudan.'

'Mengistu was ousted in a coup,' mutters Jane, 'and the Ethiopian government would no longer support the South Sudanese refugee camps.'

'We were forced to cross the river at gun point and many did not make it because of the crocodiles.' I am next to Manny and I see his eyes darken with pain as he looks down for a moment. His hand, resting on the table tightens round his fork and pushes it into the wood like a weapon. I reach out and take the fork and he relaxes his fist.

'We walked many miles. Planes dropped water for us but we had no food. We walked through southern Sudan into Kenya to a camp called Kakuma. We stayed there for a long time with many other Dinka boys. The camp was divided into sections. In other areas there were Nuer and Acholi and smaller tribal groups. We had food and water but we were often hungry. Pastors came and started schools and churches for us so I was able to carry on with my studies. I also gave my life to the Lord Jesus.' I smile at him; it is so good to know that Manny shares the Christian faith. It is difficult to imagine that this confident man endured such hardship. Like me he never knew parents when he was growing up and yet somehow the Lord Jesus has brought him through it.

'Maria, did you know this story before today?' asks Rory.

'No, I remember that Manny was not with us for the last time in Nimule. His family were living there by then but they told me he'd stayed behind to look after the goats. They deceived me.'

'I guess they didn't want to frighten you,' says Manny. 'They thought that I would come back again. If I'd known they had survived I would've walked to Nimule. We thought everyone had been killed. Some of the boys had seen hundreds of corpses in the streets. We didn't dare go back.'

The waiter arrives with the desserts and coffees. The sun has set and lights are coming on around the harbour. The last few rowers are hauling their boats up onto the slipway. A cruiser full of people creates a wake that rocks the barge sufficiently to move the cutlery, and we hold onto our plates as the sound of drunken singing pierces the peaceful chatter of the restaurant. My body sways to the motion of the barge but in my mind I am back in those terrifying years in South Sudan when every family we knew had lost relatives or seen them killed or captured.

'So tell us how you made it to the US,' prompts Rory as the drunken hubbub outside subsides.

'News came that the United Nations was going to select boys to go to America. There was a pamphlet stating that there would be education and support available but you had to apply. I was still with Kuol and Ngang so we filled in the forms and waited. Then we had to answer many questions to prove that we had walked all the way to the camp fleeing the fighting. They started putting the names of those who had been accepted up on the notice boards. One day after many weeks Ngang, Kuol and I were on the list. They gave us a sweatshirt and put us on a plane to Washington. We had a booklet to read about how to live in the US and find work.'

'So you went from a refugee camp in the Kenyan bush to Washington?' says Rory.

'Yes. It was an adjustment!'

'How did you manage in such a big shift of circumstances?'

'We made mistakes. We sent all the money they gave us to friends in Kakuma, and then we could not pay for our electricity at the end of the month. Local people helped us with cooking and shopping. It was crazy because we had never seen so many foods to buy before. Kuol and I kept setting fire to things when we cooked but Ngang was better at it. He was the last to find work so did most of the cooking for us for many months. I worked in a canning plant and then in a warehouse.'

'But you were able to carry on with your education?' Jane asks.

'No, that was much harder than we expected. We had to take the General Education Development tests and it was difficult to find a class at times when we were not working. I was fortunate because the manager of the warehouse made adjustments to my schedule. When I had passed the GED tests I was promoted and I was able to save money to start studying the law but it has taken me many years to qualify. We were given local sponsors and Jack Nutley and his wife, Ann, helped me through my tests and gave me a room in their house for many years. When I had qualified they helped me to apply for the job in Baltimore.'

'Amazing that you managed to work and study law at the same time,' responds Jane. I am too overcome to speak. I see the boy I remember in Nimule and it is hard to believe that it is the same person; yet in my bones I recognise the movements of the child in the man and deep in his eyes, under the pain of hardship, I glimpse the merriment and sense of fun we shared as children. I thought I would never feel like that again but as I watch Manny and listen to him answer their questions I can feel a spring of laughter welling up inside me.

'I think we had better settle up,' says Rory. 'It's getting late and you must be tired. We'll run you back to the guest house.'

'Maria and I are going to be very busy getting everything ready for the opening and the anniversary celebrations tomorrow,' says Jane. 'Why don't you have a bit of a lie-in and then come over to Avon View House at lunch time and we can show you round. We can arrange some lunch, can't we, Maria?'

'Yes, of course.' I would like to prepare Manny the best meal he has ever eaten but I have many guests to bake for tomorrow. I hope there will be another time.

'I have a gig at a pub in North Street tomorrow night,' says Rory, 'Come with me; I can pick you up from Mrs. Jackson's.'

'The only problem is,' continues Jane, 'how are we going to get you to the house tomorrow lunchtime? I have to pick up leaflets from the printers as well as arrange the displays with Paul.'

'I can walk,' offers Manny.

'It must be a good hour on foot,' says Jane.

'No problem!' says Manny. We all laugh, our voices

mingling joyfully together. It seems ridiculous that we are worrying about his ability to walk for an hour after the story he has just told us.

....

The next morning I pause at the top of the main staircase in Avon View House and look out of the long central window above the doorway. I have been running like a crazy lizard all morning, darting into cupboards, scooping up overlooked rubbish and tidying the kitchen ready for tomorrow. We have been clearing and cleaning the house for weeks but there is always so much to do at the last minute.

Jane is in the hall below with Paul and Ellie putting up the panels that will show the story of the Olaudah Trust. The sun suddenly breaks through and streams onto the tiled compass on the floor bringing the alternating black and cream tiles into sharp relief. Jane's phone rings and she holds the pop-up display board she is assembling steady with one hand while she answers. The doorbell sounds and she casts a frantic eye around as I run down the staircase. For a brief moment I sense the many other women who have run down these stairs over the years to greet a visitor; I have seen their pictures on the walls, elegant ladies in long frocks, groomed young women in straight fringed dresses – the ghosts of the past floating around me as I run down the last few steps and across the tiled floor. I press the button and the glass doors swing open to admit Manny who has been standing in the front porch.

'Are you expecting me?' He laughs as I seize his hand and drag him over the threshold. He looks around.

'My dear friend,' he says, taking both my hands, 'whatever your journey has been you have arrived at a good place!' I nod and lead him by the hand to the back of the hall towards the kitchen area. Jane waves her phone as we go past and mouths:

'See you in a minute.'

I have made sandwiches and a salad for all those who are working here this morning. Andy is in the office on the other side of the stairs, finalising the running order and speeches for tomorrow. Rory and his band have arrived and are rehearsing in the dining room. While the kettle boils I lay the table so that as people come in they can eat quickly. But no-one appears for several minutes and there is time for Manny and I to sit together. I tell him of my years as a captive servant in Juba and then in Slough. I do not tell him about the colonel, and being "wives". I still feel shame at what happened even though I had no choice. I do not know how he would react. He seems shocked even at the little I have told him.

'I did not know such things were happening,' he says, 'those of us they call "The Lost Boys" have tried to piece together the story of our country from our own stories and from the Sudan newspapers. We thought all our womenfolk were either dead or safe with the family.'

'The worst time was when I was left in Slough and I thought I had no hope of finding my family,' I tell him. 'I was tricked and captured again. I was very frightened to be in a prison. But I was able to train as a hairdresser. The Lord Jesus brought good out of it in the end.'

'You have done well, Maria, and now you are in a responsible position for this important project.'

Everyone starts to arrive for lunch and I am busy making sure they have everything they need. There is a buzz of conversation and people are curious about my visitor.

'So, Manny, have you managed to see much of Bristol?' asks Paul.

'I only arrived yesterday but I went out to supper last night with Jane, Rory and Maria and saw the harbour area.'

'What do you think of this project?' asks Paul.

'Impressive; I'm looking forward to hearing more about it.'

Jane has finally made it into lunch. She comes over to greet Manny briefly and then turns to me.

'I can hold the fort here for a bit, Maria, why don't you show Manny the house and explain about tomorrow.'

I lead him back to the hall and up the main stairs.

'This house belonged to the Hamilton family but they have built a new home and have given this one to the Olaudah Trust,' I tell him. We pause at the top of the stairs and look through the bare trees to where David and Glycella's elongated cube of a house nestles into the slope of the land. The slate roof of the porch catches the light and the sight of the water tumbling over the edge into the pool below is breathtaking.

'Wow! That's quite a house,' comments Manny.

'They are unusual people and very generous. They could have sold this house for millions of pounds but they want to support the Trust and other local charities.'

'So what's in it for them?' There is a new note in Manny's

voice, perhaps the lawyer's tones he uses when he is working.

'There's been a tragedy in the family and they don't want to live here, but they don't wish to sell it either, so we rent it for a very low rate. The Trust helped them free children who were captured from Glycella's home in Uganda. Glycella is a family lawyer working to protect children. She says slavery is a crime against the family.'

'I look forward to meeting her. And her husband?'

'David worked in Nairobi and is involved in many projects in Kenya, Uganda and now in South Sudan.'

I show Manny the bedrooms that have been converted into studio flats for the men. I take him to the top floor and show him my apartment looking out onto the Avon Gorge.

'Wow, that's like having the Pennsylvanian Grand Canyon in your view!' I can see that he is impressed. 'So what is your work, Maria?' he continues.

'At the moment, I look after the house and the renovation work. As soon as we have clients I will take care of the girls and young men when they arrive; make sure they eat, wash themselves and stay clean from drugs or alcohol. There will be a nurse dietician to help and we will refer them to counselling as necessary.'

'How do the clients know you are here?'

'In the UK there is a referral process, led by the Salvation Army. Some of them will be referred to us in London; others will be from local anti-trafficking agencies. It will be my job to manage the bookings and keep the house running smoothly.'

'This is a big role, Maria, are you enjoying it?'

'I managed the girls in the hair salon in London and this is no different in many ways. I can work hard and help my family; that is what matters to me.'

We leave the apartment and I take him downstairs to the main reception rooms.

'Who will use these office spaces?' asks Manny.

'We have several local organisations who are hiring them. The first one comes on Monday week. It will be part of my work to check that they keep to their contract to begin but as we get more organisations in we will need to recruit another member of staff.'

'Have the legal requirements been looked into?'

'David Hamilton and another member of the project

board are dealing with most of that, and Glycella is making sure that the arrangements for the clients are correct.' Manny's normally smooth forehead is creased with a frown and his eyes are withdrawn into his inner being. He is deep in thought for a moment or two and I wait for him to return.

'I would like to help,' he says, 'but American law is very different to how things work here.'

'It is no problem, we have many supporters here.'

We go out of the door by the kitchen onto the lawn and I explain that we are hoping to rent some of the office space to an organisation that will train disabled youngsters in the growing of organic vegetables and flowers. Manny stands in the middle of the lawn with his hands behind his back, tipping his weight back onto his heels as he looks up at the house towering above him.

'I sense the spirits of people who have lived here; it is good, I think.'

'Yes, this has been a place where people are happy and I hope we can make it the same for the people who will stay here.'

It is eight in the evening before the last display is up at Avon View House, the breakfast room and kitchen tidied and signs put up at the gate and entrance. Jane's phone stops ringing, Andy finalises the programme with each of the speakers and Paul announces that the chairs have all been set out in the boardroom and a leaflet placed on each one. I have scrubbed the front step three times today and am weary but as we turn off the lights in the hall I feel a glow of satisfaction; it looks beautiful and I sense the spirits of the house are at peace.

Andy and Paul are heading back to their families for the night so Jane and I make our way to the pub alone. We have left the car in a side street and walked the last few hundred metres. The "pub" is a small warehouse, stripped back to wooden floors and brick walls. Rory and his band are on a low dais at one end and the space between the musicians and the bar is packed with bodies, jerking and stamping to the music like a machine that has slipped its fan belt and is running out of control. In the middle of the crowd of gyrating bodies the dark figure of Manny can be seen. A second button is undone at the neck of his shirt and a flap of fabric has escaped one side of his belt. His hips thrust to and fro swivelling in time to the band and his head jerks rhythmically in the opposite direction. Facing him a girl with long blond hair and a very short skirt is matching him move for move as if they were linked by some invisible chain. On the platform Rory and the band play faster and faster while other people spin and weave around the two figures in the centre of the floor.

'Wow, Manny's in the groove,' comments Jane, 'and Rory's fuelling it!' She waves towards the platform and Rory gives a quick nod in our direction.

Something that fluttered to life in me this afternoon dies stillborn. How can I have been so foolish to think that the bond between Manny and I as children is still there. Why would a hairdresser, whose looks were lost many years ago through harsh treatment, attract him when he can take the pick of sophisticated professional girls? He probably already has a girlfriend in Baltimore. Someone vacates a table and I collapse onto a wooden chair.

'Maria, are you OK?' asks Jane.

'I'm tired.'

'Me too, I wasn't expecting such a lively gig. Let's have a drink; stay there and I will get us both a juice.'

She pushes her way to the bar and I try to ignore the dancing figures but the music goes on, getting faster until it reaches a crashing climax and those still standing raise their hands to clap the band. Rory gestures for silence and then announces that the band will take a short break. He gives Manny a "thumbs up" and points him to our table as

Jane arrives with the juices.

'Good evening, ladies. How are you?' In spite of the crush of bodies and exuberant partying Manny still produces the slightly formal English we learned in South Sudan, tinged with an American accent.

'We are fine,' says Jane, 'but you look as though you could do with a long cool beer.'

'Yes, you're right,' he laughs and heads to the bar. I watch him as his lithe figure weaves between the groups chatting on the dance floor and then stands tall and spiky at the bar.

'He seems quite at home,' says Jane.

'When we were children he was always the one to start up a drum beat and get the singing and dancing going.'

'And you were too.'

'Yes, when I was a child, but I haven't danced for many years. The music has gone from my spirit.'

'No, not gone,' says Manny, arriving at that moment, 'just buried, it will come back.' He drains his glass and sits back in his chair, breathing deeply and wiping his face with a cotton handkerchief. Rory comes through a door at the back of the dais, weaves across the centre of the room, where the crowds are thinner and gives Jane a quick kiss on the cheek.

'We're on for another half hour and then I'm done,' he says. 'Are you all ready at the house?' Jane nods. Other band members appear on the dais. Rory ambles back to join them and they start playing and singing a gentle ballad. The pace picks up again as the band moves into a well-known song with a strong relentless beat. Manny's foot taps impatiently on the floor and he gets up and extends a hand to Jane and me.

'Come on, forget your work and enjoy the beat,' he says and sways backwards onto the dance floor pulling us with him as if we were small tugboats failing to hold back the prow of an ocean liner as it slips its moorings.

I feel immobilised. The only parties I have been to for years have been church events and Christmas socials. My feet are tied by invisible threads and my legs are stumps of wood rooted to the floor. Manny continues backwards ploughing through the shifting bodies and I am dragged in his wake until we are close to the band. Then he starts that pattern of small steps forwards and backwards, slightly shifting position each time, which we used as children long ago. Jane follows to begin with but as the beat gets faster she laughs and gives up, joining Rory on the dais. The physical memory from long ago is reviving from the soles of my feet upwards. It is as if the self-control that has anchored me for years is shifting and swaying in the deeper currents of music and remembered patterns of my girlhood. I look up at Manny – Bol was his childhood name – and start to turn and twist as my feet follow the ancient rhythm: step, step, forward, back, hips swaying, head poised, hands clapping. I have forgotten where I am. The lights are dim and I feel again the velvet warmth of the African night, the mesmerising beat of the drums and the whirring of wings as crickets salute the moonlight. The sweat is pouring down my back, and my forehead and cheeks are soft and moist. For the first time in many years I feel as though I am alive, glowing, resonating to the songs of the African soil. The drum rolls faster and faster and Manny and I match each other's rhythm beat by beat, moving across the dance floor. I am laughing and singing Dinka words that have been buried deep inside me. I have lost all sense of my surroundings except for the urge to keep the beat, step with inner synchronicity, feel the music. The snare drum cuts in with a higher more rapid note and a clash of cymbals and Manny winks at me and then goes into the loose limbed 'stick dance' that we used to do as young children. Legs akimbo, elbows and knees bent we dance like puppets raising an arm and leg on one side then on the other. The snare drum stops but the crowds around us have taken up the beat, clapping in unison as the music rises to a crescendo and ends in a long drum roll. The drum dies away but the hand clapping continues getting louder until it breaks down into applause. I realise we are the only people on the floor, the rest are standing or sitting, clapping and cheering, their glasses raised in salute.

'See, you still have the beat of Africa,' grins Manny. He tucks his shirt in, does up a button, smoothes his hair and with a gentle hand on my elbow leads me back to the table. People ask us where we learned to dance like that but Manny just smiles.

'We trained at a special school.' He says.

....

I lie in bed that night unable to sleep but content to watch the moon rise slowly through my window. After a while I get up and look out at the narrow silver ribbon of the river and the steep mottled cliffs on either side of it. Different soil – greyer, wetter, but the same reverberating rhythm is carried through the rocks of the earth's centre to beat in England as strongly as it does in South Sudan. Tonight I recaptured that beat and felt again the dance that cruelty tried to silence.

17 THE ANNIVERSARY

The Avon and Somerset Anti-Slavery Partnership began in 2009, initiated initially by Unseen in partnership with Avon and Somerset Constabulary and Bristol City Council.[17]

The recently laid gravel at Avon View House contrasts with the glossy leaves of the rhododendrons; the lawns on either side look trim, though our volunteer gardener, Mark, says they are in poor condition; he promises a better sward in the spring. It is a shame we cannot afford to repair the fountain in the centre but at least it is no longer leaking rusty water across the drive.

The freshly painted woodwork accentuates the windows and porch, even on this dull November day, and the gloss black of the gutters and drainpipes delineates the height and breadth of the building.

Patches of brighter terracotta show amongst the brown of

---

[17] http://www.aspartnership.org.uk/avon-and-somerset

the roof tiles, where replacements have yet to weather in. As I turn the car and park to one side near the rhododendron bushes Maria comes out, a thick cardigan wrapped round her dark skirt and jumper.

'Good morning, Jane, how are you?'

'I'm good, Maria, excited that the day is here at last!'

'Yes, I am so happy. Andy and Paul are in the kitchen having a cup of tea. Will you join them?'

'Yes, but no tea for me!'

I follow her up the steps and into the hall. There is a warm smell of new wood, polish and freshly baked cakes. The compass mosaic in the floor gleams with reds, creams and oranges I have never noticed before. The hideous carved wooden ships prows at the end of the balustrades are so highly polished that the curls of the mermaids' hair look freshly hennaed. The stair treads have been brushed and the pile is no longer flattened but upright and soft.

'Maria, you must have been up all night cleaning!' She looks embarrassed.

'I was late,' she laughs, 'the carpenters didn't leave till six o'clock and there was all their mess and dust to clear up.

'Well, it looks amazing.' As we turn into the passageway to the kitchen Glycella's house keeper, Agnes, comes towards us with a huge vase of autumn leaves and chrysanthemum flowers.

'Mrs. Hamilton thought this should go to the right of the entrance, the other side from the coat hooks,' she says, her voice muffled by the foliage.

'There is a stand ready for them,' confirms Maria, and we continue through to the kitchen.

'Jane, long time no see, the great day is here!' Paul wrings my hand heartily, and the tea in the mug in his other hand slops dangerously and threatens to overtop the rim. Ellie removes it, placing it firmly on the worktop and then turns and we kiss on each cheek.

'Ellie, so pleased you can be here to organise us.'

'No worries, Jane. Maria has it all in hand.' I look round the kitchen where every worktop is covered with cake tins and plastic food boxes containing an assortment of cupcakes, tarts, cookies and other delights visible through the translucent sides.

'And the fridge is full of bread for the sandwiches,' adds Ellie.

'Something smells wonderful,' I say. Beyond us Maria is bending down lifting scones out of the double oven at the far end.

'This looks fantastic, Maria. Do we have enough help to get it all to the dining room?'

'Yes,' she responds. 'Agnes is staying all day and we have two local girls who have just completed their catering course at the college arriving at one.'

It all seems calm and well organised. I breathe a sigh of relief. There will be plenty of challenges today but the housekeeping side seems well under control.

'Right, Paul, when you have finished your tea we can get the displays up. Did you pick up the box of booklets?' He gulps down the last mouthful with a grin, gestures to a package in the corner and picks up one of the three large cylinders standing beside it.

'Ready when you are, boss!'

'Ellie?' I look across to her and she holds her palms up to me, level with her shoulders, fingers spread and waves them as if she was in the finale of a dance troop show.

'Save your energy!' I laugh. 'You will need every ounce of it today.'

We erect the first panel and sunlight pouring through the hall window falls in a golden line across the tiled floor and shines a spotlight onto the plastic surface. This is the panel which I prepared showing the growth of Bristol as a port in the seventeenth century and the *Phoenix*, the ship owned by the Hamilton ancestors, leaving the quayside in Princes Street. There is a brief history of the family, the growth of their trading and insurance business and the building of the house in 1860, with an early photo taken before the ballroom wing was added. Flanking the other side of the staircase is the panel Paul has prepared illustrating the abolition movement in Bristol and London. He has included a portrait of Hannah Moore, the poet and abolitionist. The last panel has the story of Maria's life and the work of the Trust today including statistics of the number of victims rescued and supported into work. We set up a table beside this panel and arrange copies of the booklet Rory has produced of Maria's story.

My phone rings, and the doorbell peals at the same time, but Maria is on her way and I see her cross the hall from the kitchen, press the button and greet Manny. They retreat to the kitchen laughing with excitement.

We tie a wide ribbon to one of the ship's prows and stretch it across the stairway ready for the opening ceremony and stand back admiring our work. I hear a car door and Rory and the band enter, staggering under the weight of their instruments.

'Morning, Jane, where do you want us?' He gives me a quick conventional kiss on the cheek but every nerve in my body responds. I touch his hand lightly and say,

'Paul, Ellie, this is Rory.'

'And my band mates Archie, Cliff and Theo,' adds Rory. We shake hands.

'Over there between the panels and the coats,' I tell him. 'Leave a space for Maria and the staff to get through to the dining room but the guests won't be going that way till after you've finished playing.'

'You want us to play between two and three?' checks Rory.

'Bit earlier; can you start at quarter to two so that you're playing when the first guests arrive and then finish an hour later? Andy wants to get people seated before three if possible so that we can start the speeches promptly.'

'Fair enough. Chairs?' queries Rory.

'There are stacking chairs in the dining room.'

I point the way and leave them to arrange the chairs and unpack their instruments. Paul has wandered off to help Andy in the boardroom.

'Ellie, what do you need for welcoming people?'

'Table and chair will be fine, Jane. I can use that one.'

I help her move the heavy oak table so that it is diagonally placed by the front door opposite the musicians. I leave her to sort out what she needs while I consult my list and remind myself what else needs to be done.

I've laid out all my instructions for the day in the small room to the side of the hall that Tom, the security guard has been using. The room is no wider than my outstretched arms and one wall is completely taken up by a window with a wide sill, which has been acting as my desk, and a plastic chair with a padded seat and back. Behind me are the shelves that used to house the Hamilton family silver, soon to be converted into filing space for our clients' records. I lean my elbows on the sill and gaze out down the drive. This is my moment of quiet before our big day starts. Rory's car is parked in front of the porch and Cliff is closing the rear door with one hand whilst holding the tangled metal frames of several music stands tightly to his chest with the other. Agnes is pinching the dead leaves out of the flower tubs on the front steps and rearranging the foliage; a squirrel runs across the drive and sits on its haunches in front of the window, balancing on the narrow stone edge of the flower border. It has a pine cone between its paws, and is carefully stripping off layers and munching on the nuts hidden within. The tiny paws work their way down the cone, teeth gnawing furiously as the larger, more delicious pine nuts at the bottom are revealed.

My mind wanders back over the preceding months – the initial meeting with David Hamilton in his office, my first visit to the house and the conversation with Anka, my growing awareness of its history as I worked through the archive material, and the hectic months of surveys, plans and refurbishment. Now the Trust has a permanent base where we can provide a home for those who haven't had a place to rest for many years. It has been an exhausting, bewildering process at times but, like the squirrel, the layers have been peeled back and I can savour the treat. I close my eyes and let the sounds wash over me, the band practicing, Maria and Ellie discussing arrangements for serving welcome drinks in the hall, Agnes and Cliff chatting on the front steps, the rooks cawing in the trees and gently, beneath it all, the soft sighs of the house as new wood settles, old floorboards creak and the clatter and thud of footsteps echo across the tiled floor. Rory's voice intrudes for a moment, directing the band as they practice, and I dream of our future together. We discussed a date for our wedding last night, Rory wants to press ahead quickly but I need time to get used to the idea. I would like to meet Rory's father and for him to meet my brother's family.

The door knob to my sanctuary rattles and I come to with a guilty start as Andy peers round the door. I haven't looked at my lists – I'll just have to wing it!

'Jane, can you come and have a look at the boardroom and see what you think?' As he speaks my phone rings; it is Sally Walters apologising that she is going to be a little late but will arrive by three in time to give her speech. My moment of peace is shattered; the rest of the morning passes in a whirl as we prepare for the many friends who have helped us with this project to celebrate its completion.

....

'Good afternoon, can everyone hear me?' Andy asks. He is standing on a small dais borrowed from the band and erected by Paul and Rory at one end of the boardroom. The tall French windows down one side are casting shafts of afternoon sunlight onto the crowd of people, glasses in hand, who have filed into the room. Anka Hamilton is seated on a chair opposite the first of the windows, with David and Glycella beside her. Mike Trent is next to them; he is thin and pale and grasps a stick. His wife seated beside him looks tired and anxious. Beyond them is a representative from the City Council planning department and an empty chair for Sally Walters. Nearby Maria has gathered together a giggling group of girls and is talking quietly to them; they are the clients from the London office who are moving in here next week. Nina is part of the group and looks well and relaxed; we are hoping that she will be able to help Maria settle the other girls now that she has overcome her own health problems. My parents are sitting behind them with Fi and Anna. I hope my brother will be here but there is no sign of him yet. Next to them are Ellie and her husband, Paul and his family and Andy's wife and children. Matt Williamson from the Record office is here and with him the architect and the contractor, and then there is a group of people from the organisations who are renting office space here, craning their necks eagerly to see Andy and gazing with interest through the windows where the sloping lawns of the garden and the surrounding shrubs are visible. The volunteers who have helped clear the garden and spread the gravel talk excitedly to each other in one corner. The local vicar is chatting to a representative from the Salvation Army and behind them are three young women from Maria's former workplace, with Jon and Sara from her church. Finally, planted firmly in her chair with an air of consequence, and resplendent in a plum coloured suit with a row of sparkling gems on her bosom is Mrs. Jackson, with her husband, a quiet self-effacing man, who nevertheless exudes an air of strength and capability. Tom, Mark and others I do not recognise are seated with them, probably local neighbours who have responded to Andy's invitation, and last of all the band squeezed in against the rear wall. There is a burble of assent in response to Andy's question so he continues:

'Welcome to you all; we are grateful that you are able to be here to celebrate this twenty fifth anniversary of the Olaudah Trust and grand opening of Avon View House as a respite centre for victims of trafficking.

'Please bear with me if you have been associated with the Trust for some time, but I would like to explain how it originated and a little of the work we do, for those who do not know us well. The Trust was set up in 1990 by Mike Trent, who I am delighted to say is able to be with us today. Mike's vision stemmed from a period as a geologist, exploring for oil in Unity province of what was then part of Sudan. He was successful in finding substantial oil reserves and as a result was much feted by the business elite in Khartoum.

However Mike's interest in the area went beyond its mineral resource and he became intrigued by the number of young people working in the homes of the families he dined with. He was told they were orphaned as a result of the fighting. A man of compassion, Mike began to investigate their plight with local journalists and aid workers and was informed that many of them were in fact taken from their families as an act of retribution against the rebel army fighting the government. These young girls and boys were in effect slaves, taken from their homeland and transported down the Nile to provide labour for the families of Khartoum. When Mike's contract ended and he returned to the UK he set up this Trust, naming it after one of the first victims of the transatlantic slave trade to write about his plight, Equiano Olaudah, a leading figure in the abolitionist movement of this country. It is as a result of Mike's determination to prevent this traffic in young lives, to influence governments and to support its victims that we are here today. Thank you Mike for all you have achieved.'

He turns towards Mike Trent clapping and we do the same as Mike gets shakily to his feet and acknowledges the tribute, raising both hands, still clasping the stick, above his head and then collapsing back into his seat exhausted. We clap and cheer and I observe his wife surreptitiously mop her eyes whether with emotion or strain, I do not know.

Andy has handed the microphone to David Hamilton who now stands at the front of the dais. His appearance is unassuming and his manner mild and subdued but there is that latent energy about him that, without a word being said, brings the room to silence.

'Good afternoon, ladies and gentlemen. I would like to add my own tribute to Mike Trent for his work and vision in setting up the Olaudah Trust and for all that has been achieved over the last twenty-five years. You will see from the panels in the hall that several hundred young people have been rescued from trafficking in this country and in central Africa, many of those have been supported by the Trust into worthwhile occupations. We have one of them with us here today; Nina has been with the Trust since March and will be helping us with new clients as part of her NVQ programme in Social Care. We wish you well, Nina.' There is a flutter of applause and some murmuring, which David allows for a moment and then continues:

'I would also like to commend the Trust for the way in which the refurbishment project has been managed and in particular the efforts of Jane Taverner. Jane has been effective in her leadership of the planning committee, energetic in her pursuit of funds, and tirelessly diplomatic in her dealings with contractors, planners, inspectors and many others involved in this complex project; Jane, thank you for your dedication and commitment.' To my embarrassment there is another round of applause in which David himself joins and even Andy can be seen clapping behind him; I notice Sally slip quietly into the seat adjacent to Mike.

'Many of you will know,' continues David, 'that my family lived in this house for generations, indeed my brother and I were brought up here and remember the many social occasions and festivities organised by my mother, who is also with us today.' He gives a slight bow towards Anka, and those who know her clap. 'I cannot avoid the fact that this house was built using funds drawn from the slave trade. But branches of my family have also been involved in the Abolitionist movement and our original house in Orchard Street hosted many meetings, often attended by Hannah Moore, whose picture is on one of the panels in the hall. It is a great pleasure to this generation of Hamiltons, my wife and I, that the house can be used for the work of the Olaudah Trust and we look forward to many years of association with the Trust.

'Finally I would like to thank Bristol City Council and in particular, Mike Green from the Planning Office, and Sally Walters, the City Council lead on trafficking. Thank you for your interest and your support. I know that we have already received several referrals of young people who have been trafficked into the Bristol area and we look forward to working closely with the Avon and Somerset Anti-Slavery Partnership to tackle the evils of this global trade. I will hand the microphone to Sally in a minute but before I do so it is my privilege and pleasure to hand the key of Avon View House to Andy Kernow to receive on behalf of the Olaudah Trust.' He picks up a presentation box from the table behind him and presents a large gold key to Andy. There is prolonged applause as the key is handed over. David rejoins Glycella and his mother and Andy takes the microphone again.

'I now invite Sally Walters from Bristol City Council to say a few words and then lead us out to the hall for the opening ceremony. Could I ask those of you in the centre of the rows to remove any bags from the gangway? Thank you.' There is a moment of shuffling as his request is obeyed and Sally comes onto the dais.

'I am pleased to be with you this afternoon,' she announces. 'Bristol City Council is delighted to be involved with this project…..' My attention starts to wander; my feet are sore and my back is aching but there are no seats left so I lean against the door jamb. Through the windows I can see Camarg and his friend, Paul, and Glycella and David's two boys playing football on the lawn. Then I scan the heads in front of me. My Dad is whispering something to Mum. They both look happy and relaxed and I sense their pride. Mum was cautious the weekend I took Rory to meet them but he and Dad talked politics straight away and Mum was gradually won over by his attention to her at lunch. Several rows behind them Mrs. Jackson's permed head of hair is nodding in agreement with whatever Sally has been saying. I glance to my right and catch Rory's eye and he winks and does a surreptitious thumbs up. He is right; it is going well. Beyond him Manny stands ramrod straight; his gaze fixed on the back of Maria's head.

'...for a long association with the Olaudah Trust.' Sally is winding up and I take a deep breath and try to marshal my thoughts. Andy takes the microphone, invites us all to follow and then escorts Sally out to the hall. There is a slight hiatus while Andy, Sally and David adjust their position to face the press photographer. Sally cuts the ribbon to loud cheers then everyone relaxes filling the house with a rising crescendo of chatter. Some opt for a tour; a few linger by the displays or leaf through the booklets for sale; others head straight to the dining room for tea. Views are expressed, cards exchanged and acquaintances made. I find my father in the dining room deep in conversation with David about politics while my mother is talking animatedly to Glycella. The Jacksons seem to have paired up with Mark, our volunteer handyman, and I pass them a plate of cake, hoping that Mr. Jackson will be a useful contact for any repairs. Maria remains calm and organised throughout keeping a constant supply of tea, sandwiches, scones and cake flowing from the kitchen. She seems unconscious of Manny's presence hovering near all afternoon ready to carry trays, clear cups or make space for more food but there is a fluidity in their movements that speaks of comfort in each other's presence.

Darkness falls and we assemble on the balcony of the first floor to watch a fireworks display provided by Mike Trent. As rockets shoot upwards and sprays of brightly coloured sparks fill the sky I feel Rory's arm encircle my waist and pull me towards him.

'An excellent day! Well done you.' I twine my hand in his and indicate with my head where Maria and Manny are standing together. Their eyes follow the rockets upwards and both throw their heads back and laugh as the sparks shower down. I hear fragments of their conversation

'...Nimule in the New Year...' Manny is speaking and I catch part of Maria's response.

'...duties here... save the money...' The rest is lost as a large rocket explodes with a bang. A shower of golden sparks cascade down over the garden accompanied by 'ooo' and 'aah'. Is Manny still planning to visit his family? How can I arrange things so that Maria can go as well?

'They have both suffered so much,' says Rory quietly. 'I hope they have a chance of happiness.' I squeeze his hand, pleased that he confirms the mutual attraction I see as they reconnect with each other.

Later that evening the guests have departed; Rory and the band are dropping Manny back at Mrs. Jackson's; Andy, Ellie and Paul have set off on the long drive back to London. Only Maria and I are left clearing up the last few remnants in the kitchen.

'It's been a special day, Maria; you did a wonderful job organising the tea.'

'I enjoyed it; many people said they liked the house and what we are doing.'

'Did Manny have fun?'

'Oh yes, he doesn't want to go but his flight is booked for Sunday evening.'

'You must take the day off tomorrow and spend time with him.'

'I cannot do that, Jane; in our culture if a man and a woman wish to be together there must be an agreement between their families.'

'But here in the UK it does not matter.'

'I do not want to cause my mother or my uncle to be unhappy. And Manny will not do anything dishonourable until he has spoken to my family. He will go in the New Year. Then a number of cows must be given to my uncle because he is the head of our family.'

'But you are Christians; surely you do not still follow that practice?'

'It is our culture.'

I am appalled, both Maria and Manny have lived in the west for decades and been separated from their families yet they still feel bound by this ancient tribal custom of paying a bride price. I go to bed in the tiny bedroom next to Maria's apartment wondering what can be done.

I wake in daylight to the sound of car tyres crunching on the gravel. This room has a gable window overlooking the drive so I wrap myself in the duvet and stagger out of bed to see who it is. Rory, Camarg and Manny are getting out of the car so I hurriedly put a sweater on over my pyjamas and stumble down the back stairs and across the hall. There is a sweet smell of cooked banana coming from the kitchen.

'Hi, Janey, we thought you might need some help with the clearing.'

'Oooh, I've slept late. Come through to the kitchen, Maria is cooking, let's have some breakfast.' We sit at the table in the middle of the kitchen eating chapattis and fried banana and drinking large quantities of tea. Maria's face is flushed and excited and her hair, usually so carefully dressed is standing out from her face in tightly coiled tendrils. We are on stacking plastic chairs which are too low for the table so all we can see of each other is shoulders and faces; Camarg's cafe-au-lait skin and deep brown eyes, Manny's dark high cheek bones and black eyes sombre in repose but lighting up with a wicked sparkle when he laughs, Rory's narrow brown face, lined with sorrow but with a wide mouth that curls up to meet his eyes when he smiles, Maria's dark face, usually so still and composed but now creased with laughter, her head flung back and jaw wide as she laughs at Manny's teasing.

We joke about the mishaps of the day before – the lengthy speech that sent everyone to sleep, the football that went crashing through the open kitchen door just as David was leading a group of local residents out into the garden, the plate of scones dropped jam side down as the photographer from the local paper came round the door of the dining room. But through the laughter and the chatter I sense a feeling of achievement – a day that showcased the work of the Trust, publicised the potential of the house, gave thanks to the Hamilton family and built relationships with local people. With the last chapatti gone, the fried banana a memory and the teapot drained for the second time we reluctantly clear the dishes and set to work on the rest of the house. I hurriedly wash and change into jeans. By the time I come down the chairs are stacked neatly against the wall and Manny and Camarg are playing football outside, while Maria is standing on the verandah laughing.

Rory is leaning against one of the French windows stroking his beard thoughtfully. As I go over he puts an arm round me and draws me into his shoulder.

'Those two have really got something.' He comments, looking at Manny and then Maria. 'Did you see the way they danced on Friday night?'

'Yes, of course I did. I suggested that Maria take the day off and go out with him but she wouldn't do that. She says it is against their culture and that her family must pay a bride price. But he goes back to Baltimore tomorrow and they may never see each other again.'

'You've got another trip to Juba in February, haven't you?'

'Yes, not definite yet but I'm hoping to attend a conference of the women's movement and visit the Bishop of Torit again.

'Janey, I've been thinking; the work on the book is going well but I need an insight into South Sudanese life if I am to do Maria's story justice. How would it be if I came with you? I could pick up a bit of local colour in Juba and see how the Dinka in Nimule live. What do you think?'

'I'd have to ask Andy but I don't think he'll have any concerns. He can't stop you getting on the same plane as me!'

'We could go a couple of days early and visit my father on our way through Nairobi.'

'I would have to talk to Ellie about the flights. We book the cheapest and sometimes that is through Dubai rather than Nairobi.'

'Well, here's another thought. Could we take Maria as well? We need some pictures of her with her family.'

'Oh Rory, that's a great idea. She told me this morning that Manny is planning to go in the New Year to meet with her uncle to discuss the bride price. It would be unbearable for her to be waiting in the UK for that conversation to happen. I'll put the case to Andy and perhaps somehow we can find the funds to help her.'

'So what about us, Janey? No bride price, just a date.'

'How about Easter? It is early next year, end of March. We could have the reception here the weekend after Easter and then go away kayaking for a few days and Camarg could go to his grandma for the rest of the school break.'

'Whoa,' Rory staggers backwards as though I had hit him in the sternum. 'I'm not sure about the kayaking bit,' he says. 'Where did that come from?'

'Just testing!' I say. He laughs and kisses the top of my head.

'Easter it is!

18 MARIA RETURNS

The birds fly as they celebrate

Hovering like spirits unknown.

God called them here deliberately,

To this land of many wonders.

Ethiopia, Cush or the Sudan,. [18]

It is the end of the dry season and the riverbeds are parched. I watch women bent double digging holes in the sand to capture the last few drops of water. In the distance a line of camels sway through the scrub with ungainly

---

[18] *Beyond the rivers of the Sudan* by Abe Enosa frontispiece *But God is not Defeated* , 1999

strides, their backs loaded with sacks of grain. Banana palms leaves, shredded by wind and sun hang ragged, and the startling red of a flame tree lights up the ochre and tan palette of the bush. Memory jerks back to following Peter into darkness as arcs of fire fell on our village and ignited our homes. My ears fill with the screams of people, the thud of boots marching on Torit and the roar of our soldiers as they fought against overwhelming numbers.

'Maria? Is it how your remembered it?' asks Jane.

'Yes, so good! All the colours and the heat.'

The taxi rolls smoothly along the strip of tarmac, which glistens like treacle. We slow to a halt behind a line of ankole cattle churning up the dust on the margins of the road. The driver hoots and the herdsman persuades his animals into the bush so that we can pass. Their ribs are visible and their heads droop with the weight of their long horns. Surely cows were fatter and stronger when I was a child.

The vehicle picks up speed and we pass through a village. Grass-thatched huts whizz past too quickly – compounds like the one I was brought up in. There are no fences; the space between each tukul visible from the road and the daily life of the household revealed – washing draped over bushes, scrawny hens pecking the dust, meagre stockpiles of millet laid out on wooden platforms high above the ground, children playing, and young women pounding corn for the family supper, their arms working rhythmically as they raise and drop the heavy pole that powders the grain in the wooden bowl at their feet. The relentless daily sound that is the heart beat of Africa.

'They don't have many stores,' says Manny.

'United Nations are reporting famine.' says Jane.

Rory is silent, a smart-phone fastened with an elastic band onto the head rest in front of him and a small keyboard on his knee. He alternately stares out of the windows and then types rapidly.

We stayed in a guest house in Nairobi for the last two nights. Manny and I walked in Uhuru Park while Jane and Rory visited his father. We flew to Juba and now are on the road to Nimule. Manny is in the back of the eight-seater taxi, squeezed against the window by a large mother and her teenage child. Rory, Jane and I are in the middle seats with two young men in the front by the driver. I am pressed into the corner of the seat, too squeezed to be able to talk over the noise of the engine. I feel as though I am in a dream. After all the sad years of waiting and hoping and praying, I am back in my country. I catch Manny's eye. His face looks calm, his forehead smooth and blank. I wonder if he shares my anxiety about what lies ahead. Will we recognise our loved ones? Will they welcome us? I know that Ma is longing to see me because she has told me so many times. But what about my brother and sister; will they want me back after all that has happened? And the community, will they welcome me? I am not the innocent child that played around the New Jerusalem church. Manny and I have been practicing speaking Dinka, reminding each other of forgotten words and easing our mouths and brains round once familiar phrases. Will they find us foreign?

'Driver, can we take a break at Gordon Mountain?' asks Jane. The taxi climbs the steep hill topped by a communications tower and then pulls into the side of the road behind three small rusty cars. We extricate ourselves one by one through the side door of the vehicle. Our fellow passengers open cans of soda but we follow a stony track up the side of the hill. It is too low to be a mountain and as Manny and I follow Jane and Rory I wonder why Jane has insisted on this detour. It is mid-afternoon; the heat of the day has built up and the air has become hazy and heavy with dust. We can see little more than a few metres of dry grass and thorn bushes ahead of us.

The land levels out and shapeless mounds of brick appear.

A sudden gust of wind parts the haze and I catch site of an Egyptian kite swooping down behind an incline ahead of me. Jane comes to an abrupt halt and flings her arms wide.

'General Gordon's lookout!' she proclaims. I come alongside her and look over a steep precipice dropping to a wide valley below us where a braided ribbon of grey brown turns an astonishing right angled bend to thread its way northwards.

'Bar el Jebel,' I whisper in awe.

'The White Nile!' Rory exclaims. 'My father has told me of this.'

'Nimule!' breathes Manny, his eyes scanning the township laid out astride the bend in the river. We are each in our own way moved by the site of the White Nile flowing eastwards through Uganda and then turning abruptly north to continue its journey to Khartoum and Cairo.

We stand mesmerised watching four kites catch the up currents on the mountainside and soar and swoop over the valley one after the other. Their flight seems effortless, the skilful tilting of a wing, the calculated incline of the neck as it balances the spread tail feathers; first one then another rises above the precipice and falls back and my spirits soar with them. The river stretches away from us to the north and to the west, calm and untroubled, a sleeping lion, dangerous when roused. Our land has seen many troubles but it has a potential that will one day grow to maturity if only we can build in peace.

The kites leave as suddenly as they appeared, and I follow Jane and Rory back down the hillside with the whispering sound of the wind lifting their wings in my ears. Manny is behind me.

'The birds are a sign of freedom over our town, Maria. Nimule never fell,' he says. 'There was fighting all along this road but the SPLA held on, that is why so many of our people fled here.'

'How do you know?' I ask him.

'We keep in touch and share news, those of us who ended up in the US.' As my feet bump down the rough track I realise that I have been too isolated from the story of my people, too anxious to survive and to pay for my small flat. I hope my family don't find me dull and stupid.

The taxi drops us at the side of the Gulu to Nimule road, near General Gordon's church, where Pamela is waiting for us – a small lady with streaked grey hair and a determined stride. We follow her along the main road past cafés and shops, our nostrils filled with stale cooking oil and dried chicken, picking our way over broken pavements and cracked steps. Pamela pauses and we line up beside her along the busy road, lorries rumbling past us, overloaded cars weaving between them. There is dust everywhere, in the cars, in our hair and on the fruit laid out on roadside market stalls; I think longingly of London streets so clean and sparkling. There is a brief break in the traffic and we run across and leap the knee-high pavement edge on the other side. Pamela leads us through a gap between the tin roofed houses and along a narrow path across an open area of coarse grass where boys in ragged shorts kick a ball and shout with excitement. On the far side we enter a wide lane. There is no concrete here just a thoroughfare of grey sand between bamboo fences. My heart starts to thump with excitement. I recognise this! My eye catches Manny's.

'We are near,' he says. We turn a corner and there are the dark red metal doors of the New Jerusalem church, the green roof and the three giant trees beyond with their buttress roots, where as children we used to play hide and seek. Young people wearing bright green tabards step out from under the trees. They line up in front of two small tukuls opposite the church. A drum beat starts and they sing, chant and dance a traditional Dinka welcome song.

Their bodies move in unison, their feet perform the intricate forward step, step, back step in total synchronicity and at the end of each segment of the song their hands raise in a single joyful clap. Adults step out from the church and line the track on either side of us. More children appear carrying plastic chairs, which they place carefully in a line under the trees. Manny is already moving in time to the rhythm and raising his hands to clap. Rory is joining in too while Jane, Pamela and I stand politely, hands clasped in front of us. I feel so strange; when I was last here I was one of the choir, and Manny was the drummer leading us in welcome songs for important visitors. Now we are the visitors who are being honoured in this way. Once again shame clutches my heart; they do not know what my life has been. The choir finish their song with a loud clap and start another, "Jesus number one". They sing and I can feel my bones tingling to the ends of my feet. I love my church in London, and in Bristol I have been going to a church with a good band. English people who know the Lord Jesus are kind and read the Bible stories but they cannot sing and dance in the way that even a small child in my country can.

The bishop in his shiny purple shirt, with a jewelled cross hanging over it, steps out from the trees. He raises his hands to stop the choir. The drum beat slows and dies and the voices fade to a final clap. As we applaud the bishop steps forward, with two others accompanying him, and shakes Pamela warmly by the hand.

'Greetings, dear friend.'

'Greetings, Bishop Michael.'

'You will sit?' He indicates the row of plastic chairs under the trees and we settle ourselves, Bishop and Pamela in the centre with the Olaudah Trust to their right and the bishop's party to the left. The choir disperse and people bring more plastic chairs making a circle around us. A young man works his way along the line offering us a bottle from a crate of sodas. The Bishop stands.

'We thank Almighty God for bringing these friends who left us as children back to us. We praise him for his mercies. Amen' He turns to us. 'Now you introduce yourselves; please start with you, Miss Jane.'

'Jane Taverner from the Olaudah Trust. We are working to eliminate slavery along the White Nile. We help people who have been trafficked to the UK.'

'Pamela Spinner from Doves of Peace. As you know, we have just finished leading a conference on peace and reconciliation and healing.'

Soon it will be my turn and I will have to say something. I cannot see if my family are here. There are many faces staring back at us, perhaps a hundred people; which of them is my mother? There is an elderly lady at the back under the trees with a group of younger women. Many are wearing dresses of bright blue fabric with "Mothers Union" printed on it. The men are sitting on the chairs in front of us. Is one of them my brother? Is my sister here? I thought I would recognise them instantly as I did with Manny.

'Rory Odhiambo, researching a book on the work of the Olaudah Trust.'

'Manny Deng, son of Deng Bol. I was taken to the United States from Kakuma Camp as a young man and I'm now a lawyer in Baltimore.' There is an audible gasp from the women. Now it is my turn.

'Maria Kuol, daughter of Peninah, I am the manager of the Olaudah Trust centre in Bristol. I was taken by the Sudanese Armed Forces to work as a servant in Juba, then taken to London.' There is another gasp and the women make a low sound deep in the throat. I remember that sound so well – wordless sympathy and support.

'Now I introduce our leaders,' says the bishop. 'Archdeacon Jonah of Nimule District, Pastor Samuel of this church, Simon, bishop's chaplain and Mothers' Union pastor, Dorcas.' The people on his left rise as he says their names and come down the line shaking hands with each one of us and lastly the bishop does the same. The wait is agonising. I just want to see my family but this is South Sudan where politeness and welcome are paramount. After the bishop has shaken our hands all the men rise to do the same and then the women and there is a buzz of conversation as everyone greets us warmly. Manny and I are doing our best to respond in Dinka and I am thankful that we practised. The bishop holds his hands aloft; the hubbub subsides and people return to their chairs.

'We will take you to your people,' he says. He takes Manny by the arm. 'Please to go with Archdeacon to the church office. They are waiting for you in there.' He puts a hand on my back and pushes me forward. 'Pastor Dorcas will take you, Maria, to your family, they are waiting in that small tukul.'

I follow Dorcas across the sandy street feeling the hot grit seeping into my sandals and stoop under the low roof of the tukul. There is a smell of cut reeds and clean linen and I pause while my eyes adjust to the low light inside. The tukul has three tiny windows, one of which is partially shuttered. The walls and ceiling are lined with fabrics of many different patterns, barely visible in the darkness; the effect is both sumptuous and subdued.

Three figures rise from the low sofa in the corner and one of them steps forward with hands outstretched.

'My darling daughter!' She folds me in her arms and holds me to her. I am taller than she is now. I bend my head to receive her embrace. I smell her rather than see her. I am flesh of her flesh and bone of her bone. Her cheeks feel soft and cool, criss-crossed by a thousand fine lines that tell the story of the hardship and suffering of her life. As my arms go round her I can feel that her back is crooked and one hip higher than the other. She smells of lemons and cooking fire smoke and I feel as if I am sinking back into the security of my childhood years – a weary traveller home after a long journey. As my eyes adjust to the dark I see deep into hers and there is nothing but immeasurable love.

'Ma!' Tears spring to my eyes and we are both crying. 'I thought I would never see you again. I thought you were dead.'

'We never gave up hoping.' She speaks at the same moment that I do and we laugh and hold each other at arm's length for a moment and then hug again. I do not ever want to let her go and the hug lasts for a long time. I can feel her hands pressed into my back and her arms around me. She feels like a fragile bird. After a long while she breaks away again and says:

'Your brother and sister are here.' I look further into the gloom and there they are. My brother Peter steps across the red felt covering on the floor and takes my hand, then he envelops me in a hug. He is stick thin and his lower body is slightly lopsided; I can feel the unevenness of his gait even as we hug.

'God bless you, Adut, you have come back to us.' He releases me and steps back making way for Deborah. She is as tall and poised as ever and her hair is plaited into an elegant bun that enhances her high cheek bones but as she hugs me I can feel every bone, and deep lines edge her mouth and brows. She is only four years older than me but it seems more.

'I wanted to run after you... but I was afraid... Rosa...' She holds me tight and we are back in that torrid shed with Rosa lying on the floor in front of us. 'I knew you must be in Juba. They let me go to market sometimes. But I never saw you.' Her voice is stilted, broken.

'I never went out. They never let me.' We cling to each other and I remember afresh all that my wonderful sister said to prepare me, strengthen and inspire me so that I was able to endure.

'You found Seme again?'

'Yes we have five children now.'

'Five children! God has blessed you!'

'Yes, perhaps too many! Seme has no skill except soldiering. It is difficult to find work, but we manage with our uncle's help.'

'And Aaron and Joel are they here?' I ask.

'Aaron is in Bor,' says Deborah. 'He is worried about cattle raiding. Joel is in Juba. We have not seen him for two rains.'

'And you, my daughter?' says Ma. 'Tell us about you.' So I tell them about being captive in Juba and Slough, my attempt to escape and being recaptured. 'I did not know that I was doing anything wrong.' As I am speaking a cow starts to low outside the back window of the tukul and her mournful sounds make a sad accompaniment to my words.

'I thought it was a job but they were evil men, who took advantage of me, and I was sent to prison.' My family make that low noise of sympathy. They do not condemn or scorn me.

'In prison they taught me how to speak and write English, and how to cut hair the western way. One day the governor called me to his office. He said I should not be there and that he would get me freed. He said I must study so that I was ready to have a job. So I worked very hard and passed many tests. When they released me some people helped me to find a job at Lucille's doing hairdressing. I became the manager and now I manage the Olaudah Trust project in Bristol.'

'You have acted with courage and wisdom, Maria,' says my brother.

'The Lord has blessed you,' says Ma.

'You have done well,' says Deborah. 'Many people here want education but the schools are closed. Only in the church, if the bishop arranges it, then you can train as a pastor or an administrator but there is no pay in these jobs.' They do not think me dull or stupid, or bad. I hear the note of envy in Deborah's voice and am upset that my lovely sister has not had the opportunities I have.

There is a soft tap at the doorway. Dorcas carrying a flask, and a lady in Mothers' Union dress carrying a tray of cups enter bent double as they stoop under the thatch and cross the raised threshold. They place the tray and flask on a low table in the corner. The Mothers Union lady bows silently and leaves. Dorcas says:

'If you need something, you call. There will be dinner soon.' She waves a hand towards the area under the trees, bows and ducks back under the thatch.

We cluster round the table and help each other to tea. They want to know what happened to me after I was separated from Deborah. Ma questions me about the household.

'Did they ever... you know...' This is the question I have been dreading. I look across at Deborah. I wonder if she has told Ma what happened with the colonel. Deborah's dark eyes look back and she shakes her head very slightly. I take a deep breath.

'The master was a very religious upright man. He would not allow his business friends to touch me.' My mother lets out a sigh of relief.

'You were fortunate, my daughter, to have a good master.' I look at the lines of suffering etched on Deborah's face... I will ask her later what happened to her and perhaps share my fear of Mohammed.

'Life is good in Nimule?' I ask. I know immediately from

their glances that this is the wrong question. Ma takes my hand and Peter opens his mouth, pauses for a moment and I see his ribs rise as he draws breath deep into his lungs.

'The Sudan Armed Forces never took Nimule but there was fighting along the Nimule–Juba road for many years. The town was bombed. Many people fled over the border into Uganda and are living in the refugee camps.'

'We do not always have enough to feed the children,' says Deborah, 'and for adults there is one meal a day.' There is no emotion in their voices; they are simply stating facts.

'Peter was part of the reconciliation process after Independence,' says Ma.

'But when fighting broke out in December 2013 all that had been agreed was ended and there is no more money now,' Peter adds. I look at their faces creased with anxiety, at the furrows of hardship and worry on Deborah's face and I am ashamed. All this time I thought I was the one in difficulty but for my family life has been worse.

We drink the tea and they tell me about my nephews and nieces, how good uncle Amos has been in sharing his house and helping with food and clothes.

'We are grateful for the money you have been sending,

Maria; it has helped us to give something to Amos and to many who have less than we do.'

My heart is breaking as they speak. I have so much, my lovely apartment at Avon View House, my clothes and more food than I can eat. The Trust has sent me on courses for hygiene, safety, and first aid. I have been given many good things while my family continues to suffer. It is very hard to know what to say, except that I love them and I will do what I can to help.

A bell sounds.

'Time to eat,' says Peter. 'Are you ready, Maria? Deborah?'

We have one last lingering hug and then walk out to face the people. There is a loud cheer as we emerge from the tukul and some of the women ululate. It is dusk and the light is fading rapidly as it does in my country. The stars are coming out and I gaze up for a moment at the soft velvety sky, still with a tinge of pink over the church office where Manny has been meeting his family. I wonder how his reunion has gone. I will find out later but now we must join the crowd round the cooking pots on the table.

....

This is the biggest party of my life – even the wrestling match celebrations when I was a child did not match today. People from the compounds around the church have joined in, drums announced returnees from far away, and many from the surrounding refugee camps have arrived; soon there are several hundred people eating the goat stew, corn pancakes, rice and greens that the Mothers' Union ladies have prepared. As some leave others come and another pot of stew and one of rice, cooked on the open fire in the compound behind the church, are brought over. There is singing, dancing and endless hand shaking and questioning.

'You have come from UK. From US?'

'We remember you. You are tall!'

'Do not forget us now you are rich!'

Rory and Manny join in the dancing to loud cheers. I sing and clap with my mother and sister, then, linking hands with younger family members, join the dance 'You are still a good dancer, Maria,' say the older women. 'You have not lost your dancing feet.'

Now it is past midnight; the moon is high in the sky; its pale light filters through the leaves making silver patterns on the packed earth beneath. The Mothers' Union ladies have cleared the dishes and carried off the many empty bottles of water and soda to burn in the morning. People have drifted away, leaving a few dozen still chatting under the trees. Rory is talking with the bishop and Peter about peace, politics, the future of the country; their voices rising in excitement and then falling away again. Jane is sitting on the low wall that surrounds the east end of the church talking quietly with Dorcas. Manny and I have been explaining to the archdeacon and his wife how we came to leave our country and what brought us back. They too get up to go and we are left on our own. The lamps have gone out and the night is black and soft. There is a bright star low in the sky over the church office and the sandy street glows pale grey. Now that the chatter and dancing have ceased I can hear the familiar sounds of the African night, the whirring of insects, chirruping of crickets, the soft rustle of animals moving in the thatch. This is a beautiful time, when the heat and the rush of the day are over and the air moves sweetly. I can talk to Manny at last.

'Your family, they are well?

'My father is old; he lives with my eldest brother now.'

'And your Ma?'

'We think they went to Central African Republic but

don't know where they are now.'

'I am sorry.'

'Three of my brothers are lost. None of them returned from the fighting. They thought I had perished in the massacre in Bor.'

We sit together gazing upwards and soaking up the beauty of the night. As my eyes adjust I start to see a myriad of stars, stretching deep into the heavens.

'It has been better for us than for them,' I murmur. 'We have had education, work, and food. It has been much harder for them.' There is an exclamation from the group of men behind us and laughter. Then I hear Peter say quietly,

'All this country needs is peace.'

'Maria?' I look at Manny's face shining in the dark. His eyes are bright and his eyebrows raised in a question. 'I spoke with my father and your uncle Amos today. They have agreed to a discussion about cows.' He gets up and starts to walk down the street and I follow. He is teasing me.

'About cows!' I exclaim. He stops and turns to face me.

'Maria, will you marry me?'

'Yes, Manny.'

'Will we help to rebuild this nation together in whatever way we can?'

'Yes, we will do that, if the Lord blesses us.'

'If peace comes, if the Government of National Unity is formed, I would like to try for a legal job in Juba. Would you come with me?'

'Yes. I can start a hairdressing business, and maybe continue to work for the Trust, if Jane agrees.'

'So, that is arranged. I will have the discussion about cows. We will make our plans. When the time is right we will join our families together through marriage. But for now...' I feel his hand on my arm and he draws me back into the shadow of the church building. 'I love you, Maria,' and we hold each other and kiss long and deep – friends and partners for whatever the future holds.

19 A SUNNY DAY

A safe and prosperous southern Sudan will take many decades to materialize. Critics question whether the South has a generation to achieve these goals[19].

The house basks in the late April sunshine. Morning showers have cleared and the windows reflect the last few cumulus clouds drifting across the sky. Birch trees toss their hair in the light breeze and send kaleidoscope patterns onto the lawns beneath. Shaggy clumps of daffodils, their flowers long over, quiver and shake their seed heads. In the polytunnel fresh green shoots of lettuce, radish and tomato seedlings are soaking up heat and water as their roots form. The garden is poised for growth.

On the other side of the lawn, close to the verandah, two heads of dark curly hair are bent over the screen of a tablet together, one face dark and narrow, the other rounded and

---

[19] *Sudan, South Sudan and Darfur, what everyone needs to know* by Andrew Natsios, 2013 page 219

pale.

'Riek Machar, the rebel leader, has returned to Juba, Jane. He's agreed to take part in the discussions for a government of national unity.'

'At last! Now there might be some progress.'

'There's still fighting to the south west. They will be focused on getting that under control. The twitter feeds are asking for more UN forces to be brought in.'

'Once there is stability the Trust will be able to set up orphanages and training programmes.' She pauses. 'I dreamed about the giant again last night, Rory, but it was different this time- the figure surrounded by the families of Nimule rather than striding off into the bush. I recognised Maria's mother and uncle and some of the young people. They were reaching up to pull away the weed and untangling the ankles from the chains. Then I saw Peter, wearing a bishop's robe, say a prayer. Maria and Manny were leading the way along the road to Juba with the giant following and the people dancing and singing. Manny was beating a steady rhythm on a drum. It was as though they had entranced the giant into following them to the city.'

'I think the dream is very profound, Janey. Only the people of a country can lead its spirit. We do everything we can to help but only they can bring in the message of justice and peace;' He looks at the twitter stream on the tablet in his lap and sighs. 'but first the leaders must lay down their desire to be the "Big Man" and all the greed and corruption that goes with it.'

Jane ruffles his hair and kisses his brow, and he turns to her.

'You were so lovely in that cream dress holding the roses with the gorge behind you – like a beautiful angel.' he says.

'I was feeling impatient because the photographer kept taking more shots of me and all I wanted was to get back to our guests!' He laughs and they kiss.

The shadow of the roof creeps across the lawn. The breeze wafts through the open windows and brings with it the laughter and merriment that filled the garden three weeks ago.

What a gathering of family and friends! Rory's father from Nairobi, and his mother-in-law and friends from London; and Jane's family from the length and breadth of England, elderly relatives who had gone to immense trouble to make the occasion; local friends and colleagues including the Hamiltons; Camarg pressed into service as an usher and looking very self conscious in a brown jacket and trousers; Anna as Matron of Honour and Fi as Chief Bridesmaid in orange and yellow silk with red roses in their hair and Poppy, hand held tightly in Anna's, as a diminutive bridesmaid beside them. Rory's band, augmented by extra musicians serenaded the newlyweds. The hall was filled with flower arrangements in every shade of red, yellow and orange, framed by fronds of deep green palm leaves. The young couple walked up the drive hand in hand and, like another couple two centuries ago, he lifted her over the threshold. Then the house resounded with the merriment of the wedding feast. Guests seated themselves in the panelled dining room and laughed and joked and toasted 'Rory and Jane' before the couple left for a holiday in the Bahamas, which, Jane assured him, would include some kayaking.

The sun is setting but the heat of the day remains. The

timbers ease and shift slightly as the damp of winter evaporates. Roof tiles, cloaked in moss, breathe in the warmer air and spiders lodged there for months, scurry away looking for somewhere more congenial to hide.

Good times have returned to Avon View House. First the anniversary and opening day in November and then Christmas with its special magic, so lacking in the years of dereliction. Young men and women, full of anticipation, yearning for love to repair their damaged lives gathered round a small pine, cut from the garden. Their laughter filled the hall as they decorated the tree, sang Christmas songs and giggled together. In the kitchen the good fairy, whose magic transformed the house with the sparkle of cleanliness and the warmth of love, brought together the ingredients of a perfect Christmas.

Now on this warm spring day the fairy herself looks out from the window of the attic apartment to the deep channel of the Avon. The oblique rays of the sun gild the cranes along the dockside at Portishead and glitter on the widening waters of the river, where it fans out and enters the Bristol Channel.

She turns back to face into the room, dark face and wiry hair framed by the white weather boarding of the attic.

'What do you say, Maria?' asks the equally dark figure perched on the table in the corner. 'Are you ready to try your hand in Juba?'

'It's an opportunity, Manny. We've talked and prayed about returning to our land. Our country needs people to rebuild and try new things. What are they offering; is this work you can do? Would it help our country?' He looks down at the paper in his hand.

'It is the department of Gender, Child and Social Welfare; they want to plan how they can protect women and children. They have written because I have experience of family law. The interview is on the tenth of May. My fare will be paid. You could come with me and look for a place to have a hairdressing shop.'

'We could arrange to marry in Juba and then our families and our US and UK friends would come!'

'We could have one of the cows for the feast!' They link hands and laugh, dancing across the wooden floorboards as they did across the dry sandy ground many years ago. The eaves of the old house wrap around them and the trees bend in to listen. The brick walls glow red in the setting sun and the window panes flash a reflection onto the craggy sides of the Avon Gorge. Deep in its valley, the river picks up their dreams, and carries them towards Africa. It will be a long journey, through adverse terrain, pitting their love and skills against the dark spirits that engulf their land.

The two dancers pause stand looking our across the gorge, hands linked tightly together.

'We will pray to the Lord Jesus.' says Manny. 'He has kept us safe so far and He will guide us on the path ahead.'

'Yes, He will, we will trust Him.' and they stand quietly together watching the light fade. It is dark now in South Sudan but a new day will dawn and Maria and Manny will pack their bags, say 'goodbye' to their friends and make a new life in the land the rivers divide.

Go swift messengers.

In the second Maria of South Sudan novel Maria looks for her sister, Rachel, and her brother, Joel.

For more information go to:

https://mariaofsouthsudan.wordpress.com

or follow on Twitter @TishMason1

or at the Facebook page for MariaofSouthSudan

ABOUT THE AUTHOR

Letitia Mason has a passion for mercy and justice. She fell in love with East and Central Africa while living and working in a *harambee* school in Kenya in 1972. She now works for Flame International, an organisation providing a ministry of peace and reconciliation in areas of conflict and trauma. She has listened to many stories of women's lives while on short term missions in South Sudan. This book is a tribute to the bravery, faith and dignity of the women of South Sudan during decades of civil war. Letitia has two sons and a granddaughter and grandson; she lives in Surrey with her husband, and two dogs.

84161218R00204

Made in the USA
Columbia, SC
27 December 2017